On *a*
COLD
DARK SEA

ALSO BY
ELIZABETH BLACKWELL

In the Shadow of Lakecrest

While Beauty Slept

On a COLD DARK SEA

ELIZABETH BLACKWELL

LAKE UNION
PUBLISHING

Published by Lake Union Publishing, Seattle

www.apub.com

Amazon, the Amazon logo, and Lake Union Publishing are trademarks of Amazon.com, Inc., or its affiliates.

ISBN-13: 9781477808900
ISBN-10: 1477808906

Cover design by PEPE *nymi*

Printed in the United States of America

To Mary Jean, Jenny and Gayle
Long-time readers, lifelong friends

PROLOGUE

April 15, 1912

Captain Rostron ordered rope set out by the deck chairs to restrain anyone driven mad by the disaster. But the crew of the *Carpathia* also busied themselves with more mundane preparations: gathering spare pillows and blankets, heating up soup, and brewing tea. Dr. McGee bustled back and forth from the medical bay, laying in supplies for an unknown number of patients. A few light-sleeping passengers poked their heads out of staterooms and asked why the engines were going so loud. The captain had insisted they not be told. No use in starting a panic.

They'd all find out soon enough.

In those frantic hours before dawn, it didn't feel quite real. The *Titanic* sending out distress signals? Loading her lifeboats? There wasn't anything heroic about the poky *Carpathia*, yet the Mediterranean-bound liner was now speeding to the rescue, more than fifty miles off course. Lookouts stationed on the bow scanned the treacherous obstacle course before them, cheeks stiffened by the arctic air. Chunks of ice dotted the water in shades of white and blue, an awe-inspiring sight to anyone not trying to steer through them.

The sky was softening from black to gray when one of the officers saw the first lifeboat. A gangway door was opened and ladders hung down for those strong enough to climb; the others would be lifted up in slings. The lifeboats were undermanned, and the *Carpathia*'s officers were cautious, making each approach and unloading a drawn-out affair. In all, it took four hours to unload the boats, each filled with a ragtag assortment of millionaires and immigrants, some in hats and fur coats, others in what looked like nightclothes. The only thing they had in common were the life belts fastened around their chests.

And then, when the *Carpathia*'s deck was crowded with stunned passengers and exhausted survivors, one last lifeboat emerged from the sea's icy camouflage. Weaving erratically, it made pitifully slow progress as the bent figures at its oars struggled to bring it flush with the *Carpathia*'s side. Three stout American women climbed up the ladder first—clearly sisters, by their family resemblance. A twitchy-faced British woman clutched the hands of two small children and looked relieved at a steward's offer of tea. An elderly lady, assisted by her nurse, had to be pulled up in the sling; she was the only one who managed a smile.

When the officer in charge turned to greet the next passenger, his heart sank. The creature standing before him looked like a character from a fairy tale, a frost maiden carved from snow. Her dark-blonde hair was frozen in icicles around her homely face, which showed no emotion at all. A man's coat hung limply off her slender frame. The officer asked the girl her name, and she stared at him, bewildered. He looked at the girl's homespun dress and patched stockings. Lord have mercy, she wasn't even wearing shoes. Third class. And a foreigner.

"Votre nom?" the officer asked, trying French. Then, adopting the time-honored English strategy of speaking louder in order to be understood, "Your name!"

The girl stared at the officer, who found the blankness of her features unsettling. "Anna Halversson," she said.

The officer steered the girl toward a steward and whispered, "Find that boy Olaf, in the kitchens. We'll need a translator."

When the officer returned to his position, the next three passengers were already aboard, and for the rest of his life, the pitiful tableau they formed was the first image that sprang to mind when he thought of the *Titanic*. The handsome young man in his evening dress, eyes haunted, one hand pressed protectively against his companion's back. There was a girl hovering nervously behind them—a maid, by her cowed bearing and black dress. And then there was the lady, swathed in a fur coat over a shimmering green gown, a vision of ruined elegance. She looked done in, her thick auburn hair cascading in a tangle over one shoulder, a dull burgundy gash blighting her cheek. Yet there was a nobility to her suffering. She was young, the officer realized, younger than she appeared at first. Too young to have learned that the world can inflict harsh blows on even the most charmed lives.

"Your name?" the officer asked, his manner markedly more respectful than it had been toward the third-class girl.

"Mrs. Hiram Harper," the beauty replied. The officer was surprised to hear the flat American tone; he'd assumed by the woman's bearing that she was English.

"Charles Van Hausen," the gentleman said.

So, not her husband, as the officer had assumed. He jotted down "and maid" after Mrs. Harper's name, and nodded dismissively at the girl in black. Proper names were not required for servants. He directed the passengers to the first-class steward waiting to escort them further, then turned to see a young woman staring at him with disconcerting directness. Quite lovely, he couldn't help but note, though her disheveled hair and white-cold skin gave her an eerie wildness that distracted somewhat from her beauty. She couldn't be past her early twenties.

The officer asked for her name, yet she kept staring, as if the question were beyond comprehension. She didn't look like a foreigner; she was quite respectably dressed, though most likely second class rather than first.

The officer repeated the question. This time, he saw her struggle to respond. It must have been the shock. It left some people quite unable to speak.

"Charlotte Evers," she managed at last. Her voice was more refined than her clothes: British, well bred. "Mrs. Reginald Evers."

Then, to the officer's astonishment, the woman began to cry.

PART ONE:
BEFORE

CHARLOTTE

Charlotte hadn't believed the *Titanic* would sink. Even at the very end, when glass shattered and a hand thrust her forward, she'd still assumed they'd all be saved. She'd stepped out into the icy night, grabbing at the arm a sailor offered for support. Stiffened by pride and anger, she'd taken a seat in the middle of the lifeboat, refusing to look back at what she was leaving behind.

Now, Charlotte's eyes scanned the upper deck of the rescue ship, looking for the man she both loved and loathed, the only person who'd ever truly known her. From the very beginning, Reg saw past Charlotte's fluttering eyelashes and false modesty, to the scheming beneath her meek exterior. *You've the face of an angel*, he'd said, not a week after they'd met, *but a devilish soul*. Laughing, as if it pleased him. Reg didn't pull Charlotte into a life of crime; she chose her own path, herself. But Reg applauded her along the way. He alone understood what she was capable of.

And she hadn't even said goodbye.

Charlotte Digby was a beauty. Everyone told her so, even when she was too young to know what it meant. In time, she learned to heighten the effect by widening her deep-blue eyes as the faces leered down, offering a charmingly hesitant smile that made her chestnut ringlets quiver. Her looks, she quickly came to understand, were her greatest asset, an advantage to be leveraged. People assumed her perfection was a sign of inner purity, a surprisingly common belief that put them off their guard.

Charlotte inherited her good looks from her father, who'd been lost at sea before she was born. Charlotte's mother spoke of him as she would a natural disaster: a storm that upended her life before passing on, leaving her to sweep up the pieces. Charlotte grew up on the fringe of respectability, in a small but spotless house paid for by Mr. Hepworth, the father of Charlotte's two younger brothers. They called him Papa, but he was always Mr. Hepworth to Charlotte, a seemingly small matter of etiquette that told her everything she needed to know about her status in the family. There was a Mrs. Hepworth, who lived somewhere in the country and either didn't know or didn't care that her husband kept a separate household in south London. Perhaps she was relieved to be spared his physical demands. On the nights Mr. Hepworth was in residence, Charlotte pushed her face into her pillow so she wouldn't have to hear the ridiculous, piglike grunting from her mother's bedroom.

Such domestic arrangements may have been denounced from a pulpit, but in practice, Charlotte's childhood wasn't marred by scandal. She lived on a street where neighbors acknowledged each other with nods but never invited each other over for tea or questioned the story you chose to tell about your life. Charlotte had no idea how precarious her position was until a coldly worded letter arrived from Mr. Hepworth's lawyer, informing her mother of Mr. Hepworth's sudden death and the provisions of his will. School fees for Charlotte's brothers were to be paid in full, but there was nothing left to Mother or Charlotte; their house—rented, never purchased—would revert to the landlord at the end of the month. When Charlotte's mother burst into ragged sobs,

Charlotte knew she was mourning the loss of Mr. Hepworth's money as much as his companionship.

The boys were packed off to school, their faces pale but composed as they boarded the train; at eight and ten years old, they already had the look of men resigned to their fate. Charlotte and her mother moved into a room above a cheese shop, a sour-smelling space with a single, lumpy bed and leaky windows. Their rent was paid in labor, and they scrubbed cheesecloth and counters until their fingers and knuckles pulsed with pain. Charlotte was thirteen years old, growing up and filling out. She was always ravenously hungry. Now that Mother could afford meat only once a week—a gristly joint that was stretched into watery stews and soups—there was never enough food to fill Charlotte's grumbling stomach. But Charlotte also hungered for other comforts of her previous life. A new dress to replace the one whose sleeves no longer covered her wrists. A silk ribbon to distract from the shabbiness of her hat. When she saw young women her age prance across the street, their pearl-buttoned boots peeping out from beneath jaunty dresses, Charlotte felt a gnawing ache.

Life-changing decisions could be made on a whim, a lesson Charlotte would remember in the midst of the Atlantic, many years later. For months, Charlotte stared longingly at the apples on the fruit-monger's cart whenever she passed by the market. Until one day, for no particular reason and with no advance thought, she stopped and stepped closer. When the fruit seller turned to a customer, Charlotte's hand darted forward, swiping an apple and sliding it into the fold of her skirt. A cart rattled past, blocking her path and forcing her to stand in place as the fruit seller turned in her direction. Charlotte's arm trembled, and the apple's red skin peeked out, betraying her.

There was no denying what she'd done. Charlotte's eyes prickled with tears; her lips parted to offer an excuse that her mind was too dull to produce. The fruit seller's scowl softened.

"Go on, then," he muttered.

The reprieve was so unexpected, and her relief so overwhelming, that Charlotte couldn't move. She stared at the man, as he stared at her, and she felt his gaze as a physical sensation, a warmth that emanated from his admiring eyes. It was the first time she realized her beauty would allow her to sin and be forgiven. Or, better yet, never be suspected of sinning at all.

Thinking of her face as protective armor made stealing easier the next time. And the time after that. Not that Charlotte didn't take precautions. She only ventured into markets well away from home, at the busiest times of day. In a matter of months, she had progressed from snatching buns out of maids' shopping baskets to pickpocketing, brushing up against well-dressed gentlemen and feeling for the chink of coins in their trousers. On these occasions, there was no need to skulk about; she looked the men straight in the eye as she stumbled against them and slid her hand into their pockets. A few even tipped their hats to the pretty girl who apologized so sweetly, even as she clutched their money behind her back.

Charlotte hoarded her earnings for months, but it was only a matter of time before the temptation to spend it won out. When she came home with a length of poplin for a new dress, she told her mother it was a gift.

"A lady saw me admiring it in the shop window and bought it for me, out of Christian charity," Charlotte said. "It's an unpopular color—the shopkeeper offered it to her at half the price."

The fabric was a rather ostentatious shade of blue, and the shopkeeper had been willing to haggle. The price had dropped after a few blinks of Charlotte's woeful eyes. But there'd been no generous stranger.

"Aren't you lucky," Mother said, her tone suspicious. "Sure there's nothing more to it than that? There's plenty of so-called gentlemen who'd take advantage of a girl like you."

Charlotte was tempted to boast that it was the other way around, that she was the one tricking the gentlemen. But that would be asking for a slap—or worse. Mother's pride was the only thing of value she still possessed, and she'd extract a harsh punishment if she found out what Charlotte was up to. It was a protectiveness born of self-preservation, not love. Charlotte was a bauble she hoarded, kept shiny and pristine until she could be married off for an appropriate sum.

"Time you put that face to good use, in any case," Mother continued. "I've been thinking you're the right age to start in service."

Service? Working as a maid meant scrubbing and groveling and emptying chamber pots from dawn until dark. Charlotte had no intention of succumbing to such a fate, no matter how grand the house. The following day, she returned to the fabric shop and asked the owner if he knew of any dressmakers who'd pay her to do piecework. To her surprise, he offered to hire her instead.

"Be good for business, having a pretty thing like you about," he said, with a sly smile.

He kept her at the front of the shop, greeting customers. Even other women, it seemed, liked to be welcomed by an attractive face. The well-to-do clientele were the wives and daughters of factory owners and bankers who needed wardrobes for country weekends and formal dinners, and Charlotte studied them as their fingers stroked the silks and velvets. She listened to their murmurs and later repeated their words: *Quite lovely, don't you think?* and *This will do marvelously for Delia's coming-out.* She mimicked their expressions and their posture, the way their lips and teeth snapped together. A south London accent wouldn't get her where she wanted to go.

Charlotte learned other lessons as well. How many fondles to allow Mr. Thornton, the shopkeeper, before wriggling away and asking what his wife would think of such behavior. How to use such incidents to increase her pay while keeping her reputation. How to smile one way at a demanding female customer and another way at the woman's shy, unmarried son. A future beckoned, with a husband and a house and children, the kind of future that would be a victory, given her upbringing. In the meantime, she continued to steal when the opportunity presented itself. A pudgy middle-aged man walking along Clapham Common, his watch chain trailing from his coat. A sour-faced old fellow who'd stuffed a few pound notes in his pocket without folding them first. Each successful theft felt like a gulp of fresh air after a lifetime spent in smoke-filled rooms. Complacent with success, she grew careless in picking her targets. And that carelessness led her to Reg, which led to everything else.

He looked like any other likely prospect. A gentleman of means, out for a Sunday stroll in freshly shined shoes. His green suit was a shade brighter than most men would wear, and he walked with a springy step that told her he took pleasure in being noticed. A dandy, Charlotte thought, easily distracted by simpering admiration. When he pushed aside his jacket and slid a hand into his front trouser pocket, she saw the bulge in his waistcoat and knew she'd found her mark.

Charlotte followed him into the park, around the fountain where children were racing wooden boats. She lingered by a tree as he stopped and smoked a cigar, then picked up her pace when he resumed his walk through an alley of trees. She pitter-pattered until she was almost running, a seemingly distracted young woman focused solely on her destination. She hurried on until—thump!—she'd bumped into his back, throwing off his balance so he stumbled forward and then teetered back against her.

"Oh dear!" Charlotte cried out in mock distress. Her mouth formed a perfect round O.

"Gracious."

The man had the kind of face whose bold features all fight for attention: dark eyes framed by prominent eyebrows; a large, fleshy nose; a thick-lipped mouth and dimpled chin. The overall effect was striking rather than handsome, but there was something appealing in the way he looked at Charlotte, as if she were just the person he'd hoped to see.

"Pardon me," Charlotte said, looking down, her entire body cringing in mortification.

"Have no fear—I am quite unharmed." He had a musical voice, the words sliding up and down in register.

Charlotte bobbed her head. "Good day."

The man took a step sideways, just far enough to block Charlotte's path.

"Where are you off to in such a rush?"

The first flicker of worry tickled Charlotte's chest. Her success depended on speed: getting what she wanted and getting away. The longer she spoke to this man, the more time he'd have to realize what she'd done.

"My mother, she's sick," Charlotte said, with genuine apprehension. "I'm off to the doctor for her medicine." She heard the flimsiness of the lie as she said it.

"Your poor mother, at death's door." The man sighed melodramatically. "Is that why you need this?"

In a single swift motion, he grabbed her upper arm and twisted it, bringing Charlotte's right hand up and forward, still clutching his leather billfold.

Charlotte had an arsenal of weapons: her shaky voice; her terrified expression; her feet, if he'd let go long enough for her to make an escape.

"Sir, I swear on my mother's life . . ."

"Let's not bring your mother into this, shall we?" the man asked cheerfully. "Or your ten starving brothers or sisters, or the old lecher who's made an assault on your virtue. I can see from your dress that you're not destitute, and from your delightful figure that you're not starving. So tell me, why exactly did you make a play for my money?"

She looked into his face, a face that looked more curious than angry, and decided on a tactic she'd never tried before. Honesty.

"For the fun of it."

The man burst out laughing. "How charming! You're very good, you know. Most fools wouldn't have realized what happened until you were long gone."

"You're not a fool, then."

His smirk acknowledged the compliment, but he still hadn't let go of her arm. A tightly coiled energy seemed to hum through him, as if his thoughts and emotions ran at twice the speed of everyone else's.

"Let's say I have some experience in your line of work," he said. "I should haul you off to the nearest copper. Do my duty as a good citizen."

Charlotte already knew he wouldn't. She remembered what her mother had said about men taking advantage of innocent girls, and she wondered if that was what this gentleman had in mind. She was more curious than scared. How did men proposition girls they thought were in their power? How would she trick him into letting her go?

He released Charlotte's arm and opened the billfold. It was empty.

"I'm afraid your little escapade would have proved disappointing," he said. "I keep my funds far more secured." He flapped open the left-hand side of his jacket and waved a finger toward the bottom corner, where the small seam of a hidden pocket was barely visible. As if he were daring her to try again.

"It would be a shame to squander such talent," he said. "I have a proposal that could benefit us both."

Charlotte could have run. She didn't.

"There's a gentleman of my acquaintance who owes me rather a lot of money," the man said. "I had a good run at cards, and he was unable to meet his obligations. I have his signature on a paper, stating what he owes, but my attempts to collect have been unsuccessful. I have been pondering alternative methods of pursuing my claim, and I believe you could prove most helpful."

He explained his proposed solution and Charlotte's role in it. It would take only a few minutes, and she'd walk away with a pound once the debt was collected. But it meant trusting this stranger to do what he promised.

"No later than quarter to ten," the man said. "He always goes to the ten o'clock church service. Pious bastard."

Charlotte nodded.

The man swept off his hat and bowed. "Then it's time we were acquainted. Reginald Evers. At your service."

"Charlotte Digby."

Like an apprentice at a master's knee, she wanted to ask him how he'd started pickpocketing. If he'd ever been caught. But he was already stepping away, back to his mysterious, no-doubt-disreputable life. Even before he was out of her sight, Charlotte began to miss him.

On the day they'd arranged, Charlotte wore her shabbiest dress, the one she reserved for housecleaning. She told her mother she was headed out for a walk before it grew too hot, and when she reached the street corner in Kensington, she unfastened her top two buttons. Reginald had instructed her to look for a round red-faced man and his equally rotund wife, and Charlotte recognized them as soon as they came strolling along, arm in arm.

When they were nearly in front of her, Charlotte called out, "My darling! How can you be so cruel?"

The man and woman stopped abruptly, their confused stares mirror images of each other. Charlotte stepped toward them, her hands dramatically clutched.

"You said you'd take care of me and the baby! You said you loved me!"

The wife's face shifted to anger. "Who is this?" she demanded, glaring at her husband.

"I don't know! I've never seen her!"

Even to Charlotte, who knew it for the truth, his words sounded unconvincing. Perhaps he was thinking of another woman he'd wronged. She scrunched up her face to hide the fact that her sobs were not accompanied by actual tears. She heard footsteps behind her, then Reginald's voice.

"Harry!" he called out. "What's all this?"

"Reginald!" the man exclaimed. "This . . . *creature*, whom I've never met, is causing a scene. There must be a misunderstanding."

"I wasn't going to tell her, I swear!" Charlotte protested. "Only you didn't send the money you promised, and how am I to pay for our little one's food?"

Harry's wife removed her hand from the crook of his elbow and watched Charlotte with horrified fascination.

"She's lying!" Harry snapped.

"Of course she's lying," Reginald said. "You always pay what you owe, don't you, Harry?"

Charlotte watched Harry's eyes widen with understanding.

"Allow me to assist, if I may?" Reginald asked. "I would hate for your wife to suffer any further humiliation." He gave Harry a meaningful stare as he took hold of Charlotte's arm, pulling her aside.

"Yes, yes," Harry muttered, his feet shuffling on the pavement. "Much obliged. You may be assured of my gratitude."

"Why don't we toast your gratitude tomorrow? The Three Bells, at noon?"

Harry nodded curtly, and his wife scurried behind him as he hurried away. When they disappeared around the corner, Reginald looked at Charlotte and let out a triumphant laugh that made his chest shake. Charlotte felt weightless, as if a rope that kept her tethered to everyday life had been snapped. For a few exhilarating moments, she'd been transported into a different body, a different life. She and Reginald had played off each other like dancers, the lies coming as easy as breathing.

16

Charlotte had never been lonely as she schemed her way through the London streets, but she knew she would be the next time, without him.

"He'll have my money tomorrow, you can be sure of that," Reginald said. He reached into his jacket and pulled a pound coin from one of his hiding places. "Unlike dear Harry, I always settle my debts."

"That was the most fun I've had in ages," Charlotte said, fixing Reginald with her best flirtatious smile. "When can we do it again?"

And with that, an unofficial partnership was formed. She couldn't have Reginald come by the flat—Mother would know him instantly for a ne'er-do-well—but he visited Charlotte at the shop, making her laugh so hard that Mr. Thornton asked pointedly if the gentleman would be buying anything, and if not, it was time for Charlotte to sweep the storeroom. Not long after, Reginald arrived with a proposal: a friend was taking up a collection for poor orphans, and would Charlotte make an appearance at a charity drive as a penniless urchin made good? There was no orphanage, of course, and the only needy souls who'd benefit from the scheme were Reginald and his friend. And Charlotte, if she agreed.

The falsehoods multiplied from there. Charlotte told her mother she was attending educational lectures during her evenings out (where, she implied, eligible young men were in ready supply). She told Mr. Thornton her tortured feelings for him were affecting her health, which allowed her to shorten her working hours while stoking his vanity. She and Reginald concocted story after story: one day they were a missionary and his sister raising funds to build a church in China; the next they were newlyweds recently arrived from Australia, with opportunities to invest in a copper mine. Her favorite ruse starred Reginald as an earnest country vicar who was building a home for wayward young women and Charlotte as the reformed fancy girl he'd rescued. Her performance was particularly appealing to wealthy old roués, men whose consciences were susceptible to tales of ruined virtue. She'd sidle up to them with an innocent smile, even as the movements of her hips and chest hinted at the lewdness of her past. It was an irresistible combination, and donations flooded in.

For six sparkling months, they were Lottie and Reg, companions who understood each other on a primal, wordless level. With a glance or a nod, Charlotte could send Reg a message—*This fellow's suspicious*—and Reg would swoop in with a slap on the back and a whirlwind of words that rescued Charlotte from awkward questions. She trusted him utterly, yet she knew almost nothing about him. He lived in a lodging house in Chelsea, where she occasionally sent messages but was dissuaded from visiting. He had a large circle of friends—friends he played cards with (and cheated, when he could); friends he dreamed up schemes with; friends he drank with and fought with and accused of taking his fair share. But none of them knew the real Reg any more than Charlotte did; he'd even hinted, once, that Reginald Evers wasn't his real name. Like a conjurer at a country fair, he dazzled through misdirection, deflecting questions to protect his secrets.

With each swindle, discovery became more likely; defying those odds was half the fun. And then it all began to go wrong. It started with Mother, asking skeptical questions about Charlotte's lectures and wondering when the new friends she'd been making would come to call.

"You'll be nineteen next month," she warned. She'd taken to coughing dramatically to emphasize her supposedly precarious health. "I will *not* leave you an old maid. If you can't find yourself a husband, I'll do it for you."

Not long after, Reg, masquerading as "Lord Cavendish," was spotted by the brother of a man he'd cheated, resulting in a mad dash out the servants' entrance of the Empire Club.

"Time for Lord Cavendish to emigrate, I think," Reg told Charlotte the following day. "India, perhaps?"

Charlotte was disappointed; they'd been planning to go to Harrods and charge a new set of clothes to the Cavendish account.

"I'd best make myself scarce, in any case," Reg said. "I've gotten rather greedy and made myself a few enemies."

"What do you mean?" Charlotte asked.

"I'm going to leave London," he said. "Allow tempers to cool."

They were walking in Regent's Park, their favorite place to hatch plans and savor their triumphs. Charlotte had allowed herself to believe the two of them would stroll down these paths forever, in a vaguely imagined eternal future.

"How long will you be gone?"

Reg held up his hands in an amused show of helplessness. "Who can say?"

Charlotte didn't have the heart to smile back. She was angry and hurt, and all she could think was that she had to get away from all the people around them, to find a place where she could calm the dirgelike thudding of her heart. With abrupt resolve, she stepped off the path and across the grass, still damp from the previous night's rain. She could hear Reg behind her, but she didn't look back. Didn't want to face him with her teary eyes. When Charlotte reached a high point among the trees, she stared down at the muddy hem of her dress. Reg's spattered boots sidled up next to her. It must mean something, for a man who took such care with his clothes to follow her this far.

Charlotte waited glumly for Reg to speak. She wanted to tell him not to go, that she couldn't face the emptiness of a world without him. But Reg wasn't one for such sentiments.

"We've had fun, haven't we?" Reg spoke in his usual cheery tone, but the words came out hesitantly.

"The most fun I've ever had."

"You could have fooled me, from the way you're carrying on."

Charlotte knew she was supposed to laugh, but she couldn't quite manage it. Today, for the first time, she didn't want to play a part. She didn't want to be Lady Cavendish, or Pippa the orphan, or the missionary's sister. She didn't want to be pretty, devilish Lottie, who gleefully took strangers' money and laughed about it afterward. She had never realized until that moment how exhausting it had become.

Charlotte looked up at Reg, at the smile she'd seen dozens—hundreds?—of times. Reg used his smile to charm and disarm; it was his greatest weapon, and his greatest disguise.

"We couldn't have gotten away with it forever," Reg said. "Sooner or later, there would have been a copper round the corner at the wrong time, or a woman doing her shopping who recognized you at the shop. I knew, every time, that I'd have to put a stop to it sooner or later."

"I wish we'd had a bit longer," Charlotte said.

"You can still make something of yourself, Lottie. You're clever and you're beautiful. You can do anything you want."

In the early days of their acquaintance, Charlotte had been prepared for Reg to grab her or kiss her, but he never had. He'd treated her with the protectiveness of an older brother, and he was looking at her the same way now. It wasn't the money or the adventure she'd miss, Charlotte realized. It was Reg's faith in her. The way she felt when he was at her side.

All at once, in a dazzling rush of certainty, Charlotte knew what to do. She'd always thought love would overtake her like a sickness, leaving her helpless and weak. Her affection for Reg was something else entirely: a force that strengthened and sustained her. And wasn't that what every woman hoped for in a husband? She remembered the evening they'd spent acting as the Australians, selling mining shares. Their conversation had come so naturally, it was as if they were already married.

Reg was likely to laugh if she began spouting grand declarations. So Charlotte did what her body urged: she rose up on her toes and kissed him. His lips pressed back against hers; his arms encircled her; his chest pushed against her with such force that her back collided against a tree. For those few, breathless seconds, Charlotte felt how much he loved her.

Then, with a jolt, Reg released her and stepped back. He made a show of adjusting his hat, composing himself, then shot Charlotte a look of wry amusement.

"Good gracious," he said. "My apologies." As if he'd spilled his tea or bumped against her in the street.

"No," she stammered, "I was the one . . ."

"My dear Lottie, I am enormously flattered. But you must see—this won't do."

"Why?" she asked, reeling with confusion.

Reg was an expert at reading his marks; he must have known he'd hurt her. "I am greatly flattered," he said again, gently. "But you should save your kisses for someone who deserves them."

"There's no one else. You're the one I want—I know it."

"Ah, you're young! You think you aren't, but you are."

"And you're such a wise old man?"

Charlotte realized with a start that she had no idea how old Reg was. Twenty-five? Thirty? He carried himself with a confidence beyond his years.

"I am richer in life experience," Reg said. His lips twisted into a mischievous smirk. "And that vast store of knowledge tells me you're meant for a better man."

"I don't care," Charlotte insisted. "I love you. I want to marry you."

"Oh, Lottie."

Reg looked terribly sad, and understanding sank over Charlotte like a weight. "You're already married."

"No." Reg's voice turned harsher. "I am terribly sorry, but I have no interest in the chains of matrimony. I value my freedom too highly."

Charlotte realized, with sickening regret, how badly she'd misjudged her own appeal. Why would Reg, a man of the world, marry a girl who lived above a cheese shop? For all she knew, he had a harem of women who provided all the comforts he desired. He was looking at her with pity, which only made it worse. From now on, he'd always see Charlotte as the silly girl who'd made a fool of herself by kissing him.

The humiliation was total—and unbearable. Charlotte turned and ran, tears blurring her vision as she fled across the park and stumbled along the streets. How could she have put so much faith in someone she barely knew? All her memories of Reg had become tainted, like photographs splashed with water. He was a blur, a mystery that resisted being solved, and she had only herself to blame for her disgrace.

The next day, Charlotte was looking out the front window of the shop when she saw Reg approaching. She muttered a quick excuse to Mr. Thornton and scuttled out the back door before Reg could see her. She made a similarly swift escape when he returned a few days later, and after that, he stopped coming.

It was two years before they spoke again, in the spring of 1912.

～

Mother's cough turned out to be serious. For months, it worsened, from discomfort to pain. Charlotte's life was restricted, every minute given to serving customers at the shop and Mother at home. At night, she lay sleepless as their shared bed shook with Mother's groans. The Charlotte who had once shape-shifted with mischievous glee was worn out and worn down; the few times she caught glimpses of herself in a looking glass or shop window, she was shocked by her gaunt reflection. Heads no longer turned when she passed, because beauty without light veers perilously close to tragedy. Charlotte's air of suffering kept others away.

During her brothers' term holiday, Charlotte sent them to stay with her mother's sister in Devon, and when Mother died a few months later—a blessedly quiet passing after so much suffering—Charlotte's Aunt Lucy came to the funeral. It was a somber affair with less than a dozen mourners, but Charlotte was able to pay for a decent gravestone with the money she'd saved from her exploits with Reg. She'd been planning to use it for new lodgings, but Mother's death had quashed Charlotte's already limited ambitions. Seeing Mother laid to rest in a churchyard, with a proper marker, assuaged a small part of her guilt over the many lies she'd told.

Charlotte watched the way her brothers looked at Aunt Lucy as they took their tea afterward, so she wasn't surprised when her aunt offered to take over as their guardian. A farmer's wife who hadn't approved of her sister's unconventional family, she exuded a comforting maternal warmth now that Mother was no longer around to scold.

"The country air will do the boys good," Aunt Lucy said. "You'll be glad to be spared the bother, surely? Won't be long before you're married with little ones of your own."

Charlotte loved her brothers, in the detached way you love a childhood toy; though she didn't much miss them when they were away, she liked to think of them well cared for. She knew they'd be happier chasing after chickens at a farmhouse than with her in London. But Charlotte cried harder when her brothers left than she had when Mother died. With the last remnants of her family gone, she was truly alone.

Grief moved through Charlotte like mud after a hard rain, slowing her down, making every step forward a struggle. She expected the sadness to lessen with time, but it endured and deepened, a force lashing her to the past. Occasionally, startled, she'd acknowledge the passing of time—six months since Mother died; a year—only to wonder how so many days could go by with nothing to show for them. Even stealing had lost its appeal. She wasn't as quick or determined as she'd once been, and one afternoon she came dangerously close to being caught. Only a swift kick to the knees had gotten her out of a policeman's grasp, and after that, she never tried again.

What had felt like a dreamlike world of interchangeable days and nights began to take shape toward a possible future when Mr. Thornton's wife took sick. The illness, unlike Mother's, was swift, and Mr. Thornton dropped hints that his mourning would be similarly curtailed. Not long after Mrs. Thornton's passing in February, he told Charlotte how unsuited he was to bachelor life and how it brightened his days to see her kind face. Once, the idea of marrying Mr. Thornton would have made Charlotte laugh; now, it felt inevitable. The benefits were so obvious that she took to reciting them mentally: he owned his own business and home; he wasn't bad-looking for a man in his forties; she already knew all his quirks and faults. Charlotte was nearly twenty-one and didn't have any better prospects. Mrs. Thornton hadn't been able to carry a successful pregnancy, but if Charlotte had a few children straight off, Mr. Thornton would allow her to run the household as she pleased. Perhaps that would be enough.

Though Charlotte was still able to muster a forced friendliness with customers, she no longer paid particular attention to new arrivals. So she didn't realize Reg had entered the shop until he was standing directly in front of her, resplendent in a burgundy-checked suit, smiling like a child who'd found his lost kitten.

"Lottie."

Charlotte felt the anger rise up, fueled by remembered shame, but the swell was short-lived, the crackling embers of a fire that had long since burned out. She couldn't think of a thing to say.

"Let's have a chat, shall we?" Reg asked.

Charlotte followed Reg outside, carried along in his wake. Reg looked the same as ever: immaculately if ostentatiously dressed, moving with jaunty confidence. When he looked at Charlotte with bemused curiosity, it felt like a bracing ray of May sunlight after a harsh, dark winter.

"I expected to search half London for you," he said. "Must say I'm rather shocked to find you still here—I thought you'd have had a dozen marriage offers by now."

Charlotte told him about her mother's death and her all-but-official engagement to Mr. Thornton. In their glory days, she would have made the story amusing, for the pleasure of hearing Reg laugh. But that kind of vivaciousness was beyond her now. She could only recount the facts, none of them worth smiling about.

"I would congratulate you on the happy news, but it sounds as if I should offer condolences instead," Reg said. "You're not really going to marry that fool, are you?"

He looked up, over her shoulder, and tipped his hat. Charlotte turned to see Mr. Thornton tapping on the front window of the shop. With his pinched lips and raised fist, he looked like a cranky old Scrooge berating children who'd woken him from a nap. She saw him through Reg's eyes and felt a curl of disgust.

"No," she said, surprised by her own vehemence. "I don't think I will."

"Splendid. I'm delighted to have rescued you from a dreary fate." Reg flashed Mr. Thornton a wide, cheeky grin, then turned back to Charlotte. His face had an expression she recognized from days past, when he'd dreamed up a new scheme. "Run away with me."

He was teasing. He had to be. Reg was no gallant prince, and he'd made it clear long ago that he wasn't in love with Charlotte.

"Where?" she asked suspiciously.

"New York."

It was all a game, the kind of story they used to invent for fun. Except Reg sounded deadly serious.

"The thing is," Reg said, with exaggerated remorse, "I've found myself in a bit of a scrape."

"Who do you owe money to this time?" It was comforting, in a way, to find Reg hadn't changed, given the upheavals in Charlotte's own life.

"I'll not sully your ears with the sordid details," he said. "Suffice to say, I have made myself an enemy of a family that one should not run afoul of. Best I leave England for a time, until the commotion blows over. I hear America has much to offer a man of my talents. If you put on a posh act and call yourself the Earl of Nonsense and Nonesuch, everyone thinks you're rich, and you can rob them blind."

"The Earl of Nonesuch," Charlotte said. "You'll be a smashing success."

Reg grabbed Charlotte's hands, and she was surprised by the force with which he squeezed them.

"Come with me."

Charlotte heard another tap-tap from Mr. Thornton. She had thought her impulsive kiss had forever shattered the bond between her and Reg, that the trust they'd gifted each other could never be recaptured. Now his longing flooded through Charlotte like a fever. Saying yes would be reckless and possibly dangerous; she had no idea what Reg had done and who might be after him. But this, Charlotte knew with bleak certainty, would be her last chance for escape.

"What's the story?" Charlotte asked, putting on a show of doubtfulness. She didn't want Reg thinking she'd fall in line right away. "The missionary and his sister?"

"You will travel as Mrs. Reginald Evers. My devoted wife."

Wife? What exactly was he proposing?

"In name only," he said smoothly. "You know I'm not the marrying sort." Then, more quietly, "To my great regret."

Reg looked down with a flicker of genuine sadness, a gesture that silently asked forgiveness. When Charlotte nodded briskly, asking no questions and demanding no explanations, his face shifted back into its usual cheery expression.

"A ship's saloon is ripe pickings if you know what you're about at cards," he said. "As a respectable married fellow, pleasant enough but none too sharp, I'd be welcome at every table. I wager I'll earn back our passage before we make landfall. Once we're in New York, we can work out a scheme as the count and countess, or whatever you please. Just like old times."

Just like old times. Charlotte felt the pull of it, strong as the hunger that had pushed her to steal that first apple.

"We'd be expected to share a cabin," she said, looking at Reg straight on.

"Are you afraid for your virtue?"

"Should I be?"

Reg laughed, but she saw the tempted twist of his lips. He'd take whatever she was willing to give, as long as she expected no promises in return.

"I'll book us adjoining rooms," Reg said. "You can put it about that I've got a terrible snore—which, I've been told, I do. Mrs. Evers deserves every comfort."

Mrs. Evers. Charlotte had hoped to have that name, once. This might be the next best thing. She'd have a place at Reg's side, a role in the theatrical masterpiece that was his life.

"Mrs. Evers would need a suitable wardrobe," Charlotte said slyly.

Reg pulled a handful of banknotes from his waistcoat. Whatever trouble he'd gotten into, it hadn't left him penniless.

"Buy whatever you need. I'll book us tickets on the *Titanic*, leaving next week. We'll go second class, but I hear the appointments are better than first class on any other ship. As I said"—he tipped his hat—"only the best for Mrs. Evers."

And that was that. Charlotte said her goodbyes to the few people who cared enough to notice she'd be gone, and the nastiness of Mr. Thornton's spitting rebukes made it all the easier to leave without regrets. Reg had supplied her with the perfect excuse for her sudden departure: a whirlwind romance, a surprise engagement, the chance to accompany her new husband on a business trip to America. Reg's money paid for new dresses, hats, and shoes, the bags to pack them in, and a ticket for the boat train to Southampton. Reg had some mysterious matters to attend to the day before and would meet her at the pier.

On that Wednesday morning, as the train chugged through country vistas Charlotte had never seen and didn't know when she'd see again, her heart raced in the same way it had before every outing with Reg. It could all go brilliantly or terribly wrong, and she hadn't realized until then how she thrived in that uncertainty. By the time Mrs. Reginald Evers arrived at the White Star Line berth, she had perfected her part: a modest, self-possessed young wife in a simple wool jacket and skirt, her hair arranged in sedate waves under her moss-green hat. She surveyed the travelers milling around the second-class gangway, assessing her future companions the same way a gambler eyes the ponies at a trackside stable. They were a variety of ages and shapes, many of them in family groups, but they shared a common purposefulness. Their eyes were on what came next, not what they were leaving behind.

An officer began steering the passengers on board, and Charlotte looked around for Reg. He might pride himself on living moment-to-moment, but he'd never been late for a job; she could always count on him to be where he was supposed to be. Right as she was wondering what she'd do if he didn't come—he had her ticket, after all—he rushed over with a wave and dramatic exhale of breath, overpowering her with apologies before she could come out with a question or reproach.

"Ah well, Lottie, no harm done. Got your luggage all sorted?"

Charlotte nodded, and Reg took her by the elbow and hurried her toward the ship. As they joined the queue along the gangway, Charlotte was struck by the sheer size of the vessel she was about to board. She hadn't had any fear of sailing before that moment, but her chest felt tight, as if her body were forcing her to slow down and reconsider. She thought of the father she'd never known, a sailor who'd climbed on a ship and hadn't come back. A man whose only legacy was the daughter he'd never met.

The passengers surrounding Charlotte shuffled forward with polite, mostly silent restraint, though she heard occasional "oohs" and mothers commanding their children to stay close. The young man directly behind Reg seemed particularly anxious to get aboard; he kept stepping forward when there was barely space to move and bumping against Reg's back. His hands and face twitched with excitement, and his eager eyes kept shifting from the ship to Charlotte and back again. If Charlotte hadn't been so put off by his pushiness, she might have been flattered. He was quite good-looking, in a youthful, sunny way, and the cut of his clothes suggested he was well off.

An officer welcomed them aboard, then directed them to the steward who would lead them downstairs to their staterooms. Charlotte tried to keep track of where they were going so she could find her way around later, but it was all a bit of a blur. They passed a smoking room, a library, and a wood-paneled dining room with corridors leading off in every direction. Charlotte noticed the young man from the gangway trailing after them. She kept expecting him to stop at one of the cabins they passed, but he never did. Finally, the steward unlocked a door with a flourish, then handed two keys to Reg.

"The other room's right next door, to the left. The porter's already brought in your luggage. Is there anything else you need, sir?"

To Charlotte's annoyance, the pushy stranger was still hovering. He had the decency, at least, to gaze elsewhere as Reg talked to the steward. Perhaps he was lost and waiting to ask directions.

"Nothing at the moment," Reg said.

"Twenty minutes until we sail, noon sharp. If you'd like to watch from the deck, it's two flights up."

Reg nodded his thanks, and Charlotte waited for the man who'd been following them to finally leave. Instead, he stood there, staring at Reg.

"Ah."

Charlotte knew that sound. It was Reg's way of buying time in an awkward situation—the moment someone accused him of cheating at cards, or a policeman shot him a suspicious glare.

"I had hoped to do this under different circumstances," Reg said, his eyes not quite meeting Charlotte's, "but our train was delayed and there simply wasn't time."

The word "our" was the one that caught her attention. Charlotte looked at the young man, who was looking at Reg, who was looking back at him. Her confusion began to clear.

"You know each other?" she asked, right as the man demanded, "You haven't told her?"

Reg looked uncharacteristically flustered. "Georgie, give us a moment, will you? Get yourself a drink in the saloon."

Bewildered, Charlotte allowed Reg to escort her into the stateroom. A settee was set against one wall; two berths were flush against the other. Her bags had been stacked in front of a small bureau. It was nicer than any room she'd ever slept in, yet at the moment it felt as close and stifling as a prison.

Reg leaned against the doorjamb, one foot crossed against the other, a posture intended to show her he was perfectly at ease. But Charlotte knew him well enough to spot the tense set of his jaw.

"Who is he, then?" she demanded.

"Georgie's a friend."

That could mean anything. Reg had dozens of so-called friends.

"Does he have something to do with that spot of trouble you're in?" Charlotte asked.

Reg exhaled sharply, a sound that could have been a laugh if he'd made the effort. "Yes."

Charlotte felt the disappointment first, a heavy, dull pain pulling her down. It was supposed to be just the two of them. With a flush of shame, she remembered the fantasies she'd entertained over the past few days: Reg half-drunk, reaching for her; her own mock-reluctant surrender to his seduction. What a fool she'd been, to think she could ever trust him! Reg had lured Charlotte onto this journey with half truths, like one of his marks, and she had fallen for it. Her embarrassment hardened into anger.

"I know Georgie wasn't part of the plan," Reg explained, with exaggerated remorse, "only it turned out he needed rescuing at rather the last minute, and there wasn't time to check with you, and I couldn't turn my back on him. Loyalty is one of my few admirable qualities, wouldn't you say?"

It was the same way he chattered at cards, a melodious flow of words distracting attention away from what his hands were doing with the deck. It only infuriated Charlotte more.

"Why is he here?" she demanded. "For once in your blasted life, tell me the truth!"

She'd shocked him: good. Reg's smile wilted, and he looked down. It took him a very long time to decide what to say.

"Georgie is George St. Vaughn, late of Cambridge University. He is also the son of Lord Upton, second cousin to the queen, and an all-round blighter. Georgie and I were discovered in what I believe is best described as a . . . *compromising* position, in his rooms at college. Cue scandal, uproar, and calls for my immediate beheading."

The words tumbled and spun around Charlotte as she struggled to understand.

"I knew you wouldn't come if I told you before," he said. "I am very sorry."

Charlotte realized that the simplicity of his apology meant it was sincere. But that moment of compassion was quickly overpowered by dizzy uncertainty. What was he saying? What did it mean?

"Georgie'd be recognized in first class, so he's traveling as my brother."

"Your brother." Charlotte nearly spit out the word. "So, we're to be a happy family?"

"We could be."

Charlotte stared at the face she knew so well, the face of a man she didn't know at all. *A compromising position.* She didn't know how it was possible for two men to do such things, only that it went against nature to do it. Her first impulse was to leave. There was still time; she could pick up her bags and stalk off the ship. Back on the train, back to London, back to Mr. Thornton.

"Please, Lottie."

Reg's plea cut through the haze of wounded pride. If she stayed, she'd be condoning behavior she could think of only as sinful. She'd have to pretend she didn't care. Yet even that humiliation, she realized, was preferable to returning to her old life.

Charlotte nodded, briefly and painfully. "I'll do my bit."

Reg reached out to her—for a pat on the shoulder, a squeeze of the arm—and she twisted away.

"Go find your *brother*," she snapped. "We'll be off any minute."

Charlotte missed the celebratory departure from Southampton, the waves and shouts between deck and shore. She sat alone in her cabin, palms clenched around her knees, as the coals were shoveled and the engines sprang to life. She spent hours in that cabin during the days that followed, fuming and squeezing back tears. For the steward's benefit, she had to rumple the sheets on the upper berth each morning and wet her husband's towel so it looked used. But of course Reg never slept in her room; he spent every night with Georgie, and she tortured herself with thoughts of what they might be doing.

Her fellow passengers, she gathered later, were dazzled by the *Titanic*'s grand appointments and air of glamour. For Charlotte, all those public spaces were merely backdrops to an unending, excruciating game of make-believe. At every meal, during afternoons in the lounge, or on deck, she played the dutiful wife, pretending to find Georgie's company tolerable. He was an overgrown child, all eager smiles and self-amused giggles, shooting glances at Reg the way a puppy begs for scraps at the table. His attempts to befriend Charlotte were laughably clumsy. When he tried to butter her up by telling her how highly Reg thought of her, Charlotte was too tired and frustrated to summon a polite response.

"He thinks of you as a sister," Georgie insisted.

"Yes, we had quite jolly times together. Until you came along."

Georgie looked so wounded, like a child that'd gotten a slap instead of a pat, that Charlotte almost felt guilty. Then he went off on a story about his mother's sister's horse, and her moment of empathy passed.

Reg was the only member of their unconventional trio who never seemed ill at ease. He befriended businessmen and won handily at cards; he boasted that the sea air was doing him good, and he felt better than he had in years. He fawned over his "dear wife" in public, but never gave Charlotte a private opportunity to ask what would happen when they arrived in New York. She'd pictured herself and Reg on a spree across America, like the outlaws they wrote about in the papers, stealing from millionaires who wouldn't even know they'd been robbed. Now, there was Georgie to consider. Georgie with his grating laugh and exasperating need to be liked; Georgie who wanted Reg all to himself.

So when the dreadful night came, and the steward rapped on the door and informed her that the captain had ordered all women and children to the lifeboats, Charlotte wasn't frightened. She was already miserable; this was merely another trial to be endured. Reg came for her soon after—his shirt and trousers rumpled—and Georgie hung behind, looking similarly bedraggled. She tried not to think about the fact that they'd obviously pulled on their clothes in a rush.

"What's happened?" Charlotte asked Reg as he fussed with her life belt.

"Something's wrong with the ship," Reg said.

"It's just a precaution, though, isn't it?" Georgie asked. "They're not actually launching the boats, are they?"

Honestly, Charlotte thought. She caught a cringe of annoyance pass across Reg's face. *Good.* She and Reg walked up to the deck in silence, ignoring Georgie's prattling. When Charlotte stepped outside, her face prickled in the arctic air. She looked at the row of lifeboats, which hung from ropes that were secured to metal davits jutting up and out from the ship. Sailors and officers were huddled around the boat nearest her, arguing. She heard a sharp creak as the boat was winched partway down, then came to a shuddering stop. The water looked impossibly far away. The crewmen's obvious unfamiliarity with the lifeboat's mechanisms was hardly reassuring.

Passengers were gathered in small groups around the boat, but Charlotte was never able to explain, afterward, the calm that prevailed amid the commotion. No one was screaming or panicking; families were separating with polite farewells, pecks on the cheek, and sometimes no words at all.

"You watch," an elderly lady said decisively. "They're going to row us out, then row us right back."

The even-more-elderly gentleman beside her pursed his mouth, his bushy mustache squirming like a caterpillar. Everywhere around Charlotte, couples were having offhand discussions about whether to go or stay, as if they were planning a summer holiday. *Cornwall or the Lake District?* No one was stepping forward to get in the boat.

Reg pushed Charlotte forward, with Georgie right behind. The officer at the helm of the boat nodded to Charlotte, then looked sternly at Georgie.

"Women and children only."

"He's only a lad . . . ," Reg wheedled.

"Step back," the officer ordered.

Charlotte was in no rush to climb into what looked like a poor shelter in the vast ocean, and she fell back alongside Georgie. The sailor nearest her muttered a curse as he tried to maneuver the ropes; either the boat was stuck, or he had no idea what he was doing. When a man called out that boats were being launched on the other side, most of the people around Charlotte moved away.

What happened next came so quickly—Reg pulling them toward the stairs, tossing his coat around Charlotte, and muttering in her ear—that she could barely remember how they came to be standing in the enclosed second-class promenade, three floors down from the lifeboats.

"No one will know," Reg was saying, and Charlotte suddenly realized what he was asking of her. "With your hat and coat, he could pass. Say he's your sister . . ."

"Absolutely not!" Georgie protested, all injured pride. "I will conduct myself as a gentleman!"

"You won't be a gentleman if you're dead!"

The force of Reg's anger froze Charlotte in place. She felt the rough wool of her hat against her fingers, the weight of Reg's coat on her shoulders. A single lie, to add to the thousands she'd already told. A lie that might save a man's life. She looked at Georgie's hated, bewildered face. She heard the quiver in Reg's voice as he softly murmured, "Lottie." It was the first time she'd ever seen him frightened.

And Charlotte knew what she must do.

US SENATE COMMITTEE ON COMMERCE

Titanic Disaster Investigation

Thursday, May 2, 1912

Testimony of Mrs. George McBride, First-Class Passenger

Senator Smith: Was there any panic as the lifeboats were boarded?

Mrs. McBride: Not at all. It was very orderly. An officer supervised the loading, and he escorted me on board, followed by my two sisters. We were able to step in without any inconvenience.

Senator Smith: How many were in your boat when it left the ship?

Mrs. McBride: Perhaps a dozen. I didn't count.

Senator Smith: The boat was built to carry the weight of sixty-five people. Do you know why it was lowered at less than half capacity?

Mrs. McBride: I couldn't say. We waited quite some time before the officer gave the order to board. When my sister and I entered the boat, the officer called out, "Any more women?" but there was no reply. We dropped down in great fits and starts, and one of my sisters was convinced we'd all be tipped overboard.

Senator Smith: How many sailors were in your boat?

Mrs. McBride: Two.

Senator Smith: How would you describe their conduct?

Mrs. McBride: One of them was a very rough fellow. He waved his oar all around, and I said to him, "Why don't you put the oar in the oarlock?" and he said, "Do you mean that hole?" He'd never held an oar in his life. He also smoked a pipe against many of the ladies' objections. We were quite upset that our safety had been entrusted to such a man.

Senator Smith: And the other sailor?

Mrs. McBride: I had no complaint with him. He seemed quite comfortable rowing and steering, and he was properly deferential with the passengers. I had great confidence in him until the disagreements broke out.

Senator Smith: What disagreements?

Mrs. McBride: There was some confusion as to what we should do, after the ship was gone. It was not always clear who had charge of the boat.

Senator Smith: Would it not be the senior crewman?

Mrs. McBride: Yes, I suppose.

Senator Smith: What was the nature of these disagreements?

Mrs. McBride: It does not matter now. We were all quite upset. It was very dark and very cold. We did our best in trying circumstances. We survived.

ESME

Afterward, people would always ask Esme where she'd been when the ship struck the iceberg. Had she heard the impact? Did she know what had happened? She learned to deflect questions by saying she'd been in bed, asleep. The momentous event had passed her by, unnoticed.

It was partially true; she had been in bed. But she wasn't asleep, and she wasn't alone. When the *Titanic*'s starboard flank scraped against the ice, with a sound that one passenger later described as rolling over a thousand marbles, Esme was curled up next to Charlie, her arm draped over his chest, smiling as he twisted a finger through her hair.

Soon, the honeymoon would be over, and she'd be back in Philadelphia. Esme was amazed by how essential Charlie had become, in so short a time. Every thought she had meandered toward him; every breath she took in his presence restored her. She had been stockpiling sensations during their nights together, crafting memories she could draw strength from later. As the first surge of water poured through the *Titanic*'s hull, sealing its doom, Esme was thinking: *I love him so much it hurts.*

She heard a faint metallic groan, and Charlie turned his head toward the door.

"What d'you think that was?"

Esme was still floating in the haze that overtook her after giving in to Charlie's whispered urgings. Before, she'd always put up a show of being reluctant and shy. At first, anyway. That night, with her home-coming looming ever closer, she'd flung herself against him as soon as the stateroom door was closed. She'd nuzzled his neck as he attacked the buttons of her dress, her skin prickling in anticipation of his touch. She hadn't cared how she looked or what she did, because Charlie was the man she loved, the person who knew her best in all the world. How could something that brought them both such joy be wrong?

Esme glanced at the gold pocket watch Charlie had placed on the nightstand: 11:43 p.m. They didn't have much time. She swept her fingertips across his lips. Charlie was elegantly attractive in his evening clothes, or when tipping his hat to ladies on the promenade deck. But the sight of him like this—cheeks flushed, his dark hair mussed, bare shoulders and chest peeking out from the sheets—made her nearly sick with longing. And it was more than simple physical attraction; Charlie was clever and witty, affectionate and kind. When he fixed his inquisi-tive eyes on Esme, it was because he wanted to truly know her, as no one else ever had.

Esme kissed Charlie's cheek, hoping to draw back his attention. He absentmindedly stroked her back. Even now, after all they'd done, he didn't take for granted that she was his; he always waited for Esme to signal when and where he could touch her. Esme pulled him toward her, and Charlie tucked the covers around their bodies, molding them together in a private cocoon. Esme knew she'd have to ask him eventu-ally about their future, about what they'd do when the *Titanic* docked in New York. But with Charlie's arms encasing her, and her heart racing, she could only kiss him, over and over, with frenetic pleasure.

The steady hum that had been a constant backdrop to the voyage suddenly stopped, leaving an eerie silence. Charlie froze.

"The engines are off."

He pulled away and sat up. Esme heard muffled voices in the hallway. A door opening.

"Maybe they're broken," Esme said. "And it will take days to repair them, and we'll have that many more evenings together. Sounds rather blissful, doesn't it?"

"Little goat," Charlie said affectionately. It was the nickname he'd given her the first time they kissed. "You don't want to go home, do you?"

Esme shook her head. Thinking of home, and what it meant, brought on an overpowering despair. She didn't trust herself to speak without crying.

Hurried footsteps thumped closer and gradually faded away. Someone else passed in the opposite direction, talking quickly. Esme thought she recognized the voice of Mr. Trumbell, the steward, though she couldn't make out what he was saying. Charlie slid out of bed and pulled on his drawers and undershirt.

"Do you think it's serious?" Esme asked.

"Of course not," Charlie said, but not in a reassuring way. "You'd better get dressed, too. With all this commotion, it's going to be harder to get to your room without being seen."

With Charlie's help, she managed to get herself halfway respectable. The evening gown she'd bought in Paris sparkled in the lamplight, but there wasn't time to arrange her hair properly, so she pulled it over one shoulder. Taking a diamond-and-velvet bracelet off her wrist, she tied it around her hair at the nape of her neck so it wouldn't hang loose. Then, after Charlie had peeked outside and declared the coast clear, Esme crept down the hall and up the stairs to her husband.

—

Esme had intended to be a good wife. It was the position she'd been raised and groomed for, her life's work. She'd never be the richest girl in Philadelphia society or the most beautiful. She didn't have the lustrous eyes and lashes of Faith Hodges, who sat languidly at parties while the boys swarmed around her. But Esme was pink-cheeked and vivacious, able to talk to anyone and make them feel flattered by her attention. Esme, everyone agreed, was fun; parties and outings turned brighter when she was there. Esme was conscientious in her duties: she sat through French lessons with the forbidding Madame Guilldot and learned to play piano well enough to entertain her father's friends after dinner. But she drifted from childhood to adulthood with very little education in the practical aspects of being a wife. Esme's mother, who had died when Esme was six, was nothing more than a faint memory of rustling skirts and medicinal smells. Esme grew up knowing how to manage a household, but not how to manage a marriage. She'd never seen a successful one up close.

Esme's social debut was followed by a delicious whirl of parties and ice-cream socials. Esme enjoyed herself thoroughly, but she never lost sight of her ultimate goal. Father's cryptic hints about difficulties at the factory made it clear that she'd best marry soon—and well. Within a few months, she'd settled on two likely prospects. Theodore Yates was the eldest son of a former mayor, part of a well-established political family. Cursed with a stammer, he'd never follow in his forefathers' footsteps, but Esme found his awkwardness endearing. Theo was always so grateful when she stopped to talk to him or when she kept the conversation going even though he stumbled over half his words. He was tall and skinny, and she'd heard a few of the girls jokingly call him the "Sc-sc-scarecrow." But Esme sensed he'd be fiercely loyal to a wife who accepted his deficiencies. As would his family.

Then there was John Moss. John was the life of every party, his laughter resonating above the din of conversation. John, like Esme, was fun. He banged out music on the piano to liven up stodgy luncheons, arranged picnics in the country—with silver flasks passed discreetly among the men—and once held a séance at which he swore he spoke to the spirit of his dead grandmother. John was the one who had pulled Esme behind a tree during an Easter egg hunt and kissed her, his hands firm against her waist. Afterward, he'd smiled and put his fingers to his lips, and the fact that he hadn't declared his love for her, or gone to her father to ask for her hand in marriage, should have made Esme upset. But she hadn't been. The knowledge of that secret kiss—hinted at later with winks and long looks but never discussed—only increased John's appeal. Though she was woefully uneducated on relations between men and women, she suspected John's forwardness should make her wary, that it wasn't a desirable quality in a husband. But she was tempted by the unpredictability of a future with him.

It was while she was veering between Theo and John—between Good and Fun—that Esme's father invited Mr. Harper to dinner. She'd spoken to him briefly at some affair or other, and she'd heard about his tragic past: the death of his wife and baby daughter after only a year of marriage, the devotion to their memory that kept him a widower. But it was unusual for Father to invite one of his professional acquaintances home for supper; he usually dined with them at his club. Father told Esme that Mr. Harper, president of Keystone National Bank, had approved a loan to Father's factory, and the meal was a gesture of thanks. Esme enthusiastically agreed to act as hostess. She put together the small guest list, planned the menu along with the family cook, and arranged the flowers on the table herself.

When Mr. Harper arrived, Esme was at the door to welcome him.

"How lovely to see you again," she said, smiling brightly. She was wearing the emerald-green gown that set off her eyes, and the effect seemed to dazzle Mr. Harper.

"Miss Sullivan," he said, with a formal bow.

"Come in, come in," she urged, waving for Nora, the maid, to take Mr. Harper's coat. "We're starting out in the front parlor, this way. Mr. and Mrs. Ayres are already here. We'll be a small party but an enjoyable one, I hope."

Mr. Harper looked as if he hadn't enjoyed himself since the last century. He offered Esme a wan smile, his cheek muscles straining with the effort. Esme felt sorry for him, in the general way she was sorry for anyone who'd suffered a tragedy, but she couldn't help being irritated, too. He could make a small effort, couldn't he? He might even be handsome, in a distinguished way, if his expression weren't so miserable and droopy. She'd seen statues with more spirit than Mr. Harper.

The thought made her smile.

"Am I amusing, Miss Sullivan?"

"Not at all," Esme said girlishly. She tilted her head sideways for a coquettish effect. "I have the terrible habit of smiling for no reason at all."

"A cheerful disposition is a rare gift," Mr. Harper said stiffly.

Esme waited for the next polite observation: *Your father tells me . . .* or, *When I was your age . . .* but Mr. Harper's mouth had reverted back to a half frown. Esme felt genuine pity for him then. How lonely he must be, if he could barely manage this much conversation!

Despite Mr. Harper's reserve, the dinner proceeded smoothly, thanks in large part to Mrs. Ayres, a chatterbox who never allowed a lull to linger. As they finished the dessert course, Father prompted Esme to play piano for their guests, an offer she modestly declined.

Father leaned toward Mr. Harper and observed, "We have to watch out with these modern girls, you know. They'd rather play ragtime than Chopin."

"I'm afraid I'm not familiar with modern music," Mr. Harper said.

"Take my Esme," he said, glancing at his daughter with a mischievous look. "I'd be the first to admit she's a flibbertigibbet, always chattering about dances and the latest fashions."

"Father!" Esme admonished, but only because she thought it was the right thing to do, not because she was truly offended.

"There are some who'd say I haven't been strict enough with her. But my proudest accomplishment is to have raised a happy daughter. She wasn't always so carefree. My wife's death was a trial for both of us. Mr. Harper, you know what it is to suffer the loss of a dear companion . . ."

Mr. Harper's face seemed to droop even further, his mustache sinking down over his frowning mouth. Esme looked at her father's empty sherry glass, and the empty decanter next to it, and wondered how much he'd had to drink.

"Esme was denied a mother's love and comfort, yet she has grown into a young woman of great spirit. She is the joy of my life, and one day, I hope, she will bring equal joy to her future husband."

Father looked meaningfully at Esme, and Esme glanced at Mr. Harper's wooden, self-conscious expression, and her face went hot. So this was why Mr. Harper had been invited to dine. She would have been furious at Father's machinations if it weren't for the guest of honor's obvious mortification. He was as much a victim as she was, a realization that softened her anger.

With practiced ease, Esme summoned an expression of amused nonchalance. "I have much to learn before I'm ready to marry. Mrs. Ayres, what do you believe are the ideal qualities in a wife?"

As she'd hoped, Mrs. Ayres went off on an extended discussion of duty and self-sacrifice, with the occasional nod or grunt from browbeaten Mr. Ayres. Esme would have very much liked to hear *his* thoughts on the matter, guessing he'd rank muteness above anything else, and she stifled a laugh. When she realized Mr. Harper had noticed her amusement and seemed perilously close to cracking a smile himself, she turned away, blushing. Afterward, the men turned to their port and cigars, and Esme retired to the sitting room with Mrs. Ayres. Her anger at Father's meddling had eased. He was concerned for her future, that was all, and now that she was nearly twenty, marriage was the next logical step. Tomorrow, she'd tell him about Theo and John, and he'd be thrilled to hear she had two prospective suitors. Together, they would work out which one was the best match.

"I was surprised to see Hiram here this evening," Mrs. Ayres said, settling next to Esme on the sofa. "He declines most invitations."

"I was just as surprised," Esme said. "I don't think I've said more than two words to him before."

"Be ready to say more than that!" Mrs. Ayres let out a braying laugh. "He was quite charmed by you."

"I don't see how. He looked miserable most of the evening."

"Oh, that's Hiram's natural state. You didn't see the way he stared at you, when your attention was elsewhere."

Esme looked down modestly, pretending to be embarrassed, but secretly she wanted to know everything about the way Hiram Harper looked at her.

"He's a good catch," Mrs. Ayres continued. "Huge house, very well off. Inherited everything when his father died a few years ago. He may seem a dour old man to you, but he was considered very handsome in his time. Just between us, I was quite smitten with him! That was before I met Mr. Ayres, of course."

Despite Mrs. Ayres's self-satisfied smile, Esme could see from the woman's eyes that a part of her would always see Mr. Harper as the beau he once was, when they were young.

"There's no understanding between me and Mr. Harper," Esme said. "I hardly know him."

"That'll change, if he has anything to do with it!" Mrs. Ayres teased. "Don't dismiss him out of hand. A girl could do far worse."

The fact that Mrs. Ayres had such high regard for Mr. Harper piqued Esme's interest, for she'd always found that there was nothing like another's admiration to stir up her own. When Mr. Harper sent a card the following day thanking Esme and her father for dinner and inviting Esme to his sister's for tea the following Saturday, she sent her acceptance the next morning and sprayed the notecard with a touch of her eau de cologne. Mr. Harper was formally polite during Esme's hour-long visit, not at all the kind of man she could imagine stealing a kiss behind a tree. But his sister seemed delighted to have Esme join them, and her children were charmingly affectionate with their uncle Hiram. The Harpers were such easy company, in fact, that Esme found herself agreeing to future plans—an evening at the theater, a lunch at the country house of his sister's in-laws—and the more time Esme spent with Mr. Harper, the less impressive her other prospects began to look.

Theo's nervous attempts at conversation, once so charming, had grown tiresome, and John's antics were those of an overgrown boy, not a man. Mr. Harper had no talent for or interest in romance, yet Esme found his steadiness increasingly appealing. Mr. Harper acted like a husband should act, with quiet confidence. He was careful with his money, and therefore he'd never want for anything. Wealth wasn't Esme's prime concern—she'd never have married someone she didn't like simply because he was rich—but she did want a secure future. As Mrs. Harper, she could take trips to New York and Europe. Buy the clothes she wanted without enduring a lecture. As a married woman, she could go to restaurants and order champagne and escape the stultifying rules of her father's house.

So when Mr. Harper invited Esme for a ride in his new Ford—and her father said she could go, unaccompanied—she knew what it meant. She pulled on her traveling coat and pinned her largest hat into her swept-up hair, artfully arranging a swath of netting so it protected her face from the dust while perfectly framing her eyes. Mr. Harper escorted her into the car and began an earnest description of the motor and how it worked and why it was better than a certain other motor—very little of which she understood. As they drove, Esme did her best to look fascinated, but her natural pleasantness was tested by Mr. Harper's avoidance of the only subject that mattered. Had she been mistaken? Would he be eternally faithful to his dead wife?

At last, Mr. Harper pulled over by a park. They were in a part of town Esme wasn't familiar with, a quiet, residential area that looked nearly deserted in the early November afternoon. They were alone.

"Miss Sullivan, I must speak to you on a matter of great importance."

Esme's heart pounded, but she kept her expression calm. *Act surprised,* she told herself.

"I have grown quite fond of you." Mr. Harper said the words in a rushed monotone; he might have been addressing a meeting of his bank managers. "For many years, I have been quite content in my solitude, but I have recently contemplated a change in my circumstances."

Esme fought back a giggle. This was a far cry from the passionate declaration of love she'd always imagined. John Moss would be down on his knees by now, summoning up dramatic tears. But she found she didn't mind Mr. Harper's stiff delivery. It felt honest and true.

"I have very little hope that a young woman of your charms would consider me an ideal husband. I do promise my complete dedication to your well-being, if you would but consider my offer . . ."

"What offer?" Esme asked, feigning confusion.

"I—er, that is to say, it would give me the greatest honor . . ."

"Are you asking me to marry you?"

Mr. Harper's surprise at her bluntness gave way to relief that she'd said it. "I am. In the most bumbling way possible."

Esme looked at Mr. Harper, her prospective bridegroom, a man she'd never addressed by his given name. She saw the streaks of gray in the hair above his ears, the creases in the skin beneath his wary eyes. All his features had a mournful cast, from the natural downturn of his mouth to the slight stoop in his shoulders. She found herself wanting above all else to make him happy.

"Of course I will," she said simply. And the delight that brightened his face silenced any lingering doubts.

"You have made me the happiest of men," he said.

"Silly thing, don't you know you're supposed to kiss me?"

Esme leaned forward and offered up her lips; Mr. Harper hesitated a moment, then pressed his mouth against her cheek. The kind of peck her father used to give her at bedtime. Esme laughed, and Mr. Harper looked at her in bewildered delight.

"I suppose I can call you Hiram now." She sounded it out again with deliberate emphasis. "Hiram. A very upstanding name."

"Esme." The sound of it seemed to almost overwhelm him. "Esme, my dear girl."

It was the same endearment her father used, which made her want to laugh again, but she repressed her amusement. His hand wrapped around hers, and she shifted her body closer, until she was pressed up against the solid mass of his hip and leg.

"When we're married, will you let me drive the motorcar?" she asked.

He looked baffled by the thought of a woman at the wheel, and she squeezed his fingers to show she was teasing. The momentousness of what had just happened made her giddy, and she wished they weren't in such an isolated spot. She wanted to spread the news like a town crier: *I'm going to marry Hiram Harper and live happily ever after!*

⌒⌒

Esme never expected the regrets to come so soon. Her two-month engagement was a blur of parties and congratulatory hugs, and Esme thrived at the center of the storm. She showed Hiram off like a piece of new jewelry, calling him an "old dear" and "the sweetest man." She could tell her friends were surprised someone like her had settled on someone like him, but Father's contemporaries—who'd experienced twists and turns of fortune—were enthusiastic about a match that combined youthful enthusiasm with practical business sense.

"She's always been headstrong," Esme heard Father confide to a friend one night over glasses of whiskey. "It'll do her good to have a husband who knows what he's about. She'll keep him on his toes, too, eh?"

Over one of many celebratory suppers, Mrs. Ayres told Esme she couldn't be more pleased. "Hiram's been alone too long," she said. "I've been telling him that for years."

Esme fought back the temptation to joke that Hiram proposed solely to avoid another of Mrs. Ayres's lectures. Better to smile sweetly and endure Mrs. Ayres's advice on the social obligations of a new bride. Esme listened half-heartedly, confident that it wouldn't take much effort to make a success of her marriage. As long as she kept Hiram happy, she could do as she pleased.

Hiram and Esme had a Christmas wedding, with garlands of holly hung on the church pews and a service that ended with "Joy to the World." They'd booked a delayed honeymoon in Europe, not wanting to make the Atlantic crossing in winter, so their first days as man and wife were spent at the Ayres's weekend house in Bucks County. There'd be a housekeeper to see to their meals, but otherwise they'd be alone to "get acquainted," as Mrs. Ayres put it. Esme was a touch apprehensive about the exact ways they'd be getting acquainted, and Mrs. Ayres had been uncharacteristically perceptive of Esme's concerns.

"There's nothing to fear," she said. "Be grateful you're marrying a man of experience. Two young newlyweds with no knowledge of such intimacies have a much more fraught time of it."

For one mortifying instant, Esme thought Mrs. Ayres was about to describe her own wedding night. Fortunately, the woman was more interested in pontificating than reminiscing.

"Do what Hiram tells you, and cheerfully. He admires your vivacity, you know."

"I've wondered . . ." Esme hadn't planned on revealing her deepest fear, but Mrs. Ayres was the only person who might set it to rest. "If Mr. Harper will find it difficult. Our relations as man and wife may provoke memories of the first Mrs. Harper."

"Don't be silly!" Mrs. Ayres admonished. "Nellie was a sweet little thing, but so shy she could barely put two sentences together! You're much better for Hiram."

Esme had often wondered about Hiram's first wife, whom he never spoke of, and she took a selfish satisfaction in knowing the woman had been a bore. After a vague description of what actually happened in a marital bed, Mrs. Ayres assured Esme that having an older husband was an advantage in this instance, for he'd insist on his rights far less often than a man her own age. That, Mrs. Ayres implied, was a blessing.

In any event, Esme was so tired by her wedding night that she couldn't work up the energy to be nervous. The housekeeper served broiled fish and potatoes on trays in the upstairs parlor before unpacking Esme's trunk in the bedroom next door. Esme's trousseau was a profusion of silk and satin; Hiram had insisted on paying for it and promised even more additions to her wardrobe when they went to Paris in the spring.

Esme wasn't sure how the rest of the evening was supposed to proceed. Should she disappear into the dressing room and make a dramatic entrance in her feather-trimmed robe? She remembered Mrs. Ayres's advice and decided not to do anything until Hiram told her to. When he said he liked to read before going to bed, she flipped through the latest issue of *McCall's* until he said it was time they turned in.

"Shall I help you with your dress?" Hiram asked, after Esme had followed him to the bedroom.

Esme's going-away dress had a trail of pearl buttons down the back; she couldn't take it off herself. She'd assumed the housekeeper would assist her, as her housemaid Nora did at home.

"Oh, yes," Esme said. "Thank you."

She'd thought it would be embarrassing to get undressed in front of Hiram, but it turned out to be surprisingly easy. He was familiar with women's clothes; he knew what attached where and how to unfasten each piece. It wasn't long before Esme was down to only her gauzy chemise and stockings.

"You're very beautiful," Hiram said. Not overwhelmed, not rapturous, but straightforwardly acknowledging a fact of nature.

The usual blushes and protests Esme produced whenever she was complimented seemed inappropriate, so she only smiled. Hiram removed his jacket, trousers, and shirt, methodically placing each piece over the back of an armchair before taking off the next. Esme rolled down her stockings, dragging out the process to keep herself occupied.

Despite the well-caught fire, the bedroom was still chilly, and Esme shivered as she slid beneath the covers. It felt surprisingly natural for Hiram to huddle next to her, his hands soothingly warm on her goose-bumped skin. Hiram was a presence rather than a person, his face shadowed and his body concealed by the quilted bedspread. When he straddled her and began to push, she gasped, not in pain but perplexed surprise. So *this* was what it felt like?

Hiram stopped. "Did I hurt you?"

"Oh, no," Esme murmured, as she'd reassure a dance partner who stepped on her toes. "It's only a rather . . . peculiar sensation."

Esme sensed rather than saw Hiram's smile. "It will grow less peculiar in time, I hope."

Esme reached for his forehead and gave it a kiss. "You may proceed, sir. I'll be quiet as a mouse."

"Please don't," Hiram whispered, and then he finished what he'd started. When Esme giggled, he didn't seem to mind.

As Mrs. Ayres had promised, Esme and Hiram returned to Philadelphia much better acquainted. Esme was delighted to discover that her new husband was nothing like her father with his unpredictable moods and constant fretting over money. Hiram was generous and calm and already seemed to be shaking off some of his natural gloom, though she was a tad perturbed by his ability to eat meals with almost no conversation. She loved Hiram's enormous house and the enormous bed they shared in their enormous bedroom, but after so long on his own, he was set in his ways, and Esme was expected to adapt to his preferences.

The biggest shock came when she emerged from newlywed seclusion to rejoin society. As Mrs. Hiram Harper, Esme was expected to be modest and discreet: no more wicked laughter with her friends at parties; no more dances with unmarried men. With every dull pleasantry exchanged at staid dinners and morning teas, Esme's natural exuberance shriveled. When she mingled at the engagement party for Theo Yates, who'd managed to charm an Ohio heiress, Esme faced a dilemma completely new to her: for the first time, she could think of nothing interesting to say. Once she had children, she supposed, she'd be one of those women who talked about nothing else. She was already older than friends who'd started families, but Esme wasn't quite ready to retreat into motherhood. Not yet.

"Your mother tells me you're off to New York for your honeymoon," Esme said to Theo and his future bride, as if she'd never heard such thrilling news. Theo, to Esme's satisfaction, barely paid attention to the woman at his side. It was gratifying to know Esme could still capture his attention when she wanted to.

"We're staying at the Waldorf Astoria," Theo's fiancée said. "I've heard it's very grand."

"I'm sure you'll have a lovely time," Esme said. "Hiram and I will be in New York soon, too. We're sailing for France in March."

Theo nodded his approval. "W-w-w-wonderful. What a jolly time you'll have."

"I will do my best to make Mr. Harper jolly, but it won't be an easy task."

They all laughed, and if Esme felt a twinge of disloyalty at making fun of Hiram, it was worth it. Basking in Theo's admiration, she described her future travels with an enthusiasm she hadn't felt for ages. She and Hiram *would* have a jolly time. They had introductions to well-connected families in Paris and London, and she'd be coming home with a trunk full of brand-new French fashions. With enough good food and wine, Hiram's restraint might ease, and she'd be able to enjoy herself. As Esme looked at Theo's face, his mouth slack like a child's, she knew she'd made the right choice. She couldn't imagine Theo guiding her through Europe, ordering porters and shop assistants around with Hiram's dignified poise. She'd been right to marry Hiram, and if the realities of marriage had knocked her off balance, the honeymoon would set things right.

Instead, it would end her marriage.

After a short excursion to Biarritz, Esme and Hiram spent the second half of March in Paris. Hiram didn't blanch at the bills for gowns and shoes that arrived at their room in the Ritz, and he soon gave Esme an even more valuable gift. Sabine, a maid at the hotel, had been helping Esme with her hair in the evenings, and Esme had been charmed by the girl's cautious smiles and tidy precision. Within a few days, they'd developed a conspiratorial rapport, with Esme trying to explain what she wanted in broken French, and Sabine responding in equally atrocious English. When Hiram walked in on them laughing one evening, he asked Sabine if she'd ever traveled outside of France.

"Non, monsieur," she replied. "I would like, one day."

"Any interest in seeing America? My wife is in need of a lady's maid."

Sabine looked shocked but pleased, and Esme felt like a little girl whose father had surprised her with a pony for Christmas. Her own maid, and a French one, at that! Hiram consulted the hotel's manager, who summoned Sabine's father, and they all met in the manager's office a few days later. Holding a shabby hat, looking ill at ease beside the elegantly polished manager, Sabine's father said her family was grateful for the offer but needed some time to consider it. Hiram explained exactly how generous he was prepared to be, and when the manager translated the amount Hiram was offering, Esme immediately recognized the expression on Sabine's father's face. It was the same one she'd seen on her own father, on the rare occasions the factory showed a profit. It was soon agreed Sabine would join the Harpers when they departed for London a week later.

Sabine's sweet yet deferential presence was a boost to Esme's confidence, but her new companion couldn't make up for her steadily increasing frustration. All the shopping and sightseeing only underscored how little Hiram and Esme had in common. Esme loved music and chatty gatherings; Hiram was most content reading alone. In Philadelphia, he'd escorted her to events because it was his duty to mingle with their social circle. In Europe, he felt no such obligation.

"Tea with the Deauvilles? I hardly know them."

"That's the point, darling. We're having tea in order to get to know them better."

"Isn't that best left to you women? No need to force the husbands into it."

Esme began attending events alone, defiantly, until she realized Hiram didn't object because he didn't care. Sometimes, he wouldn't even glance up from his book when she came back to their room. It wasn't until she started talking that he'd lift his head with a distracted "Hmm?" It was a sound she came to loathe.

In London, Esme found she wasn't the only wife who socialized without her husband. Some of the women she met were outspoken suffragettes who believed they should be able to do whatever they wanted, the law be damned. It was an attitude Esme privately admired but would never have announced in public; she was content on the fringes of notoriety rather than at its center. And one of the most satisfying ways to be daring was to flirt outrageously with other men.

Charlie Van Hausen seemed crafted for that very purpose. Fresh out of Harvard, son of a financier father and socialite mother who knew all the right people on both sides of the Atlantic, he had the airy confidence of a privileged Boston upbringing. A more sophisticated version of John Moss, Esme thought, out to enjoy himself above all else. The kind of boy she might have fallen for, before she was married, and who would have most certainly broken her heart.

They chatted over dinner at Lord Riverton's Belgravia mansion, then crossed paths again at a concert hosted by the American ambassador. Esme had overdressed in a wool dress and thick stockings and began to feel faint in the crowded, stuffy room. She whispered to Hiram that she needed some air, and he nodded without looking at her. Esme slipped out of the reception hall into a circular waiting room, where she felt slightly better but still light-headed. She asked a passing footman for directions outside, and he pointed her to the back terrace.

The night was cool but sticky, the damp air preparing to solidify into rain. The terrace overlooked a formal garden, with a cherub-topped fountain forming the centerpiece of neatly trimmed hedgerows. Esme wondered half-heartedly if she should install a fountain in the garden at home. She had no real interest in landscaping, but she'd have to find some way to fill her days.

"Do you mind?"

Esme turned and saw Charlie behind her, a cigarette tucked between his index and middle fingers. She shook her head, and he pulled a matchbox from his jacket pocket. He lit a match, the flame illuminating his face. Close up, Charlie looked less boyish, with his dark, solemn eyes and enigmatic half smile. He sucked in deeply and then exhaled, turning his head to blow the smoke away from Esme.

"Would you like one?" he asked casually, as if passing the salt at dinner.

Esme laughed in surprise. "Do you know many girls who smoke?"

"You're hardly a girl, are you? You're a married woman."

Esme should have been offended. He was being shockingly overfamiliar, given their slight acquaintance. But she wasn't at all upset. The way he was looking at her—daring her to enjoy herself—took her back to those debutante days in Philadelphia, when she was the focus around which every party swirled.

"Do you know many married ladies who smoke?" she asked.

"A few," he said. Again, he brought the cigarette to his lips. Slowly, he drew the smoke in and out, showing her how to do it. "But they don't tell their husbands."

Esme wondered if it wasn't coincidence that brought him outside. Had Charlie seen her leave and followed her? She liked the thought of being pursued.

"All right, then," Esme said decisively. "I'll try."

She had never understood how men could breathe in smoke, and the process was as unpleasant as she'd imagined. But Esme very much enjoyed the ritual surrounding it. She liked the way Charlie grinned when he handed her a cigarette and demonstrated how to hold it. The way she had to lean in when he held out the match. The gestures lured them together, and when Esme winced and coughed, Charlie took the cigarette from her fingers and finished it himself. She looked at his lips, pressing down where hers had been only seconds before. The silence between them wasn't empty, as it was with Hiram. There was almost too much Esme wanted to tell Charlie, but she didn't know how to start.

The distant sound of applause carried out from the residence.

"Your first cigarette," Charlie said, raising the stubbed end in the gesture of a toast. "Congratulations."

"Two puffs," Esme said. "I don't know if that counts."

"You can have it both ways," he said. "You can say, in all truth, that you've never smoked a cigarette, because you didn't finish. But if you ever want to shock your society friends, you can say you have."

Charlie had hit upon the very conundrum that tortured Esme every day: Would she be the respectable, dull wife that Hiram expected, or the risqué wife who embarrassed him?

"Better not to say anything at all," Esme said.

"It'll be our secret."

As Charlie looked at her, it felt like they'd agreed to something, but she wasn't sure what. Esme nodded briskly and turned; she didn't want to be seen walking in with him. Concertgoers were already milling in the hallway. As Esme looked for Hiram, she also kept a discreet eye on Charlie, making sure she knew where he was, even after she was back at her husband's side. When Hiram said he was ready to leave, Charlie was across the room, so she didn't have a chance to say goodbye. But that didn't matter. She was quite certain she'd see him again.

And she was right. Charlie belonged to a set of rich young Americans who thought nothing of sailing off to Europe on a whim, steamships and railways enabling their twentieth-century version of a grand tour. They were always in motion, to the theater or day trips in the countryside, and invitations to these excursions began arriving at Esme's hotel. Hiram, busy setting up a partnership with a British bank, encouraged Esme to go without him. It was all aboveboard: Esme and Charlie were never alone together, and she made sure he wasn't the only object of her flirtatious remarks. Somewhere along the way she started calling him Charlie, but he never addressed Esme as anything but Mrs. Harper.

A week before Esme was due to sail home, she and Hiram were invited to a house party at the country home of Lady Tiddle, née Sarah Neuberger, a distant cousin of Charlie's who'd bagged herself an English aristocrat in the Gilded Age era of transatlantic marriages. Esme begged Hiram to go, but he had no interest. He had nothing in common with her new friends and thought they were a bad influence. Furious, Esme told him she'd go anyway, though it meant they'd be apart for three days. Later, she would tell herself that what happened that weekend was Hiram's fault, that she wouldn't have looked elsewhere for comfort if she hadn't felt so lonely. Or was that just what she told herself to justify her actions? Esme had been both admonished and spoiled all her life, told to act a certain way but never punished when she didn't. She was ripe for corruption.

Over tea on the afternoon they arrived, Esme and Charlie talked companionably, like old friends. She couldn't help comparing him to Hiram, who spoke to every woman—including her—with the same aloof politeness. Charlie's attention shone on Esme like a spotlight; he remembered comments she'd mentioned in passing and noticed when she tried out a new hairstyle. And the more interest Charlie showed in Esme, the more interesting she found him.

The next day, all the men but Charlie went shooting.

"I'm a terrible shot," he said bluntly. "I'll stay warm and dry indoors, thank you very much."

The other female guests flitted around him like butterflies drawn to a rare, exotic flower. Charlie enjoyed the attention, entertaining them with stories of his pranks at Harvard, some of which Esme suspected were exaggerated for effect. Charlie caught her eye, acknowledging her doubts, and she took a triumphant pride in being able to understand him with a single look. After luncheon, Lady Tiddle led a tour of the home farm. They spoke to the estate manager for a few minutes, then went to admire the animals. Most of the ladies gathered at the henhouse to coo over a batch of newborn chicks, but Esme saw Charlie leaning over the side of a pen, alone. She walked over and saw he was watching a scrawny young goat, struggling to walk on spindly legs.

"Poor thing," Esme said. "Look at him, trying so hard."

"He reminds me of you."

Esme's chest tightened in hurt surprise. Before she could respond, Charlie was apologizing, looking genuinely repentant. Whatever he'd meant about the goat, it had slipped out unthinkingly, from the heart. Which made her all the more curious to know what he meant.

"I was watching this fellow," Charlie said, "and he looks so fragile, like he's going to topple over any minute, but he keeps on going. And you don't look anything like a goat. You're so much prettier"—a compliment Esme would remember and savor later—"but you have that same expression sometimes, when you think no one's looking. Putting on a brave face, so no one sees how much you struggle."

The observation was so unexpected, so true, that Esme didn't know what to say. She stared at the goat and its trembling hooves. Saw herself laughing gaily at parties, while her stomach sank with dread at the thought of returning to the hotel and Hiram. She heard the other women's voices and the clatter of their footsteps on the gravel path as they headed toward the barn. She and Charlie should join them. She would, very soon.

Not looking at Charlie made it easier to talk. "You're right. I feel quite lost sometimes."

"You'll find your footing soon enough," he said quietly. "Just like our young friend here. It's myself I'm not sure about."

"Yourself?" Esme asked. Charlie wore his confidence lightly, never boastful but accepting attention and praise as his natural due. "I shouldn't think you have a thing to worry about."

"Oh, my path's perfectly clear," he said, and she knew him well enough by then to catch the resignation in his jaunty tone. "Join the firm with Father, marry a woman picked out by my mother, give my life over to making money, and with any luck, I'll spend the next fifty years smoking cigars at my club and shaking my head at the state of the world."

"It sounds like a very bright future."

"Not to me."

Esme felt an invisible barrier dissolve. He'd shared this confidence because he trusted her. She suddenly felt ages older. Charlie was young enough to still have choices, unlike her.

"What would you do, if you could?" she asked gently. Esme could picture a thousand futures for Charlie. An explorer in a South American jungle. A bohemian artist sketching in a Parisian café.

"That's the problem, I'm afraid. I don't have the slightest idea."

There was no easy answer to that. Esme was about to suggest they join the others—it seemed the most gracious way to end the conversation and save him further embarrassment—when it began to rain. The downpour was immediate and intense, pummeling them with raindrops sharp as splinters. Esme saw the other women dashing into the barn, a good quarter mile away. Then she felt Charlie's hand on her upper arm as he pulled her into a nearby shed.

The rain beat down on the roof in a pulsing staccato, and drops of water slipped through the boards onto Charlie's hair and Esme's hat. Tools and farm equipment were stacked against the walls and piled on shelves, and there was a lingering odor of mud and rust. The wind had whipped up along with the storm, and Charlie slammed the door shut to stop the water blowing inside. As soon as they were alone, in that tight, hushed space, Esme thought of John and the tree and the secret kiss. Charlie was watching her the same way John had watched her, with a tentative smile. But this time, Esme was the one who stepped forward first, and she was the one who slid her hands around Charlie's waist.

The first kiss was hesitant, a tremor before the earthquake. His lips asked a question—*Are you sure?*—and she answered. *Yes.* Esme had never known kisses could summon such urges. Desire passed with a shudder through her chest and stomach, and she wrapped herself around Charlie to bring her pounding heart closer to his. When Charlie's lips moved along her neck and the base of her throat, they left a trail of heat on her skin. She felt reckless and possessed, thrilled by her own daring.

Charlie was the first to pull away, exhaling in a half laugh, half gasp. "My God."

His eyes looked unfocused and wild, and Esme could see he was shaken by what they'd done. Uncertainty weakened her—was he angry?—but such worries were quickly cast aside when he reached up and gently pulled off her hat.

"It's soaking," he said, tossing it next to a pile of metal buckets.

"So is your hair."

Esme smoothed it back from his forehead, and she could tell he was forcing himself to keep still and maintain his self-possession. She placed her hands on his cheeks and waited. Slowly, almost reluctantly, he wrapped his arms around her back and leaned into her.

"Esme." He lingered over the name, seeming to savor it. "What a marvel you are."

"A marvelous goat." She tilted her head and smiled to show she was teasing, and he tapped her nose with one finger.

"I should never have said that. You're a lamb." He brushed his lips across her forehead. "Soft and sweet."

Esme rose to her toes so their mouths could meet. She wanted to hear him talk like this, gentle and confiding, but she also wanted to kiss him, over and over and over.

"I don't mind," she whispered between caresses. "That goat's rather darling."

"My little goat," Charlie murmured, and laughter rippled through them like a cleansing force, washing away their hesitation. If love could bloom in a shabby shed, it must be real.

Or so Esme told herself later in the dining room, when she could barely stand to look at Charlie with the memory of his kisses so fresh. The rest of the visit was torture. They managed a few rushed conversations, in the upstairs corridors and while walking the grounds, but it was impossible to find time alone. She had to sit with him at cards, at meals, on the train back to London, laughing gaily as she fought the urge to touch him. Two days before she was due to sail home, Charlie sent a note to her hotel that he'd hired a car for the afternoon, if she could find an excuse to join him. Esme concocted a story about a picnic, knowing Hiram disapproved of meals being eaten anywhere but a table. Strangely, she felt more guilty lying to Hiram than she did kissing Charlie. What she and Charlie had done in the shed was secret, unseen. The story she told Hiram was a more direct betrayal. He trusted her so completely—or cared so little?—that he didn't even ask where she was going or when she'd be back.

Charlie drove with youthful recklessness, pushing the car as fast as it would go, shouting people out of the way with such cheerful enthusiasm that he received laughs instead of scowls. He'd ordered a hamper of food from his hotel, and they ate on the grounds of an Elizabethan manor outside of the city. Afterward, venturing into a copse of trees, they kissed and tittered as Charlie's hands wandered over the curves of Esme's legs. He'd taken off his jacket, and she could feel his shoulder muscles clench when he held her. In Charlie's embrace, she felt more at ease than she ever had in the silent house she shared with Hiram.

How could she ever go back?

In a week, she'd be in Philadelphia, and Charlie would return to Boston not long after. It was closer than London, but not nearly close enough. Esme had no relatives or friends in Boston; she had no excuse to visit. Before long, Charlie's mother would have her way, and Charlie would be married, cut off from Esme forever. She could have cried with frustration. Why had she and Charlie only discovered each other now, when they had so little time together? It didn't occur to her until much later that she had dared to kiss Charlie precisely because he was a relative stranger, in a foreign country. Separate from her real life, and therefore safe.

Impulsively, Esme said, "Come with us."

Charlie looked perplexed. "To Philadelphia?"

"To New York. We're booked on the *Titanic*—no one will think twice if you change your plans because you want to sail on the new ship. You're due back in a few weeks anyway, aren't you?"

"Are you that fond of me?" he asked. His voice had shifted from its usual joking tone.

"You fool. I'm desperately in love with you."

Esme meant to laugh, to lighten the weight of what she'd said. Instead, she had to scrunch up her face to keep in the tears. Only Charlie's gentle kisses could convince her to open them, and then they didn't speak for a long time.

Esme had intended to be good. She thought she'd be satisfied with a few kisses on a deserted deck at night; she pictured a bittersweet yet decisive goodbye. But Charlie was like a sickness to which he was the only cure, infecting her until she was listless with anyone but him. The first night aboard, when Hiram said he was ready to retire at nine o'clock, Esme told him she'd made plans to play bridge in the Café Parisien. The lie slipped out so easily that she didn't feel even a twinge of guilt. On her way out, she stopped in the adjoining maid's room and told Sabine she'd be visiting a friend in stateroom 34, down the stairs on C deck.

"If my husband wakes up, come fetch me," Esme said.

"Yes, madame." If Sabine suspected what Esme was up to, she was clever enough—and loyal enough—not to let on.

And so, that first night, Esme snuck to Charlie's stateroom, terrified she'd pass someone she knew. But she didn't—proof, perhaps, that her escapade was meant to be. Charlie opened the door as soon as Esme knocked, and she reassured him by hiding her own nervousness. She turned off the light, and the darkness made it easier for them to move from kisses to touches to clothes strewn across the floor. Despite uncomfortable thoughts of Hiram that lurked in the background of her consciousness, Esme didn't believe what she was doing was wrong, because her senses responded to Charlie in a way they never had to Hiram. This was the man she should have married, her body told her. The man she was meant to be with forever.

Esme came to Charlie the next three nights, confiding thoughts in the dark she'd never revealed to anyone else. The nighttime hours passed dizzyingly fast; the daytime hours were misery. Esme made polite conversation with Charlie when they passed on the deck, as she would with any other acquaintance. But it seemed half of Philadelphia society had booked passage on the *Titanic*, and Hiram insisted they dine with the Thayers and the Wideners, well-connected couples who would further his career. Beneath her cheerful smiles, Esme wanted to scream. She'd be seeing these same people at dinners for the next thirty years; why couldn't she spend these hours with the man who meant more to her than anyone else? She and Charlie tried to arrange meetings when they could, but there were always other people nearby, potential eavesdroppers who would notice any untoward behavior.

Once, they managed to sneak a few touches in the library, as Charlie pretended to recommend a book and intertwined his fingers with Esme's when he passed it to her. She shifted closer, until her hips pressed against his legs, dizzy with the urge to kiss him. From the corner of her eye, Esme noticed an old woman leaning forward in her chair, watching them. Esme leisurely stepped backward, not wanting to look suspicious by moving too fast.

Charlie whispered "Later" to Esme, and walked away, giving the curious woman a bright smile as he passed.

"On your honeymoon, are you?" the woman asked.

"How did you know?"

"Oh, I can always tell. You look so happy together."

Esme couldn't help smirking. She was on her honeymoon, and she was happier than she'd ever been—with a man who wasn't her husband.

"Aren't you kind," she told the woman. And she decided to wring every drop of happiness she could from these last days, without regret.

That Sunday night, after the engines had stopped, Esme snuck into her cabin to find Hiram gone. It was the first time he hadn't been in bed, asleep, when she returned. Esme knocked on the door to Sabine's room, then opened it when there was no response. Her maid had dozed off in bed, still dressed.

"Sabine," Esme whispered. "Where's Mr. Harper?"

Sabine blinked her eyes open and sat up, disoriented. "Madame?"

"Mr. Harper. He's not here. Did he go out?"

Sabine shrugged. "I am sorry . . ."

"Never mind."

Esme closed the door and returned to the stateroom. Hiram's book was on the nightstand, but his bathrobe was missing from the hook on the back of the door. She went out to the hall, where she heard voices and footsteps on the stairways, noises all the more prominent in the unusual silence of the ship.

Esme walked down to the reception room at the foot of the Grand Staircase, where knots of people had gathered. Hiram was talking to one of the dining-room stewards, looking like an eccentric grandfather in his robe and slippers, and Esme felt the urge to turn away before he noticed her. How could she be chained to such an old fussbudget for the rest of her life?

Hiram caught sight of Esme and waved.

"Where have you been?" he asked, rushing toward her. "You said you'd be in the café."

Esme dodged the question. "What's going on?"

"We seem to have scraped past an iceberg."

For the rest of her life, Esme would cringe when she remembered the relief that swept through her. In that moment, she was thrilled the ship had run into trouble, because it would distract Hiram from wondering where she'd been.

"Scraped?" Esme asked.

"There's a man in the smoking room who grabbed a piece of ice for his drink."

"The ship's all right, though?"

"I expect the captain's checking her over. He's an old hand at Atlantic crossings—he'll have it worked out soon enough."

Esme glanced at the groups lingering around them, men and women in a full range of dress, from formal gowns to pajamas and shawls. Charlie wasn't there. A man wearing a dark-blue officer's uniform walked halfway up the stairs to address the room.

"Ladies and gentlemen, Captain Smith has ordered all passengers to put on their life belts." As voices rose with questions, he insisted, "Only a precaution, I assure you."

"What's going on?" demanded a stern older gentleman. Some captain of industry Esme had been introduced to, though she couldn't remember his name.

The officer repeated stiffly, "All passengers are to retrieve their life belts and report to the boat deck."

The announcement caused a flutter of reaction, more of complaint than concern. Esme followed Hiram back to their stateroom, where he secured Esme's life belt before putting on his own. He rapped on Sabine's door and told her to put one on as well.

"Wait for me in the lounge," Hiram told Esme. "No sense standing outside in the cold until we know what's what."

"Where are you going?"

"Back to the smoking room. See if anyone's heard more news." He handed Esme the fur coat he'd bought for her at Harrods. "Take this with you."

The lounge was half full, and Esme strolled across the room, looking discreetly for Charlie. Acquaintances greeted her with smiles and tips of the head. It was all very polite, like a formal reception, with everyone making an effort to appear unruffled.

An officer appeared in the doorway. "All women and children to the boat deck. We are loading the lifeboats."

The curt order shattered the room's calm. The disparate groups of people melded into a single mass as they followed the officer up the stairs that led outside, their voices ringing out in sharp bursts.

"What does he mean?"

"What's happened?"

"I'm not going anywhere without my husband."

But Esme stayed put. She had to find Charlie. They might not be able to converse in private, but just seeing him, in the midst of all this confusion, would steady her. Motioning Sabine to hurry, she looked upstairs in the Palm Court and smoking room, then hurried up to the gymnasium, where two men were riding the stationary bicycles with forced enthusiasm. A long-faced man—Mr. Astor?—was sitting with his wife; he'd cut open a life belt and was showing her the cork inside. Esme walked out to the boat deck, bracing herself against the cold. In the distance, two levels down, she saw figures shuffling across the outdoor space reserved for third-class passengers. A few were throwing something back and forth, and Esme realized it was a piece of ice. There were chunks of it littering the deck. A girl whose kerchief barely covered her tumbling red hair shrieked at one of the men, who shouted back, and they both erupted into cawing laughter. All very juvenile, but Esme couldn't help thinking it also looked like fun.

"Esme!"

Charlie ran up to Esme, panting and flushed, his lopsided hat covering one eye. The sight of him dissolved the worry she hadn't even realized she'd been carrying, leaving her wobbly with relief.

"Are you all right?" Charlie asked. He was standing so close, his breath warmed her frosty cheek.

Esme nodded. Charlie was here. It would be all right.

"I'll take you to a lifeboat." Charlie's hand moved out involuntarily, but he stopped it just before touching her arm.

"I don't want to go," Esme said, knowing she sounded like a sulky child, needing Charlie to convince her.

"You must," he insisted. "I heard we're taking in water below."

"Aren't there compartments that keep it out?" There'd been a discussion of the ship's construction earlier that night, when she and Hiram had dined with Captain Smith, but Esme had ignored most of it. She'd been too busy trying to catch Charlie's eye across the dining room.

"Oh, we'll stay afloat for a while," Charlie said. "They've sent out wireless messages, and other ships are on the way. But I'd feel better if you were in a lifeboat. Just in case."

The exchange had an unreal quality, as if they were reciting a melodramatic scene between a dashing hero and his reluctant damsel in distress. Esme still didn't believe the ship was in serious danger. She felt a gentle tap on her shoulder and turned to see Sabine pointing at an approaching man. Esme was dismayed to see it was Hiram.

"There you are!" he chided Esme. "I couldn't find you."

He'd changed into his brown wool suit and overcoat, making him look more presentable than he'd been earlier. But he'd worked himself into a very un-Hiram-like state of agitation. The muscles of his face were drawn tight, and when he locked his arm with Esme's at the elbow, the force was so strong that she momentarily stumbled back.

"You were supposed to wait in the lounge," he snapped.

"I wanted to see what was going on," Esme said. How like Hiram, to expect her to be as rigid and self-disciplined as he was.

Hiram gave Charlie a brief nod. "Mr. Van Hausen, thank you for looking after my wife."

It was all too absurd: Hiram thanking the man who was cuckolding him. Esme let out a nervous, inappropriate laugh.

"I was about to escort Mrs. Harper to a lifeboat," Charlie said easily, as if he had nothing to hide.

The deck was already less crowded than when Esme had first walked out. A few seamen were working the davits that held the lifeboat nearest them, the last one left on deck. A semicircle of passengers stood watching, curious onlookers taking in the show.

"It's an awfully long way down," Esme murmured.

"You'll be perfectly safe," Charlie reassured her. "We'll all have a laugh about it when we arrive in New York. I'll arrange a dinner at Delmonico's."

Hiram pushed Esme forward.

"Go!" he snapped, and Esme stared at him in exaggerated shock. He'd never raised his voice to her, ever.

"What's the rush?" she protested. "Charlie says we'll be rescued."

"One of the officers told me the *Olympic* is coming," Charlie explained.

"The *Olympic* is five hundred miles away." Hiram's words had the brusque frustration of a parent disciplining his wayward children. "Things are much worse than you think."

He reached into his jacket and pulled out a fountain pen. Leaning down, he placed the pen on the deck, and Esme watched it roll steadily away from them.

"We're sinking," Hiram said. "I have it directly from the purser. We have a few hours, at most. Probably less."

As if to punctuate the warning, an explosion of green light erupted above them. Esme wondered who would set off fireworks at a time like this. She saw Charlie's face, lit with a ghoulish glow, his mouth falling slack with understanding.

"Distress rockets," he muttered.

Sabine was pressing her intertwined hands against her mouth, trying not to cry. For the last six weeks, Esme had treated her maid like a puppy or doll: something to be played with when it suited her and otherwise ignored. But Sabine was a person, with thoughts and feelings, terrified and far from home. Esme remembered Sabine's father, and the way he'd thanked her for giving his daughter a better life. Until now, Esme hadn't thought it was possible for the hulking liner to sink. But Sabine's fear had ignited her own, and dread crept like a poison through Esme's bloodstream. If Esme didn't get in a lifeboat, Sabine wouldn't either. And they both might die.

What had felt like a choice a few minutes earlier had become a necessity. Esme reached out for Sabine's hand and brought her forward.

"*Venez,*" she said. "Come along."

The officer in charge of loading the boat was strutting around imperiously, but he didn't seem to have a clear idea what to do. Two crewmen stood at either end, fiddling with the ropes, while others leaned against the davits, waiting for orders. The officer pointed to the female passengers gathered around him with a simple "In you go," and Esme saw more than one woman frown disapprovingly at his far-from-deferential tone.

This can't be how it ends, Esme thought with growing panic. How could she say goodbye to Charlie in front of all these people? It was all happening too fast: Sabine stepping gingerly into the boat; Hiram's hand against Esme's shoulder blade, nudging her on; one last glance over her shoulder at Charlie. He gave her a solemn nod, granting her permission to leave. He looked resolute, and tragic, and unbearably handsome.

Esme turned away, swallowing the misery that threatened to engulf her. A man was reaching out to her from the lifeboat, a common seaman by his uniform, and she grabbed hold of him, half climbing and half stumbling inside. She mustn't look back—that would have destroyed her—so she looked outward, at the stars glittering on the horizon. They were the only indication of where the sea ended and the sky began.

"Any more ladies?" the officer called out.

There was no reply. Esme glanced around at her companions in the boat. They numbered no more than a dozen, women of various ages, scattered on four benches with ample space between them. Esme saw a man and a woman on deck, engaged in a heated conversation; the woman eventually stepped back, out of sight. Esme couldn't see Charlie, but Hiram was still there, pacing back and forth, looking exasperated. She wondered if this would be the last time she ever saw him.

"Might the gentlemen board?" Esme called out. "We have room."

The officer shook his head stiffly. "Captain's orders. Lower away!"

The crewmen at the davits went to work, but the lifeboat didn't budge. After another false start, one of them told the officer it was jammed.

"How?" the officer asked, incredulous, and Esme felt a sickening lurch of fear. What if the boat went crashing into the water? Suddenly, a rope loosened and one end of the lifeboat jerked down. Terrified, Esme clutched the bench to stop herself sliding off. A little boy fell with a thump into the bottom of the boat but was quickly scooped up by his mother, who pulled the child into her lap and clutched him tight with both arms.

A rope on the other side shifted, and the boat evened out, then continued its unsteady progress downward. Esme looked up and saw Hiram at the railing, curiously calm. The creases in his forehead had smoothed out, and she remembered their first meeting, how he'd struck her as an old-fashioned courtly gentleman. *A gentle man,* she thought wistfully, as he gave Esme a look that said both thank you and goodbye. Esme held up one hand—a gesture of affection? of dismissal?—and he lifted one of his in response. Esme knew she should say something, but she couldn't think of the right words, and all of a sudden, she was staring at a line of rivets drilled into the ship. The deck was out of sight; the moment had passed.

They were passing a glass-enclosed promenade when Esme was startled to see a face staring back at her. It was a woman wrapped in an oversized dark coat, her large, arresting eyes holding Esme's attention. The man next to her was wearing a garish, flashy suit and banging his fists against the glass. The sound was muffled, but Esme could sense his near panic.

"Stop!" the younger crewman called up to the deck. He carried himself with the dignity of an officer, despite his common sailor's uniform. "We've a woman here!"

The boat jolted to a halt, and Esme and her fellow passengers tilted forward.

"What now?" the other crewman barked. He was the kind of sailor usually kept out of passengers' sight; his face and beard were smeared with coal dust, and his clothing was dark with soaked-in grime. "Is she going to walk through glass?"

"We must do our duty," the first crewman said. He hollered up to the deck, and when the officer leaned over the railing, he shouted out his request that another woman be allowed to board.

The woman in question was looking at Esme with a determined sort of expectation. There was something about the woman's stare—those penetrating blue eyes—that commanded Esme's attention. Esme tried to smile reassuringly, but her face froze midway, because suddenly there was Charlie, on the other side of the window, running up to the woman and talking to her with intent concentration. Then Charlie looked out, at the boat and at Esme, his expression bright with purpose.

For a moment, Esme's heart soared. Then the grief of losing Charlie returned tenfold, and her heart clenched with the anticipation of going through the pain of parting yet again. Esme could barely nod as he waved his arm out and down, motioning everyone in the boat to duck their heads. She couldn't stop looking at him, even when his foot crashed through the window and glass shattered, sending a shard toward her face. She didn't realize she'd been cut until she wiped at her cheek and saw the blood on her fingers.

The older crewman stepped into the center of the lifeboat, tipping its balance and making the passengers cry out in concern. He held an oar through the hole Charlie had created, and Charlie took hold of the other end. The lifeboat edged closer to the *Titanic*, leaving only a foot-wide gap. Bracing one elbow against Charlie and reaching out to the crewman with her other hand, the woman climbed into the boat.

"Thank you," she said, in a cool British voice. She sat on a bench in the middle of the boat, sitting defiantly upright, looking ahead rather than at the man she was leaving behind. And then Esme's interest in her vanished, because Charlie was reaching out, less than an arm's length away. She leaned forward and slid her fingers between his. Charlie's breath swirled toward Esme in gossamer clouds, and she gulped it in. When the boat dropped down with a creak of the ropes, Esme felt everything that was true and good slipping from her grasp.

Did she pull? Did he jump? All Esme knew was that Charlie was suddenly beside her, his limbs and hers tangled on the floor of the boat. She clung to his arms when he pulled her up to sit, right as they touched down in the water. As they pulled away from the *Titanic*'s shockingly crooked silhouette, another rocket illuminated the night. The light lasted just long enough for Esme to see Hiram on deck, watching with dignified calm as his wife and her lover rowed away.

US SENATE COMMITTEE ON COMMERCE

Titanic Disaster Investigation

Wednesday, April 30, 1912

Testimony of Mr. Charles Van Hausen, First-Class Passenger

Senator Smith: After you were awakened by the sound of voices, what did you do?

Mr. Van Hausen: I came out of my stateroom and spoke to a steward, who told me there was an order for passengers to put on their life belts. I spent some time looking for my friends, Mr. and Mrs. Harper, and I found them on the boat deck, near one of the lifeboats.

Senator Smith: There was no panic or confusion?

Mr. Van Hausen: No. An officer was directing women and children into the boat. Mr. Harper escorted his wife forward, and she took a place along with the others. Mr. Harper and I remained on deck as the boat was lowered, and we heard a shout from one of the crewmen. A woman on a deck below wanted to board, but the window wouldn't open. I offered to go down and help her. I broke the window and assisted her into the boat. Very soon after, I was asked to enter the boat.

Senator Smith: Who made this request?

Mr. Van Hausen: Mrs. Harper, and a few others.

Senator Smith: Passengers?

Mr. Van Hausen: The crewmen appeared to welcome my assistance. I don't believe either had much experience in manning a boat.

Senator Smith: Could your lifeboat have carried more passengers?

Mr. Van Hausen: Yes, I suppose so. But I can't say how well we would have fared with a full load. It would have made it much more difficult to maneuver.

Senator Smith: You were the only male passenger?

Mr. Van Hausen: Yes.

Senator Smith: We have heard from other witnesses that a man was seen disguising himself in a woman's clothing in order to enter a lifeboat. Could such a subterfuge have taken place in your boat?

Mr. Van Hausen: Absolutely not. I saw no evidence of cowardly behavior.

Senator Smith: A crewman in your boat, Mr. Wells, has testified that you paid him ten dollars after you were rescued. What was the reason for this payment?

Mr. Van Hausen: Mr. Wells was very angry at the loss of the ship. He said everything he owned was at the bottom of the ocean, and his pay would be stopped from the hour of the sinking. I gave Mr. Wells and Mr. Healy the money to buy new clothes and other personal items when we arrived in New York. It was a gift.

Senator Smith: So you did not pay them in exchange for being allowed to board the lifeboat?

Mr. Van Hausen: No. Absolutely not. What kind of man would that make me?

ANNA

The first time Anna Halversson drowned, her seven-year-old body slipped into the water like a rock tossed in a tranquil pond. Shocked and disoriented, she fought the downward pull of her drenched skirt. Then a hand grabbed her arm, the fingers digging into her skin so hard that their imprint remained as purple-gray bruises for days afterward. Papa hoisted Anna into his boat, the same way he pulled in a fish, and rubbed her face briskly. Only the quickness of his breathing told her he'd been scared.

That was the day Papa decided Anna would learn to swim.

"Why?" Mama asked, as if Papa had suggested teaching her to fly. "Anna fell because she was careless. She's learned her lesson."

"I won't take her out again until she can swim." Papa rarely raised his voice, but he had a way of clipping his words that made it clear when he was in no mood to be argued with.

Mama grunted, a familiar sound. She had countless small ways of expressing her feelings: the raise of one shoulder, a silent shake of the head, an icy stare. Life, for Mama, was an onslaught of frustrations and setbacks, and Anna wasn't sure if Mama was angrier about the swimming or the fact that Anna would be spending time with Papa, time better spent doing chores.

The Halverssons had always been farmers, not fishermen, but Papa enjoyed the challenge of coaxing a fish onto his line. Already, Anna's skinny fingers could gut and clean a perch in minutes, and the satisfied nod she got from Papa was better than any monetary reward. Papa was the center of her world, and she was grateful for whatever time she was granted in his orbit. He was always busy: planting, plowing, and helping out neighbors who were also scraping a living from the same stubborn earth. Anna's oldest sister, Frieda, had been born in the optimistic days when Papa expected a house full of boys and put everything he'd saved into buying more land; when Kirsten arrived three years later, Papa began envisioning future sons-in-law who'd work by his side as his weather-beaten hands stiffened. Anna was a surprise arrival after ten barren years, and Mama always accused Papa of spoiling her.

Anna's swimming lessons took place in the morning, after the cows had been milked and the pigs fed. She wore bloomers under a shabby dress handed down from Frieda, a dress that would otherwise have been taken apart for scraps. She learned to keep her head up and tuck her skirt under, leaving her legs free to kick. Though the icy lake water pricked at her skin, she pushed her way forward, eager to be rewarded with Papa's smiles.

The Halverssons weren't well off, but they owned their own land, unlike many others in their small Swedish village. Mama often held up the Anderssons as a family who had it far worse. Mr. Andersson eked out a living as a hired hand, and Mrs. Andersson was bony and pale, more a spirit than a flesh-and-blood woman.

"God's plan is mysterious, isn't it?" Mrs. Andersson asked Anna once. "Your father, with three daughters, must mourn the lack of a son. And here I am, with two fine boys, and I would give anything to have a little girl."

Anna wasn't sure how to respond. Would it would be disloyal to admit Mrs. Andersson was right? Papa loved Anna and her sisters, in his quiet way, but disappointment had marked him, like a scar or a limp.

Mr. Andersson was known to be stubborn, and there were some who said the accident was his own fault. He'd pushed his poor horse as if it were an Arabian racer; who could blame the old nag for throwing him off? *God punishes the proud,* the gossips whispered, but Anna thought God had better things to do than meddle in the affairs of country folk. Their lives were beneath his notice.

Mr. Andersson's death served no larger purpose, other than increasing the misery of his family. Sickly Mrs. Andersson sat forlornly in her ramshackle one-room house, shunning the few kindly women who came to visit, and her sons, Josef and Emil, walked miles each day in search of work, though Emil barely looked strong enough to lift a pitchfork. The network of family bonds that would have propped up any other family had long since withered; Mrs. Andersson came from fishing folk up north—none of them anxious for more mouths to feed—and Mr. Andersson's only brother had emigrated to America years before. The Anderssons were alone, and even sober, penny-pinching Mama felt sorry for them. When Frieda married a schoolteacher and moved to Stockholm, and Kirsten was promised to a young farmer more interested in expanding his family's property than working Papa's land, Mama proposed an arrangement: Josef and Emil would be brought on as Papa's new farmhands, in exchange for food and a payment when the harvest was in.

Never having had a brother, Anna found it odd, at first, to spend so much time in the presence of young men. They had such a different way of moving, such different smells. Twelve-year-old Emil was awkward and bashful, with crooked teeth and a protruding nose. He could barely make it through a complete sentence without tripping over his words and seemed more comfortable with pigs and cows than other people. Though he was only a year younger than Anna, she developed a protective kind of sympathy for him. She was grateful, too, for his help with the chores, which left her with free hours she wouldn't have otherwise.

Anna spent far too many of those spare hours watching Emil's brother, Josef, trying to sort out her complicated feelings. Unlike Emil, Josef kept his distance from Anna and the house; he was out with Papa until sundown, proud to put in a full day of work. At sixteen years old, his shoulders were filling out, and his face was hardening into sharper angles. His eyes, when they met Anna's across the supper table, were clear and blue, like the lake in summer. Slowly, promisingly, he began raising his hand in greeting when he spotted her across a field. Rather than walking silently past her, he would stop and ask what she was doing as she watched the sunlight hit a cobweb, or searched for animal shapes in the clouds.

"You see more than the rest of us," he told her one day.

Was it a compliment? Anna's dress was sticking to her back after an afternoon pulling weeds and peeling potatoes; her cheeks were flushed with the heat. She wanted to turn away, and yet she also wanted to stare at Josef's face. He actually looked interested in what she had to say.

"Surely everyone sees the same things?" she asked shyly.

"Ah, but most don't take the time to look."

Josef smiled, and Anna felt joy and hope and terror cascade through her, all at once. Anna knew she didn't have much to offer—she was plain, with limp, dark-blonde hair and a splotchy complexion—but Josef was looking at her as if they'd exchanged a confidence. And though she couldn't think of anything else to say, and Josef was soon hoisting up his hoe and turning back to the fields, she felt they'd come to an unspoken understanding.

Anna guarded her admiration for Josef like a hidden treasure, but when she finally confided in her friend Sonja, Sonja said it was obvious to anyone with their wits about them that Josef and Anna were meant to be married.

"I've seen the way he looks at you after church!" Sonja teased. She was petite and vivacious, with a bubbly laugh that drew others toward her. "He'll be going to your papa before you know it."

Anna had not been raised to believe in passionate love; her affection for Josef was simple and direct, like Anna herself. By the time she was seventeen, when Papa started dropping hints about the next generation and grandchildren running among the chickens, Anna took each look Josef gave her across the table and every nod they exchanged in the barnyard as an acknowledgment of their arrangement: *Yes. I choose you.*

Then came the letter from America, the first of two that would change Anna's life. Josef's uncle Tomas wrote that there was plenty of good-paying work in the lumber mills of Minnesota; he'd saved up enough for Josef's passage, if he wanted to come.

Josef read it out loud to the Halverssons. "What do you think?" he asked, eyes lively with delight.

Anna wanted to say, *No.* Or, *I don't know what my life will look like without you.* But she only nodded as Mama tut-tutted and Papa leaned over Josef's shoulder to read the offer for himself. While they were distracted, Anna quietly excused herself and ran to the hayloft to cry.

Josef expected Anna to be happy for him, so she pretended to be, all the way through his send-off at the train station. Mrs. Andersson and Emil looked as miserable as Anna felt: Josef's mother lamented that she might never see her son again, and Emil was jealous that he wasn't going to America, too. At first, Josef's absence was unbearable; Anna found herself looking for him, in the way she had for years, and feeling a fresh disappointment every time she realized he wasn't there. From time to time, Anna thought of confiding in Emil, who must miss Josef as much as she did, but he showed no interest in talking to her about such personal matters. He'd grown nearly as tall as his brother but was wiry rather than brawny, his arms strong but thin. His face fell naturally into a mournful expression and he rarely made the effort to change it.

Unlike Josef, Emil didn't seem to care what Anna was doing or thinking; he never indicated he saw anything in her to admire.

The second life-altering letter came more than a year later, a few months after Mrs. Andersson's death. Mama had informed Josef of the sad news by telegram, and Anna expected the envelope that arrived a few weeks later from Minnesota to contain polite but succinct thanks; Josef wrote the way he talked, in direct, short sentences. So Anna was surprised when Papa pulled out several pages from the envelope. She knew, right away, that this letter would be different.

Josef began with the usual greetings and his hope that his mother's funeral had been well attended. He grieved her loss and was sorry he had not been able to come. With both their parents gone, Josef wrote, he had decided Emil should come to America and live with him. The offer didn't come as a surprise to the Halverssons—they'd expected it since Mrs. Andersson's death—and Anna was sure Emil would be anxious to go. But when Papa read the words, Emil's impassive expression didn't change.

Papa silently read ahead, then he glanced up with an expression of delight.

"Listen!" he announced. "There's more. Josef says, 'I have saved enough for Emil's passage and have begun working my own plot of land on my uncle's farm. I therefore find myself in a position to marry, and there is no better wife than a good Swedish girl.'"

Papa looked at Mama, then at Anna. She became aware of each heavy breath she took, in and out. There was only one reason Josef would be writing such a thing to her parents. Only one question he was preparing to ask. Mama's mouth twitched; Emil picked at a fingernail. It was the first and last time Anna felt complete, unreserved happiness.

Papa read on. "I hope you will make my case to a young woman I have long admired. As I am not well acquainted with her parents . . ."

It made no sense. How could Josef not be well acquainted with Anna's parents? Emil glanced up at Papa, who looked equally baffled.

"I ask that you speak on my behalf to Sonja Gustafson's father."

Papa's voice drifted off. *Sonja?* Anna felt the others looking at her, each stare scorching her skin. Of course. Sonja was pretty and sociable; Sonja was exactly the sort of person a man like Josef would want for a wife. Anna had no right to be upset, for wouldn't she have made the same choice in his place?

Papa read the rest of the letter in a considerably more somber tone. Josef had already thought through the arrangements; if Sonja and Emil made the journey together, his uncle's wife would look after Sonja until the marriage could be held. He anxiously awaited an answer, hopefully from Sonja herself. At the very end of the letter were a few hastily scribbled words that made Anna's chest seize with grief: "Send my greetings to Anna—I hope she rejoices at this happy news."

There was very little rejoicing. Papa slowly folded the pages and slid them back in the envelope. Mama stared into the fireplace, her knitting needles silent. Emil pushed his chair back and walked out of the house, without a word. Anna watched through the window as he paced across the front field, tracing the furrows with his feet. He looked upset, though she couldn't think why. Later, when Anna asked him whether he was pleased to be going to America, he said yes, of course, but his expression remained mournful. How like Emil, Anna thought, to mope over an offer that anyone else in his position would have welcomed.

Sonja was the one who suggested Anna come to America, too. She and her parents had quickly agreed to Josef's proposal, the prospects for a girl in rural Sweden being limited to poor, overworked farm wife or poor, overworked servant. In America, you could buy your own land, build your own business, and determine your own future. Sonja was a kind and loyal enough friend to put Anna's feelings above her own happiness. She swore to Anna that she'd known nothing of Josef's intentions, and if the marriage would cause Anna pain, she'd call it off. Anna promised it didn't matter. She said she thought of Josef as a brother and Sonja as a sister and they were a perfect match, all of which she believed in her heart was true. Sonja confided her worries about traveling so far with only Emil for company. Wouldn't it be fun if Anna came, too? With so many good-paying jobs in America, she might even be tempted to stay.

It was just talk, at first. Anna knew she could never leave home for good; as the youngest, unmarried daughter, she was the one expected to take care of her parents as they aged. She would mash their food when their teeth fell out and empty their chamber pots when they were bedridden. But would it be wrong to see some of the world first? To be near Josef again, even if he would never be hers?

Mama was her usual doubtful self; like a stony island in a swelling sea, she fought back against change, even as it threatened to engulf her. Papa was the one who urged Anna to go, offering to pay Anna's fare and telling her she'd earn the money back tenfold in America. He'd taken out loans, he admitted sheepishly, when the harvest was poor; if she could earn a good living for a year or two, it would help clear his debts. Even Emil managed to produce a convincing show of enthusiasm when Anna asked if she should come along. Either she didn't irritate him as much as she thought, or he was simply grateful to be accompanied by another familiar face from home.

Anna knew she looked like a country bumpkin on the way to Göteborg. It was her first time away from home, her first ride on a train. But Sonja's excitement was infectious. She'd bought a booklet of English phrases and insisted they practice, giggling at Anna's attempts to form the unfamiliar sounds.

"How do you do?"

"Pleased to meet you."

During the two-day sea voyage to the port of Hull, on the train across southern England, and at the Southampton docks, Anna stared and marveled: at the noise, the crowds, and the size of the ladies' hats. But nothing prepared her for the immensity of the *Titanic*. She stepped closer to Sonja and Emil as they prepared to embark, needing the reassurance of their arms on either side.

"That's a sight, isn't it?" Emil asked. The farther they'd gotten from home, the more he'd shed his habitual sullenness; he actually looked happy.

Sonja smiled, but Anna could sense her apprehension. She felt more than a little nervous herself as they were swept into the maelstrom of third class and shunted off to their cabins. Unmarried women were housed in the back of the ship, unmarried men in the front, so Anna and Sonja exchanged hurried goodbyes with Emil and arranged to meet in the dining hall later. Anna wasn't altogether sure what kind of accommodations their third-class tickets would buy; they'd joked about having to sleep in hammocks or on piles of hay on deck. To her delight, the cabin was bright and clean, the paint so fresh she could smell it. There were two sets of upper and lower berths, for a total of four passengers. Sonja tested out the faucet at the basin and called out joyfully, "Hot water!"

A girl with striking red hair tossed open the door, followed by a shorter, bosomy companion. The redhead said something that sounded like "Hello!" but her accent was so strange that Anna couldn't be sure it was English. The red-haired girl flung her bag on the bottom-right bed, and asked Anna and Sonja a question. The two Swedish girls stared back, and their new cabinmates giggled, and finally Anna pointed to herself and said, "Anna. From Sweden."

Like a flock of chattering birds, they were soon exchanging greetings and names. The redhead was Bridget, from Ireland; the other was Mary, her cousin. They had family in New York, and their reason for traveling was so intricate and confusing that Sonja's phrase book was no help in figuring it out. But it didn't seem to matter. Being around Bridget and Mary made Anna feel like laughing for no reason. Though she didn't understand the words Bridget was using, Anna understood the essence of what she was saying: *We are young and free, and we will have the most wonderful time.*

Not all the third-class passengers mixed so easily. Countrymen tended to stick with countrymen, and Emil shared a cabin with three Norwegian men who kept to themselves. He ate with Sonja and Anna and lingered with them afterward, avoiding the smoking room where most of the other unmarried men spent their evenings.

"I can hardly breathe in there," he said. "Besides, I don't like crowds."

Bridget and Mary were traveling with a group of young men from their hometown—all of whom, confusingly, seemed to be named Brian—but Emil didn't seem interested in meeting them, or in listening to the music some of the other Irish passengers played one night after supper. Sonja's eyes looked on longingly as couples paired up to dance. Emil was walking away, expecting the girls to follow, but Sonja hung back, delaying her exit. One of the Brians rushed forward, holding out his hands in invitation, and Sonja looked at Anna. *I shouldn't, should I?* her eyes asked, and Anna silently answered, *Go on, have fun.* She turned her attention back to Emil, who was already out the door. It would be a kindness to Sonja to keep him distracted. He wouldn't be pleased to see his brother's intended dancing with someone else.

The air outside was chilly but refreshing after the stuffy, crowded hall. Anna followed Emil along the deck and paused alongside him at the railing. She expected him to ask where Sonja was, but he seemed content to stand there quietly, enjoying a respite from the noise. Anna looked out at the stars and tried to find the constellations Papa had shown her. Maybe he was outside right now, staring at the same night sky.

"Do you want to hear the music?" Emil asked. "We can go back, if you like."

"It's nice here," Anna said.

"You are enjoying the voyage?"

Anna could feel the effort it took for him to make even simple conversation. Since leaving the farm, Emil had tried to smarten himself up, smoothing down his unruly hair and making sure his shirts were neatly tucked. Nonetheless, he was still the same Emil she'd always known: tongue-tied with strangers, and awkward even when talking to Anna, despite their history together. Anna had never been much of a talker herself, but she felt like a chatterbox compared to Emil.

"Oh yes," Anna said. "The boat's so much nicer than I expected. I do miss home, though. I was just thinking of Papa."

"Yes," Emil said. The silence that followed was so long that Anna was ready to suggest they go hear the music after all. Then, finally, Emil said, "I'm glad you came."

He didn't look at her as he said it. If he was glad, why did he look so miserable?

"How do you think it will be for us?" she asked. "In America?"

She'd hoped the question would distract Emil from his mysteriously pensive mood, but it only seemed to make him more uncomfortable. He shifted his belt around his waist, as if that would help him straighten his thoughts. "Good. I hope."

Bridget would be driven to distraction by a man like Emil, but Anna was more patient. "It will be strange at first," Anna said. "But we'll grow accustomed to it, don't you think? Like the ship. The first day, I couldn't believe the food at supper. So many choices! Now, it seems normal."

Emil nodded.

"And Josef will be there."

Saying his name was an indulgence. Anna tried not to do it too often, because the thrill of picturing Josef only rarely outweighed the sadness that inevitably followed. Emil shuffled his feet, and his hand skimmed the railing until he was almost touching Anna's. She looked over at his tensed shoulders and pink cheeks and suddenly understood the reason for his twitchy unease. Hadn't she always felt similarly tongue-tied around Josef?

Poor Emil.

He stammered, "When Josef and Sonja are married . . ."

Another self-conscious silence, as if Emil were hoping Anna would guess the rest.

"Yes?" she prodded. If she didn't nudge him along, he'd never get around to saying it.

"We could marry, too."

Though Emil had summoned the courage to declare himself, he still hadn't looked directly at Anna. Remembering all too well the sting of rejection, she tried to think of the kindest way to turn him down.

"Think how many pretty girls you'll meet in America!" she said, with a teasing smile.

"I don't want to marry an American girl," Emil said. "I want a good Swedish wife."

"Like your brother."

Now it felt as if Josef were standing alongside them, an invisible but unmistakable presence.

"I'm in no rush to marry," Anna said.

"Say you'll consider it." Emil leaned toward Anna, and now his eyes were gazing into hers, pleading. She hated herself for inflicting such hurt, but it would be crueler to lead him on. Emil was a child in her eyes, an overgrown boy playing at adult emotions.

"I am grateful for your kindness, but . . ."

"It's not kindness!" Anna had never heard Emil speak so decisively. "I have wanted to marry you for as long as I can remember." Emil forged on, undeterred by Anna's shocked silence. "I wasn't going to say anything until after we were settled. I wanted to prove I could take care of myself first. But I don't want you to go back to Sweden—I want you to stay." Dropping his voice, he added, "I'll do whatever I can to make you happy."

In a rush of gratitude, Anna grabbed his hand. She wanted to tell him that she admired his honesty and would always care for him. But that might only raise his hopes. The affection she had for Emil would always be a dim shadow of what she felt for his brother.

"Emil, I can't. Josef . . ."

Please don't make me say it, Anna silently pleaded. During all those years spent together, Emil must have guessed. He'd been there when Anna trailed Josef around the farm, watching him with lovesick longing. He'd been there when Papa read Josef's letter declaring his choice of wife. Emil had to have seen the devastation on Anna's face.

"I know you hoped to marry Josef." Emil didn't look upset, only determined. "Don't you see? If you marry me, we can still be together, all of us. Josef and Sonja and you and I can live near each other, raise our children together. A family."

At last, Anna understood the full implications of Emil's offer. He knew she was in love with Josef, and he accepted it, because he understood. Didn't Emil idolize Josef just as much as Anna? Emil was accustomed to being second best.

Anna gently pulled away. She knew she should refuse him. But she wasn't ready to say no, either. She couldn't deny the emotions that Emil's declaration had stirred up, emotions that were far from sisterly. In the moonlight, Emil looked older, the angles of his face heightened, and she could see the outline of the man he would become. The solemnness that hung so heavy on him as a boy would make him look distinguished as he aged. And she knew, with utter certainty, that he would always be kind.

Could a marriage be built on a mutual love of someone else?

So many questions and no clear answers. Now was not the time to resolve them.

"I'm not sure," Anna said. It was the simplest form of the truth.

Emil's relief was clear in the speed of his response. "Wait as long as you want. We won't speak of it again till you're ready."

"We should see what Sonja's gotten up to."

Emil was as anxious as Anna to end the conversation, because he was quick to lead the way back to the stairs. They found Sonja standing by Bridget in the dining saloon, her face flushed. Sonja told them she was tired, and if Emil wondered why Sonja's face was damp with sweat, he didn't ask. Anna said good night to Emil and followed Sonja down the hall to the women's quarters. A quick, careless departure that Anna regretted for the rest of her life. Why hadn't she stayed? She'd wanted to dance, and Emil would have joined her if she had asked. She would have known what it felt like to be held in his arms, and that might have been enough to tell her whether she could one day grow to love him. If only she had that one happy memory, to counter all the others.

*

There was no dancing the next night; Sundays were intended for more godly pursuits. Still, it was impossible to suppress third class into a suitably holy silence. After supper, a pianist started banging out cheerful hymns, and the stewards turned a blind eye to the card games that were officially forbidden on the Lord's day. Anna and Emil were polite but distant with each other, and both turned to Sonja as a distraction from their unresolved future. Sonja, hungry to know more about her intended, urged them to talk about Josef's childhood, so Anna told her about the time Josef chased a runaway piglet halfway through the village, and Emil described how stubborn young Josef could be with their equally stubborn father. Each memory was a thread that wove Anna and Emil together. Before, she never would have said she had been happy as a child. She'd been loved and cared for by her parents and sisters, but her days were a constant progression of duties in which she had no choice or say. Anna saw things differently now, through Sonja's eyes. Amid all the demands of farm life, there had been moments of contentment, even of joy. Moments she had overlooked until she remembered them with Emil.

The public rooms closed at ten o'clock on Sunday nights, but Anna retired to her cabin an hour earlier to study her English phrase book. As their arrival drew closer, she was becoming more nervous about the challenges ahead: finding their way from the boat dock to the train station, making the right connections, getting directions to the boarding house in Saint Paul where Josef was supposed to meet them. Her last clear memory before the crash was of practicing the question *Is this the train to Chicago?*

She must have fallen asleep with the book across her chest, because it thumped against the floor when she started awake. Voices were chattering just outside the door. Anna looked across the cabin at Mary, who was pulling herself upright.

"What is it?" Mary asked.

Words simple enough for Anna to understand. She shrugged. Bridget and Sonja leaned down from the top berths, asking similar questions in English and Swedish. Bridget, not surprisingly, was the first to climb out of bed and go outside to investigate. When she came back, jumpy with exhilaration, Anna couldn't understand what she was saying; the word "iceberg" wasn't in the phrasebook. She heard the Swedish-speaking steward marching down the corridor, shouting, "Stay in your cabins! Back to your cabins!"

Bridget and Mary were pulling on their shoes, and Anna wondered if the English steward was giving out different orders. When the Irish girls held the door open for Anna and Sonja to follow them, Sonja shook her head.

"We should do as we're told," she told Anna.

And so they waited. Anna was never sure how long they sat there, listening to the commotion outside, wondering if the steward would ever come back and tell them what to do. It felt like hours. Then they heard footsteps clanging along the corridor, and Emil lurched through the doorway. His shirt hung loose from his trousers, and his hair was as wild as Anna had ever seen it.

"What are you doing here?" Sonja demanded. It was a serious infraction for a young man to be found in the women's quarters.

"There's water," Emil gasped between breaths. "Up front."

Anna followed his eyes as he tilted his head down. The fabric at the bottom of his trousers was wet.

"It's splashing around some of the cabins. I looked for you everywhere."

"The steward said . . ."

"You've got to get out!" Emil urged. "Now!"

Anna nodded and pulled on her shawl and boots, not bothering to tie the laces. Sonja grabbed her bag, ignoring Emil's protests. The women of the village had all given her wedding gifts—embroidered napkins and nightgowns, a beautiful linen tablecloth—and she refused to leave them behind. Anna and Sonja followed Emil toward the stairs. They passed a group of women in dark headscarves, forming a circle around a huddle of young children. One of the women asked Anna a question in a harsh-sounding language, and Anna could only shake her head. Everyone was looking for answers, it seemed, but no one had any to give.

Anna felt the icy air waft toward her as they approached the door that led outside. Emil took hold of her arm and pulled her along. As they stepped onto the deck, he asked, "Now do you see?"

Chunks of ice were scattered across the open expanse of wood and piled in haphazard towers along the railing. Anna wondered where it had all come from, and how it had ended up on the ship. A nearby thud made her jump, but a quick-to-follow laugh told her Bridget was nearby. Anna looked toward the sound and saw her cabinmate across the way, part of a loud, lively group tossing chunks at each other. Beyond them, on the first-class deck higher up, Anna could see figures looking down on the scene. Turning up their noses at such antics, most likely.

"I'm freezing," Sonja said, with an exaggerated shiver. "Let's go inside."

Emil escorted them to the dining hall, which had become the main gathering place for confused third-class passengers. A cacophony of voices, speaking a dozen different languages, asked the same questions and shared the same uncertain news. Was it true they hit a whale? Where were they supposed to go? The ship was about to sink; the ship had been only slightly damaged and would soon be repaired. Anna heard the name Marconi several times, and when she asked Emil what it meant, he told her the *Titanic*'s wireless operators were sending messages to other nearby ships.

Reassured, Anna squeezed Sonja's hand. Help was on the way.

A group of stewards walked in, their arms piled with bulky white objects. As the men were set upon by anxious passengers, they called out orders in English, their words immediately translated and murmured throughout the room: *Life belts. Lifeboats. Captain's orders.* Emil helped Sonja and Anna fasten the straps on their vests before pulling on his own.

"Let's go," he said, urging the girls toward the door, where people were already pushing against each other in their frenzy to get through.

A harried-looking steward was guiding people toward a staircase that was usually closed off by a metal gate.

"Women and children," he repeated. "Women and children." For those who didn't speak English, the message was made clear by a sailor who grabbed hold of a man who tried to pass. The sailor shoved the man away, causing a rippling effect of stumbles and shouts.

Sonja stepped away from the crush. "We should stay together," she said.

"Go!" Emil ordered her. "I'll find you later."

All around them, similar arguments erupted: fathers and mothers and sons and daughters, urging each other to go or stay. Anna had accepted Emil as her protector without question; in her world, women did as their men ordered. But leaving him there, amid the confusion, felt soul-crushingly wrong. He was family.

They bickered as the water poured relentlessly through the gash below the waterline, not knowing how little time they had left. Finally, Emil let out a frustrated sigh and said, "I have an idea."

He took them back past the dining room and up to the third-class deck. The expanse was mostly deserted, except for a few people milling at the bottom of a crane that sat midship, a crane that had been used to load baggage in Southampton. Emil strode toward them, his feet sliding on the wet wood, and Anna and Sonja shuffled carefully behind him. Emil called out to one of the Norwegians from his cabin, and the two men had a quick consultation.

Emil turned to Anna. "We're climbing up, to the lifeboats."

"We can't!" Sonja protested. "That deck is first class!"

"What are they going to do to us now?" Emil argued. "The ship is sinking!"

Belatedly, Anna understood why her footsteps had been so unsteady: the ship was leaning. Shock and fear heightened her senses, and she clutched at the crane, seeking reassurance in its solidness.

The Norwegian was already testing out footholds, moving like a spider up the steel bars. Another man, dressed in the white uniform of a kitchen worker, was already halfway up the other side. Emil motioned to Sonja.

"My bag . . . ," she protested.

"Leave it."

Sonja looked like she was about to cry. Anna wanted to cry, too, when she thought of what she'd left in her cabin. Her best stockings, her only hat, her Sunday dress. None of it valuable, yet every piece priceless, because it was all she owned.

"We'll fetch it later," Anna said.

The certainty with which she delivered the lie had the desired effect. Sonja put down her bag and took hold of the first crossbar.

Anna climbed alongside her, their hands and feet moving in a tentative joint rhythm. When they reached the railing of the upper deck, the Norwegian leaned out and helped them over.

Anna expected to be shouted at or quickly shooed off the deck. But the people she'd seen there earlier, gawking at the ice, were gone. From this vantage point, one of the highest spots on the ship, the *Titanic's* fate was chillingly clear. Its prow was pointing precipitously downward, only a few feet from the water. And the lifeboats that had hung along the edges of the deck were gone.

The enormity of the absence silenced them. The lifeboats had been their guiding light, a way to channel their fear into action. Now, there was nowhere else to go.

"The boats can't be far. We can get to them."

Emil's voice was firm, but his face made Anna want to weep. He was trying so hard to prove himself, to show he was a man who could protect the women in his care. But he was only seventeen.

The tears Sonja had managed to hold in earlier came flooding down her cheeks. "I can't swim."

"The life belt will hold you up," Anna said. "I'll help you."

Their scramble up the crane hadn't gone unnoticed, and other third-class passengers began coming over the railing. Like crabs making their way to higher ground at high tide, they scuttled toward the stern.

Emil crouched down, bracing his back against the rail to counteract the increasing slant of the deck. "We only have to hold on a little longer," he said. "Until a rescue ship comes."

Anna remembered the talk about Marconi and hoped it was true. A deck chair slid past them, and Sonja's tears swelled into sobs.

I can't tell her it will be all right, Anna thought. No kind words could blot out the horror of what was to come. Her legs ached with the effort of holding herself upright. All she could do was squeeze Sonja's shoulders and tell her the words pounding through her like a heartbeat: "Josef is waiting for us. Think of Josef."

Emil's foot was braced against Anna's, his weight pushing her down. She watched as the nose of the ship slipped into the water. Below deck, dishes were breaking in a distant clatter. But Emil's voice was steady as he told them the safest way out was to meet the sea on their own terms. To jump into it before it pulled them in.

Anna's assent was more of a sigh than a word. She was on her knees by then, with Sonja collapsed beside her. Her hand was numb from the effort of holding on to the rail. And then the pressure was eased, as Emil grabbed hold of Anna with one arm and Sonja with the other. Sonja curled her face toward her lap, but Anna watched the water inch relentlessly forward as the *Titanic* slid gently into its grave.

"Now!" Emil shouted.

They careened down the deck, splashing into the sea in a tumble of limbs. The cold shot through Anna in a burst of pain; she wanted to scream, but couldn't. Sonja floated beside her, eyes enormous in the moonlight, with Emil close behind. It was impossible to take in the enormity of what was happening: the drowning ship, the detritus floating around them, the shouts that shattered the peace of the arctic night.

"The lights," Emil gasped, his breath forming a cloud of smoke.

The cold was slowing Anna's thoughts as well as her movements. She saw an intermittent glow amid the crush of objects that surrounded her and tried to figure out what it was. A firefly? An angel? Then she remembered—as if in a dream—what Emil had said about the lifeboats. The gleam in the distance was a lantern.

Anna tried to block out the screams of the passengers still clinging to the railings, fighting to hold on to a ship that would soon abandon them. She reached down, willing her numb legs to obey her mental commands. She kicked off her boots—thank God she hadn't tied them!—and pulled up her skirt, tucking the hem into her life belt. She pushed at the water with her palms, firm and steady, just as Papa had taught her. Slowly, painstakingly, Anna swam.

But Emil couldn't keep up. He was holding on to Sonja, whose shivering lips were emitting a low, constant whimper, and his frantic movements weren't pulling him forward. He'd never be able to drag Sonja far enough.

It took all the strength Anna had to think, let alone speak.

"I'll get the boat."

Her lips felt heavy, and her cheeks were stiff; the words came out jumbled. But Sonja looked grateful—she even attempted a smile—and her effort strengthened Anna's resolve. Anna was dimly aware of crashes and metallic groans as the *Titanic* ripped apart, but she didn't look back. The air around her exploded with a roar, and the ocean surged from the impact. Salt water cascaded up and over her, and she was pulled down and around, dizzy with horror, her lungs shrieking for air. She was seven years old, in the lake, drowning. Then her head bobbed out of the water, buoyed by her life belt. She gulped in the frosty air, its chill searing her throat.

Sonja was screaming, her cries joining hundreds of others in a chorus of terror. She and Emil had been swept away by the waves, and Anna watched as they struggled to return to her side. Emil was holding Sonja, and he was breathing too hard, and Anna wanted to tell him to conserve his strength, but she couldn't move her lips. She searched desperately for the light, and when a heavy mass careened into her, she didn't even flinch when she saw it was a dead man, his face crushed to bone and blood. The sight came back to her years later, in nightmares, but in that instant she was immune to such horrors. All that mattered were those who were still alive.

Emil's face was flushed, his hair—for once—smoothed flat across his forehead. He looked so much older, as if each minute since they'd left the ship had aged him a decade. He was trying to tell her something, and Anna nodded as if she understood. She wished he would stop trying to talk; it was costing him too much effort. A gentle swell pushed him forward, and Anna could hear the rasp in his voice.

"I'm sorry," he mumbled. "I'm sorry."

On the edge of her field of vision, Anna caught a flicker of light. She twisted her head toward it and thought she saw the outline of a person. A sailor, holding up a lamp.

"They're coming," she called out to Emil. "The boat is coming."

Sonja lay slumped against Emil's chest, her head across his shoulder. Had she been hurt? Anna knew she was their only hope for rescue; she had to keep kicking and moving her arms, even if she could no longer feel them.

She thought of Josef, a hazy, golden figure in an imagined America of endless pasture. He couldn't lose his future wife and brother in one night. She would not allow him to suffer such pain. *Please,* she begged God. *Save Sonja and Emil. I willingly trade my life for theirs.*

Emil was no longer trying to swim. He glided like a leaf on the water, giving himself over to the currents, his arms floating uselessly beside him. Sonja was gone. Anna reached out and grabbed Emil's hand. Her flesh was so chilled that his didn't feel cold. It was solid and strong, a hand that was used to carrying others' burdens. A hand that would never let her go.

"Come," Anna grunted, and she kicked and kicked, her senses so dulled that she couldn't tell if she was making any progress forward. The water swirled around her like an embrace, and an oar brushed against her shoulder. A voice called out, and firm fingers took hold of her arm.

Just like Papa, Anna thought, as Emil slipped away.

US SENATE COMMITTEE ON COMMERCE

Titanic Disaster Investigation

Thursday, April 25, 1912

Testimony of Edmund Healy, Seaman

Senator Perkins: What boat did you go from the ship in?

Mr. Healy: Number 21, sir.

Senator Perkins: Who was in command?

Mr. Healy: I was, sir.

Senator Perkins: How many passengers did you have on her?

Mr. Healy: Thirteen, sir.

Senator Perkins: Could the boat have taken more?

Mr. Healy: Yes, sir. A good deal more.

Senator Perkins: Why was the lifeboat not filled to full capacity?

Mr. Healy: I could not say, sir. It was the officers who decided who would board.

Senator Perkins: What orders were you given on leaving the ship?

Mr. Healy: Mr. Murdoch, the first officer, pointed to a light in the distance and said it was another ship come to our rescue. We were to unload our passengers there and come back for more. It took some time to get the boat moving properly, and when we looked for the light, it was gone.

Senator Perkins: And the *Titanic*?

Mr. Healy: The *Titanic* was also gone.

Senator Perkins: Did you hear any cries of people in the water?

Mr. Healy: Yes, sir. Awful cries.

Senator Perkins: Were you able to make any rescues?

Mr. Healy: A Swedish girl swam up to us, and we pulled her in. That was soon after the ship went down.

Senator Perkins: Could you see others in the water?

Mr. Healy: Our lamp wasn't working properly, and it was difficult to see. I did hear voices, close by. I thought we should try to reach them, but there were objections from some of the passengers. They feared we'd be swamped if we took any more in.

Senator Perkins: Did you give the order to leave?

Mr. Healy: There were no orders given. Two men in our boat started rowing toward the other lifeboats. Only one of the lady passengers objected. The rest were anxious to go.

Senator Perkins: At that time, were you still hearing calls for help?

Mr. Healy: Yes, sir.

Senator Perkins: How long did you hear such cries?

Mr. Healy: It was quite some time.

[Witness requested a break in the proceedings to compose himself.]

Mr. Healy (cont'd): I hate to think on it, sir. It was the most terrible sound I've ever heard.

PART TWO:
AFTER

CHARLOTTE

September 1932

"You'll never guess who's bought it!" Teddy Ranger called out.

Charlotte could barely hear him over the usual cacophony of the *London Record*'s office: the chiming telephones, the metallic clack of typewriter keys, the joking taunts of the reporters banging away at those keys. Charlotte managed to muster an expression of mild interest. If anyone really important had died, Teddy would be barking out orders rather than strolling leisurely toward her.

Teddy held up a telegram. "Charles Van Hausen. Two days ago."

The sensation that swelled up inside Charlotte couldn't be grief. Twenty years had passed since she'd last seen Charles Van Hausen, and even then, they were barely acquainted. Yet the news settled into her body like an onset of sudden illness, slowing her reflexes and thoughts. An image appeared, clear as a film still, of Charles in the lifeboat, clutching an oar, his face reddened with effort and cold. It shouldn't matter to Charlotte that he was dead. But it did.

Teddy, no fool, was looking at her with the same twitchy expression he got whenever a juicy rumor solidified into fact. "Did you know him?" he asked.

"Not here," Charlotte muttered.

Turning away, motioning for Teddy to follow, she led him to the door marked "Theodore Ranger, Editor," nodding to his secretary as they passed. Once inside, Charlotte sat in the chair opposite Teddy's desk and leaned back. Were anyone else in the room, she'd be perched on the edge of the seat, primly poised, but there was no need to observe the formalities when they were alone.

"You'd think this were your office, rather than mine," Teddy chided.

"It might be, if I were a man."

"Didn't suffragette rants go out with hobble skirts? Or are they back in fashion?"

It felt, to Charlotte, like pulling off a pair of tight shoes. Here, in private, she needn't address Teddy as Mr. Ranger or defer to his opinions; she was protected by their shared history. Teddy's waistcoats had tightened in the years Charlotte had known him, just as her once-striking looks had altered with age, but they'd both reached a level of success that would have pleased their younger selves. At forty-one, Charlotte knew she was no longer beautiful, but she'd managed the next best thing. By investing in the best clothes and hairdresser she could afford, Charlotte exuded nonchalant elegance, an effect achieved only by concealing the effort behind it.

"Tell me," Teddy said, shifting abruptly into the blunt manager's voice he used in meetings. "You. Van Hausen."

"We were in the same lifeboat," Charlotte said.

The revelation obviously delighted Teddy. "You don't say?"

"We barely spoke." Best to quash his hopes and any further questions. "What happened to him?"

"I don't know, except it was sudden. He had to be about our age, don't you think?"

Charlotte nodded. He'd seemed so much older back then. It was the money, she supposed. He'd grown up being waited on, his very name conjuring up admiring nods and bows. He'd been bred with the confidence it had taken Charlotte years to build for herself.

"I'd rather not write the obituary, if that's what you were going to ask," Charlotte said.

"Oh, this calls for more than that," Teddy said. "It's a big story. One of the richest men in America, notorious *Titanic* survivor, unable to shake the suspicion that hovered over his all-too-brief life."

"Sounds like you've already written it."

"I could do," Teddy said. "But think how much better it would be with your personal touch. What was he really like? And his wife—was she in the lifeboat as well?"

Charlotte nodded. She remembered Esme in the front of the boat, swathed in fur, clutching Charles's arm. Snapping at Charlotte to be quiet, her face twisted into an expression of affronted alarm.

"Think she'll talk to you?" Teddy asked.

Charlotte shot him her coldest glare. "We're hardly friends."

"There'd be good money in it. The *New York Express* will pay through the nose for the American rights to an interview, and I'd see you were properly compensated. You'd get a free trip to New York, besides. Why not make a holiday of it? I could get you a few weeks off, if you like."

"The *Titanic*'s old news. No one cares."

"Our readers love to revisit a good scandal. You know that better than anyone."

Scandals, after all, were Charlotte's specialty. She had a talent for simultaneously celebrating and castigating society's upper echelon, turning the ups and downs of their domestic lives into melodramas worthy of grand opera. If it had been anyone other than Charles Van Hausen who'd died, Charlotte would have a column finished within the hour. Already, her nebulous thoughts were arranging themselves into sentences: "The handsome heir to a Boston banking fortune, Van Hausen miraculously survived the sinking of the *Titanic*, a fate that would haunt him in the years to come. For even as Van Hausen's rescue led him into the arms of love, he could never escape the question that shadowed the rest of his life: Why did he live when so many others perished?"

But this wasn't the sort of story Charlotte could assemble into her usual confection of clichés and trite sentiment. Writing about Charles Van Hausen would mean boarding a ship and crossing the Atlantic, something she'd avoided ever since she returned to England in the spring of 1912. It would mean confronting Esme and asking her to relive one of the worst nights of her life. Still, Charlotte couldn't help wondering what had become of them. Had Charles and Esme been happy? Had they made peace with their past?

For twenty years, Charlotte had purposefully avoided thinking about the lifeboat, but now, fragments of the past reached out, cajoling her to glance back. She thought of the Swedish girl, Anna. Mrs. Trelawny and her terrified children. Mr. Healy, the sailor, whom she'd always meant to thank properly but never did. What had happened to them?

Perhaps, at last, it was safe to remember.

"All right," Charlotte said. "Best I go without writing to Mrs. Van Hausen first. Take her by surprise. But mind you, she may very well slam the door in my face."

"Not you, my dear," said Teddy, beaming. "I have faith in your powers of persuasion. I'll have McClaren set you up at the *Express*." Teddy and his New York counterpart often shared sources and tips and encouraged the occasional plagiarism by their underlings. "How soon can you leave?"

If Charlotte was really going to America, there was one obligation she'd have to face first.

"I'll need a few days to get things in order. Let's say Monday."

"Very good. Have Agnes make the arrangements."

Charlotte stood, preparing to leave. But just before she reached the door, she paused and turned back.

"You'll have to make up a good reason for sending me. I don't want anyone knowing I was on the *Titanic*."

The only reason Teddy knew was that he'd been there, on that desolate April night when the *Carpathia* reached New York. The rain and cold kept most of the *Titanic* survivors below deck, but Charlotte and a few others gathered at the rails to watch the journey's end. The city's illuminated skyline was no match for the weather, which dimmed the lights into an indistinct haze. It was hardly the inspiring arrival Charlotte had once imagined. And she could no longer fend off the question that had stalked her for the past four days: What now? She needed money, she needed a plan, but she'd depended on Reg for all that. What would she do without him?

As the ship neared the piers, a huddle of motorboats sputtered toward the *Carpathia*'s hull. Camera flares shattered the darkness, and voices shouted out from the shadowy figures on board.

"Are you from the *Titanic*?"

"One hundred dollars from the *New York World* for an exclusive!"

"C'mon, jump off, we'll pick you up. Easiest money you'll ever make!"

The thought of jumping made Charlotte feel queasy, but she didn't turn away. There was something captivating about the men's brashness. Ever since the sinking, Charlotte had felt paralyzed, breathing and eating by rote, barely speaking. The passengers on the *Carpathia* had been kind, offering their cabins and extra clothes with expressions of hushed concern. To Charlotte, they seemed like angels, creatures who meant well but weren't quite real. She heard herself referred to as a survivor and thought the term particularly apt. All she'd done was not die. Her thoughts, her emotions, her aspirations—all had been frozen by what she'd endured.

Now, looking out at the newspapermen, Charlotte began to thaw. This was America, vigorous and undaunted, even in the face of tragedy. She didn't want to talk to the reporters—she didn't want to talk about the *Titanic*, ever—but she admired the fervor that propelled them out on such a wretched night. How thrilling it must be, rushing to the scene of dramatic events, never knowing what the next day would bring. Charlotte wished, achingly, that she could see the world through their eager, curious eyes.

As the ship drew closer to the Cunard pier, Charlotte saw that a crowd had gathered. In every direction, as far as she could see, spectators were huddled, their faces sheltered by dark umbrellas. She hadn't realized until then that the *Titanic*'s loss had reverberated across the continents, and the *Carpathia*'s arrival gave tens of thousands of New Yorkers an opportunity to demonstrate their anguish. When Charlotte walked down the tunnel-like gangway into the pier's reception area, she felt assaulted by the lights and shouts of people searching for loved ones. A steward had told her there was a ladies' charity that would assist anyone who wasn't being met, and Charlotte nodded gratefully when an officious middle-aged woman asked if she needed help. She was offered coffee, then escorted into a room filled with donated clothing. Charlotte took a simple wool dress and a pair of stockings as other newly widowed women looked through the piles for suitable mourning clothes; there wasn't nearly enough black. The women were then taken to taxicabs and driven to the hotels where they'd stay until further travel arrangements could be made.

Charlotte tried to see something of the city as they sped along the soggy streets, but all they seemed to pass were blurry lamps and darkened shop windows, men and women scurrying as raincoats flapped at their calves. When the taxi stopped at the Hotel Montreal, a knot of men in rumpled suits crowded around the car.

"*Titanic* survivor? *Titanic* survivor?"

"Any English ladies? The *Record* will pay for your story."

Charlotte recognized the accent instantly: a south Londoner who'd learned to put a polish on his words. She turned away from the voice—she hadn't seen the man's face—and hurried into the comforting warmth of the lobby, where a line of bellhops and maids were waiting with expressions of curious anticipation. Charlotte joined a group of fellow survivors, feeling disconcertingly like an animal on display at the zoo. She heard a woman admonish her young daughter, "Don't tell anyone you were on the *Titanic*."

An exhausted, apologetic representative of the White Star Line informed them that all passengers were to remain in New York for the time being, on orders of the United States Congress. The government would be making an investigation into the sinking, and potential witnesses must be available for questioning. The man led them to understand, in a roundabout way, that it was unlikely they'd be called in; the testimony of second-class widows wasn't nearly as important as that of the surviving officers and well-known first-class passengers. In the meantime, their room and board would be paid for, as would their train fare if they planned to travel on. Those who wished to return to England would be booked on the next White Star liner.

And that's what she would do, Charlotte decided with weary acceptance. What choice did she have? There was nothing for her in New York, not without Reg. She couldn't run a swindle on her own in a town she didn't know, and her craving for adventure had withered in the middle of the Atlantic. Her aunt would take her in, and she could join her brothers in the country. She'd never wanted a rural life, but it was the only place she could imagine starting over.

The *Titanic* widows breakfasted together the following morning, with most agreeing it would be best to stay indoors, away from questions and stares. The rain had let up, and sunlight gleamed through the dining-room windows. Charlotte didn't want to stay cooped up in the hotel's velvet-hushed rooms; she wanted to be outside, an anonymous figure in the bustling crowds. If this was the only time she'd be in New York, she might as well see something of it.

Two reporters were leaning against the side of the building, talking, when Charlotte came out the front door. She recognized the taller one's voice; it was the Englishman from the *Record*. Fair-haired and spindly, he straightened up when he saw her.

"You're a long way from home," Charlotte said, allowing her childhood accent to come to the fore.

The reporter's expression shifted from mild to intense interest. "I could say the same for you, madam."

The other man—American—blurted out, "Are you one of the *Titanic* ladies?"

Charlotte shook her head. The Englishman, who must have guessed she was lying but didn't let on, waved his colleague back with a gesture both dismissive and possessive: *Leave her alone; she's mine.* He sidled up to Charlotte and followed when she gave him a brief nod of acknowledgment. If he'd started asking questions then—if he'd pushed her in any way—she would have increased her pace and left him behind. But his respectful silence allowed her time to think. Charlotte remembered the spark of envy that ignited when she saw the newspapermen calling out from the water. This man offered a way into that world.

Charlotte stopped at the end of the block and spoke without looking at the reporter. "I'll talk to you. But not at the hotel. Somewhere else."

"There's a café round the corner," he said. "Would that do?"

From the word "café," Charlotte expected a tea shop, with subdued conversations taking place at dainty tables topped with equally dainty china. The establishment they entered sounded almost as raucous as a nightclub. The clientele was a cross section of New York working folk, from shop girls to traveling salesmen. Everyone seemed to be laughing or exclaiming, their conversations consisting of sounds as much as words. The reporter led Charlotte toward a back corner, where his nod to a waiter made it clear he was a regular customer.

"Let's get the niceties out of the way, shall we?" he said. "The tea here is dreadful; it will only make you homesick. The coffee's tolerable, and the lemonade's rather nice. I'll order some buns as well. I'm not sure about your appetite, under the circumstances, but I'm ravenous."

His words streamed out with barely a pause for breath. After the waiter took their order, the reporter leaned forward, giving Charlotte his full attention.

"My name's Theodore Ranger," he began, "Teddy to my friends and to you, if you'd like. I'm the New York correspondent for the *London Record*. The owners want every *Titanic* account I can get, with no limit on my expenses. If I deliver what they want, it'll be the making of my career."

Teddy might look like a schoolboy, his cheeks so smooth that he barely needed to shave, yet Charlotte saw in him a kindred soul. He made no bones about what he wanted and didn't pander to her with false sympathy. She was familiar with the *Record*; her mother used to take it, back when they could afford newspapers. Charlotte knew exactly the sorts of stories the *Record* would run about the *Titanic*: glowing accounts of first-class heroes who died bravely on deck, maudlin celebrations of their wives and children, gleeful descriptions of the treasures that sank to the bottom of the sea. The ideas came easily, almost without effort.

Perhaps she really was suited for this sort of work.

"I can pay fifty dollars for your story, if it's a good one," Teddy went on. "More, if you saw what happened to the captain or one of the millionaires."

It wouldn't be hard to come up with a convincing lie. Charlotte could tell Teddy that she'd seen Captain Smith save a baby from certain death, or heard the last words of Mr. Guggenheim. Fifty dollars would be enough to change her life, for a time. But once it ran out, she'd be back where she started: alone and adrift.

"I doubt my story's worth much," she said apologetically. "I boarded a lifeboat, and we floated about for a few hours until we were rescued." Not once did she consider telling him the rest. "But there's another way we might help each other."

Teddy looked at her blankly, waiting to be convinced.

"The women I'm staying with at the hotel are more likely to talk to me than you. I could write down what they say, then you could put it in one of your stories. I think they'd agree, if I made it sound noble. I could tell them it would honor their husbands' last hours, to share their memories. Though it wouldn't hurt to offer a payment as well."

"And you'd charge a fee for your services?"

"Yes, but it's more than that. I want to do what you do. Take me on as an apprentice. Teach me."

Teddy looked doubtful. "It's not that easy . . . ," he began.

"You've got nothing to lose by trying me out."

Charlotte gave Teddy her most flirtatious smile. Not the most appropriate response for a young widow, perhaps, but it seemed to soften Teddy's resolve.

"Show me what you can do first," he said. "If you get me something good by three o'clock, it'll be in time for tomorrow's paper."

"I'll meet you in the lobby of the hotel," Charlotte said as she stood, already pulling on her coat. She mustn't allow him time for second thoughts. "Thank you very much, Mr. Ranger."

That heady first day, Charlotte convinced three fellow passengers to talk. Despite the lack of first-class names, Teddy was pleased with the stories Charlotte brought him. One woman had seen an officer fire a gun to prevent a rush on a lifeboat; another had been reunited with her son on the *Carpathia* after thinking him drowned. That afternoon, Charlotte accompanied Teddy to his office—a gloomy room equipped with a desk, a typewriter, and a decade's worth of dust—and watched as he intertwined the words she'd taken down as a knitter twists yarn, melding single colors into an intricate pattern. Teddy's frenzied fingers turned stark facts into heart-tugging dramas, and when he was done, they dashed to the telegraph office. He transmitted his cable to London in a shorthand-like code, but Charlotte was still staggered by what it must have cost. The whole tumultuous process entranced her. *This is what I'm meant to do,* she thought.

Newspaper work required a quick tongue and a quick mind, Teddy told her, and Charlotte had both. The survivors she interviewed trusted her to tell their stories, just as the gentlemen she'd once stolen from had trusted in her innocence. No one who looked like Charlotte was suspected of having ulterior motives. As she learned how to build the framework of a story around what people said—an act of both translation and creation—Charlotte discovered that writing brought the same satisfaction as crafting a scheme with Reg. It allowed her to be someone else, someone who shaped unruly reality into a narrative with a satisfying end.

When the Senate began its investigation into the disaster, Charlotte traveled to Washington, DC, as the *Record*'s newest correspondent. There, all it took was a bashful, girlish giggle, and the other reporters ushered her into a sought-after front-row seat. In the overcrowded hearing room, she listened to the testimony of Mrs. McBride and Charles Van Hausen. They glided over the truth of what happened, of course, but Charlotte felt oddly detached from their stories. What they described seemed to have nothing to do with her, and she took no notes. It was different when Mr. Healy gave his evidence. There'd been something between them in the boat, an instantaneous trust she'd never felt with anyone else. His distress latched into Charlotte as if it were her own pain, and for one absurd moment, she wanted to leap up and defend him before all those condemning faces: *It's not his fault!* Instead, she slumped her shoulders and slid lower in her chair, hoping Mr. Healy wouldn't see her. Charlotte hadn't spoken to him since the rescue, and she was shocked at how his once-confident expression had been dulled by grief. Yet she shied away from offering a kind word, or even an acknowledgment of her presence. What was the point? Mr. Healy would always be a reminder of the past, of a night Charlotte was determined to forget. She was looking only to the future.

When the British inquiry began in May, Teddy and Charlotte were called back to London. By then, Charlotte was eager to return home—she was tired of the constant attention that came with being a foreigner—but she hadn't counted on how difficult the journey would be. When the ship pulled away from the pier, her limbs felt shaky with nerves. No one would have known it to look at her; she managed to chitchat with Teddy and was breezily friendly with the stewardess who showed her to her stateroom. But she could hardly bear to remain below deck. As long as she was outside, scanning the horizon, Charlotte was able to stave off panic, but dinner sent her into a whirlwind of fear. She pictured the floor of the dining saloon tilting, china crashing to the floor, water pouring through the cracked windows. Sleep wasn't possible the first night, not with her ears constantly alert for shouts or a knock on the door. The engines' steady hum gave no reassurance, for she expected it to cut out at any moment. The thought of passing three more nights in such agony brought her close to tears.

The second evening, Charlotte lingered with Teddy in the second-class lounge after dinner. When she caught him yawning discreetly behind an upraised hand, she asked him to see her to her stateroom. She didn't even bother with finding a suitable excuse, knowing only that every minute she spent in his company was a minute she wasn't afraid. When they reached her door, she wordlessly took his hand and brought him inside.

Teddy, like any good reporter, knew there were occasions when it was best not to ask questions. If he was surprised to be kissed by a woman so recently widowed, he didn't show it, meeting Charlotte's advances with good-natured acquiescence. She hadn't intended to pull him so close, or tug at his shirt, but once her palm made contact with the bare skin of his back, she realized that the longer she continued, the longer Teddy would stay. And so Charlotte forged on.

It struck her as rather ridiculous, all the panting breaths and fumbling with clothes, though Charlotte tried to maintain the solemnity she thought such an encounter demanded. As they collapsed onto the bed, each of them wincing as they pulled apart to adjust their twisted wrists and cramped legs, Teddy laughed. The realization that physical relations needn't be deadly serious—that the entire process might even be funny—was a salve to Charlotte's despair. She felt like a child again, all wide-eyed curiosity, and had to remind herself that in Teddy's eyes she wasn't an innocent virgin but a woman who'd experienced a marital bed. Charlotte's heart raced when Teddy maneuvered on top of her, but the act wasn't as painful as she'd expected. When Teddy had satisfied himself, he slid down to her side with a content grunt and regarded Charlotte with moist-eyed gratitude, the recipient of an unexpectedly generous gift. Charlotte felt the warmth of his body soak into hers, soothing her far beneath her skin. When he began to pull away, she asked him to stay, and he did. For the rest of the journey, she spent her nights curled up against him, sleeping more soundly than she had in ages.

It wasn't love. Charlotte found Teddy soothing, that was all, and they continued to soothe each other from time to time, whenever they were lonely or frustrated or giddily celebrating a professional success. Charlotte told Teddy early on that she wasn't interested in marriage, and if Teddy had hoped otherwise, he never let on. Charlotte knew they'd make for an uneasy domestic match, for despite Teddy's happy-go-lucky façade, he was just as ambitious as she was. When Teddy got engaged to a suitably domestic-minded woman, their physical interludes came to an end, with no regrets on Charlotte's part. By then, she'd had other lovers, men who intrigued and amused her, men she thought herself passionately in love with until their mysteries were revealed and the attraction withered. At work and in bed, Charlotte was always drawn to novelty.

Life as a newspaperwoman wasn't so very different from life as a thief. Though Charlotte no longer created characters with made-up names and histories, she still played roles, shifting her words and mannerisms to lure her subjects into trusting her. When she was talking to a cook suspected of poisoning her drunken employer, she was Lottie, the south London scrapper-made-good. When she toured the Chelsea Flower Show, she was Mrs. Evers, a respectable middle-class wife. Charlotte's stories may have been confined to the women's pages, where reporters worked without bylines, but public recognition was never her goal. What mattered to Charlotte were her own, more personal successes: convincing a reluctant subject to give her an exclusive interview, furnishing her own bedsit near Hyde Park, juggling suitors with the expertise of a circus performer so that none ever knew the others existed.

Charlotte may not have been a real widow, but she lived as one, knowing the "Mrs." gave her a social standing she'd never have as a "Miss." Her sham marriage came in especially helpful during the war, when she interviewed other women who'd lost their husbands and occasionally joined in their tears. Charlotte wrote far too many stories of young men snatched from their families too soon, as she desperately tried to conjure heroics from youthful promise and the Flemish mud where the young soldiers had died. In time, she suffered her own loss, a young officer who left for the front before her usual disillusionment set in. She knew she was mourning the idea of him more than the man himself, who would have inevitably disappointed or bored her. But that didn't make her sorrow any less real.

Teddy, somewhat unexpectedly, made a name for himself as a fearless war correspondent, a reputation that led to his appointment as the *Record's* editor in 1925. He gave Charlotte her own column and a substantial raise, and suddenly "Mrs. Evers Reports" became required daily reading for anyone who wanted to vicariously savor—while outwardly condemning—the outrageous behavior of the so-called bright young things. Scandalous divorces, young heirs fighting over Grandpapa's fortune, secret love children and paid-off mistresses—Charlotte wrote about them all with witty panache. The disillusioned youth of the 1920s were a never-ending source of material.

Charlotte transformed herself with the times, the fustiness of her Edwardian youth giving way to Art Deco sleekness. Her curly, once-tempestuous hair was subdued into sleek marcel waves, her lace-trimmed shirtwaists and petticoats abandoned in favor of sharp wool suits. As she passed through her thirties into her early forties, Charlotte lost her appetite for shape-shifting. She bought a flat in Belgravia, cultivated a circle of artistic friends, and settled into her role as the *Record*'s tartly amusing social columnist. No one ever asked about Mr. Evers. Like Charlotte, her companions had turned resolutely away from the past.

It was impossible to escape that past completely, of course, not when one's job depended on keeping up with the news of the day. From time to time, Charlotte would read about one of her fellow lifeboat passengers: Mr. Wells, the surly fireman, who was killed in the Battle of Jutland in 1916; or the old woman, Mrs. Dunning, who died not long after the Armistice. But Charlotte never made an effort to find out what happened to the others. Of all the people in the lifeboat, the only one she ever gave any thought to was Mr. Healy. During her first years at the *Record*, as she was zealously plunging into her new life, he lingered in her memory, the way an abandoned book tantalizes with its unknown ending. She'd never met another man with whom she'd felt such instant rapport. It wasn't just his looks, though his classically handsome features had made him a favorite with the female spectators at the hearings. It was something about the man himself, a deep-rooted sense of honor that offered a ballast to Charlotte's wayward soul. She'd find herself wondering what he was doing and whether he was still at sea. If he ever thought about the awful reckoning they'd faced on the lifeboat. Charlotte imagined Mr. Healy appearing on her doorstep and inviting her to tea, and the thought of seeing him again brought her a peaceful sort of satisfaction.

It was wishful thinking, in any case, because Mr. Healy never did trouble himself to find her. Charlotte could have sought him out, if she wished; the White Star Line would have records on his family and his last known address. But if she did write, what would she say? All she had were memories of emotions from years before, emotions he might not welcome or share. And so, as with all well-intentioned but potentially humiliating impulses, it was easier to do nothing.

The meeting that Charlotte had been dreading was arranged for Saturday, two days before her departure for America. The chauffeur arrived at two o'clock sharp, and Charlotte settled into the Rolls Royce's luxuriously tranquil interior for the hour-long drive to the country. In her handbag was a letter dated November 23, 1930, typed on the engraved stationery of Grainger & Sons, Solicitors. For nearly two years, it had been lying under a pile of correspondence in the bottom drawer of her desk, its silent accusation pricking at her conscience.

> *Dear Mrs. Evers,*
> *I am writing on behalf of my client, Lady Upton, wife of the late Frederick St. Vaughn, Lord Upton. In addition to her most recent bereavement, Lady Upton suffered the loss of her youngest son, George St. Vaughn, on the* Titanic. *For some time, she has wished to locate a Mr. Reginald Evers, an acquaintance of her son whose name appeared on a list of British citizens who survived the sinking. It is her hope that Mr. Evers can provide an account of Mr. St. Vaughn's last hours.*

In the course of our inquiries, we have not been able to locate an address or record of employment for Mr. Evers, and we believe it likely he changed his name or moved abroad. However, a Mrs. Evers also appeared on the survivors' list, and we are writing to inquire if you are the wife of Mr. Reginald Evers or otherwise related to him. If so, would you please write at your earliest convenience? Any information that assists in our search would be a great comfort to Lady Upton.

> *Yours most sincerely,*
> *Oswald Grainger*

Charlotte hadn't written back. How could she possibly tell Mr. Grainger what had happened to Georgie and Reg? But she hadn't thrown the letter away, either. She told herself the St. Vaughns had nothing to do with her, and a stranger's sorrow was none of her concern. Yet Charlotte couldn't help but think of the poor woman, still mourning the son who had never come home. Now that she was preparing to confront her own past, it seemed unconscionably cruel to deny a grieving mother a simple act of kindness. Charlotte wasn't prepared to admit everything; she didn't owe Lady Upton the truth. But a few polite lies might be enough to assuage Charlotte's guilt.

Charlotte had been to her share of house parties, so she no longer felt a flutter of nerves as she approached The Oaks, a mansion set at the end of an intimidatingly long drive. But her previous excursions had been jolly gatherings of bon vivants and socialites who greeted each other with kisses and shouts of "Splendid!" and "Darling!" This time, she had been summoned by a stranger, with no idea of what awaited her. The important thing was to stay calm, no matter what she might be asked. Lady Upton mustn't suspect that Georgie was anything more than a casual shipboard acquaintance.

The chauffeur said nothing as he opened the car door and Charlotte stepped out. A butler done up in full prewar livery stood in the doorway, his face a portrait of grim resolve. He, too, was silent as Charlotte walked into the entry hall, a gloomy, wood-paneled cave in which Henry VIII would have felt right at home.

"Lady Upton will see you in the morning room," the butler said, his back to Charlotte as he led the way.

Charlotte felt the disapproval coming off him like a strong cologne, and she bristled with self-righteous anger. It had been a long time since Charlotte had been subjected to such flagrant snobbery; the circles she traveled in welcomed working-class writers alongside aristocratic titles. If Lady Upton displayed the same contempt as her butler, it wouldn't be a long visit.

The Oaks had the hush of a museum, or a memorial to the dead. The morning room, with its oversized fireplace, worn sofas, and family photographs, was much as Charlotte expected, but Lady Upton wasn't. Charlotte had pictured her as an aristocratic archetype, with stiff shoulders and an even stiffer upper lip. The woman who rose to greet her, however, had the weathered face and pudgy, shapeless body of a nanny or farmwife, a woman who puts more effort into her work than her appearance. She was dressed in an old-fashioned frock that grazed her ankles, and her white hair was piled in a ramshackle heap held together with diamond pins.

"Mrs. Evers," she said. "Thank you for coming."

Charlotte's initial reservations softened. "Lady Upton. A pleasure."

Lady Upton wavered a moment, looking from the butler to Charlotte, then back. "We'll take our tea," she finally said, and as the butler walked away, she gestured toward the sofa. "Please."

Charlotte began to feel more at ease. She'd been in this situation before, interviewing old women in rooms just like this, sitting on sofas just as faded. She knew how to look fascinated when they rambled and when to nod understandingly as they complained about the latest modern outrage. She prepared herself to begin the conversation with a few pleasantries and perhaps some benign tidbits of London gossip.

But Lady Upton surprised Charlotte again. Dispensing with polite chitchat, she spoke bluntly.

"Mrs. Evers, I have lost everything I loved."

Charlotte's eyes followed Lady Upton's to the mantelpiece, where an array of silver frames had been precariously jumbled together. From one, she saw Georgie's face looking back at her. It came as a physical shock. She hadn't prepared herself for what it would be like to see him again. His eyes seemed to be staring directly at Charlotte, demanding an explanation she couldn't give.

"I no longer receive guests," Lady Upton said. "I no longer go out. I live here, alone, with memories as my only companions."

Lady Upton stood and walked to the fireplace. She picked up the largest photograph and carried it back to Charlotte. Charlotte laid the bulky frame on her lap and looked at the figures of two boys in school uniforms, posing on The Oaks' front drive.

"My George and my Tom," Lady Upton said. "The dearest boys you could imagine."

A maid arrived with the tea tray, and Charlotte, grateful for the interruption, put the photo aside. She had interviewed dozens of women who'd been scarred by the war, yet she had never been able to shield herself completely from their hurt. Every soldier who'd died had left an abyss of grief, spiraling out from those who loved him.

"I'm so very sorry," Charlotte murmured. An empty gesture, but it was important to say something, to forestall the temptation of tears.

Lady Upton took the picture and set it tenderly on the cushion beside her, the same way she once might have settled her sons before reading them a story.

"Sugar?" Lady Upton asked.

Charlotte nodded, and Lady Upton poured. She offered Charlotte a plate of biscuits, and Charlotte took two, though she hardly felt like eating. The sooner she got to the heart of what Lady Upton wanted, the sooner she could leave, and already she was worried that if this meeting dragged on long enough, she'd be asked to stay for supper.

"Your son Tom," Charlotte said. "Was he lost in the war?"

Lady Upton nodded. "At Ypres. Only a month after he joined up."

"What a terrible loss," Charlotte said, wishing there was something more she could say, knowing there wasn't. She hadn't seen a photograph of a man in uniform on the mantel, but she was sure the family would have commissioned a portrait of Thomas St. Vaughn in his military finery before he went off to the front. Most likely it was by Lady Upton's bedside, to be sobbed over each night.

"I invited a group of his school friends here a year or so after the Armistice," Lady Upton said. "The ones who'd survived. One fellow lost both legs at the Somme, which must have been dreadful, but he put on a good show. They all did, for my sake. It was so lovely to talk about Tom. People don't want you to speak of the dead once they're gone. It makes them uncomfortable. But how can you ask a mother to pretend her children never existed? The only scraps of happiness I've felt in ages are when I've been able to share memories of my boys."

Charlotte nodded, thinking she never should have come. She'd expected a brief, formal conversation, not this wrenchingly honest confession.

"I grieved terribly for Tom. Of course I did. But I was prepared to lose him, from the day he left. I even expected it, though I didn't dare say so at the time. My heart was already broken, you see, by George's death. To lose my sweet, darling boy with no warning, and not even have a body to bury . . . it ruined me."

Charlotte told herself Lady Upton's grief had nothing to do with her. But she felt the woman's anguish leak through her armor, infecting her with guilt. "He was a delightful young man," she said.

Lady Upton's face lit up. "Wasn't he, though?"

If Lady Upton was so keen to talk about her son, why not indulge her? It was better than watching her cry.

"As you know, he was an acquaintance of my husband, Mr. Evers," Charlotte continued. She had no idea how much Lady Upton knew about Reg and Georgie. Best to be circumspect. "I hadn't met him before we sailed, but Reginald introduced us on board. I remember thinking he was one of the most handsome men I'd ever seen, but he wasn't at all vain about his looks. Right off, he said he hoped we'd be friends."

In a queasy wave of remembrance, it all came back: Georgie's puppy-dog eyes, hungry for Charlotte's approval. His constant hovering. She'd been awful, barely able to look him in the face without scowling. But Lady Upton didn't need to know that. Charlotte sifted through her memories, choosing the bits that presented her and Georgie in the best light, describing strolls on deck and friendly conversations over meals. Lady Upton listened raptly, as if Charlotte's banal vignettes were a thrilling tale of suspense, for these were stories Lady Upton hadn't worn smooth with repeated recall. They allowed her to imagine that Georgie was still making his way across the Atlantic, unseen but not yet lost.

Charlotte even managed to make Lady Upton laugh. "I can't believe he told you about my sister's horse!" she said, with a disconcertingly childish giggle. "Poor Prancer. He was such a naughty one." Then the sadness swept back in, like clouds dimming a midnight moon. "He had to be put down in the end."

Death and more death. Charlotte desperately tried to think of a story that would distract Lady Upton, something amusing to keep the mood light. She'd already embellished the truth beyond recognition. She was close to inventing a conversation, when Lady Upton asked with disconcerting directness, "Do you know what happened to George? At the end?"

Finally, the question Charlotte had been dreading. She shook her head. "I left in a lifeboat, before the ship sank."

"With your husband?"

"No."

"But he survived," Lady Upton said.

This is wrong, Charlotte thought. *I shouldn't mislead this poor woman.* But she'd made a promise, and she feared the repercussions of breaking it.

"He was rescued later," Charlotte said, "by another boat."

"Did he tell you what happened to George?"

Again, Charlotte shook her head, more forcefully than before. "We didn't talk about the sinking. It was all such a shock."

"I understand. You mustn't feel bad on my account. It was such a muddle for us, as well. At first, we were told George had been saved. The next day, his name was on a list in the paper, of passengers lost. It wasn't until the rescue ship arrived in New York that we received a telegram . . ." She paused to take a shaky breath. "Even then, I kept hoping. I thought George might walk through the door and tell me it had all been the most dreadful mistake."

She was smiling and crying, all at once, and Charlotte felt leaden with shame. She hadn't expected to like Lady Upton so much. It would have been so much easier if Lady Upton had been condescending and awful. Then Charlotte could have walked away knowing there was a good reason for her lies. Now, she wasn't so sure.

"I saw Mr. Evers's name on the survivors list, and I wanted to write to him," Lady Upton said. Her voice was steady, though her eyes were shiny with tears. "But my husband wouldn't hear of it. I was allowed a month of mourning, and that was that. My husband cleared out all George's things, and I was forbidden to speak of him, as if he'd never existed. I thought it might be for the best. That I'd recover if I didn't brood. Then we lost Tom, and I barely cried at all. By then, I had no feelings left.

126

"My husband was not an easy man to live with, but I knew my place. He made the decisions, and I did as he wished. Since his death, I've found myself rather adrift. I walk through this enormous house, alone, thinking of my children when they were small, rushing down the steps or begging me to join them for tea in the nursery. My husband would have found it all terribly self-indulgent, but it makes me happy." Lady Upton managed a crooked smile. "Does that sound mad?"

"No," Charlotte said, wondering if Lady Upton was, in fact, deranged by grief.

"I'm so glad you understand." Lady Upton looked momentarily happy. "It's such a consolation to be able to talk about my boys. It feels as if they've been returned to me, in some small way."

What a sorry life, Charlotte thought. Kept under the thumb of a domineering husband and forbidden from mourning her own sons. Not for the first time, Charlotte congratulated herself for never marrying.

"The only thing that continues to trouble me is the thought of George's final hours," Lady Upton continued. "Not knowing how he died. I remembered about Mr. Evers and thought I'd try to find him. I directed our family solicitor to make inquiries, but Mr. Evers seems to have disappeared." Lady Upton's face dropped. "Oh dear, I didn't even think to ask. Is he . . . ?"

Charlotte's mind raced. What should she say? It would be easiest to tell Lady Upton that Reg was dead. The conversation would be over, and Charlotte could be on her way. Instead, Charlotte found herself shrugging.

"He's alive, as far as I know. We've been estranged for some time."

"I hate to trouble you, it's only—I can't stop myself wondering what happened. We all heard such terrible stories about people freezing to death or being trapped in their staterooms, and it would be such a blessing to know he didn't suffer. And seeing that he and Mr. Evers were particular friends . . ."

Lady Upton gave Charlotte a quick, meaningful glance. With that one look, she told Charlotte that she knew the truth about her son and Reg. A truth she would never openly acknowledge.

"They were together when I saw them last," Charlotte said carefully. "I don't think Reg would have left Georgie alone." She wasn't sure if Lady Upton would be consoled by that or not.

"Yet only Mr. Evers survived."

There was nothing accusatory in Lady Upton's tone; it was stated as simple fact. All Charlotte could think of was Reg's face when she'd refused to help Georgie dress in her clothes. The way Reg's expression had shifted from anguish to understanding. How he'd shouted when the lifeboat jerked past the windows, forcing it to stop so Charlotte could be saved. She remembered her last glance at Georgie—cowering and confused, like an abused kitten—and was shocked to remember how much she'd hated him. It felt like the savagery of a more primitive self.

"Do you think Mr. Evers might pay me a visit, if I asked?"

Charlotte tried to keep as close as she could to the truth. "He stayed in America. I don't think he's been back to England since."

"I could send a letter, if you have his address."

"We don't correspond," Charlotte said bluntly. Then, almost against her will, she offered, "I'm traveling to New York in a few days. I might be able to find him. I could try."

Lady Upton gave Charlotte a twisted smile, an expression of such determined appreciation that Charlotte felt sick. "I would be so grateful. You've been very kind to indulge an old woman like me. Hearing your stories, talking about George—it's been such a help."

Charlotte had her doubts about that. She suspected that dredging up Lady Upton's questions about Georgie's death might have made things worse. But Charlotte could no longer shield herself from Lady Upton's grief. Even the way she looked at Charlotte—with hopeful longing—was an echo of her son, and a stinging reminder of Charlotte's own selfishness and jealousy. Lady Upton wasn't at all what she expected;

what if Georgie wasn't, either? Had Charlotte given him a chance to prove otherwise?

Charlotte had never shied away from lying, when it suited her purposes. But now she felt the burden of her deceit. The arrangement she'd made on the *Carpathia*'s deck had consequences she'd never foreseen. She would carry Lady Upton's pain, deservedly so, until she could set things right. And if she couldn't, she would console herself with the knowledge that she'd tried her best. Charlotte knew, all too well, that some mistakes could never be mended.

ESME

Esme Van Hausen took her first steps carefully, making sure each heel was steady before shifting her weight to the opposite foot. She'd been so wobbly lately. The previous day, she'd nearly taken a tumble in the hall, right in front of Mrs. Gerstner. She'd managed to laugh it off, but it had been a close call. Esme couldn't afford to have the staff gossip about her more than they already did, not when her reputation was as shaky as her nerves.

Her mysterious visitor really should have known better than to show up at ten o'clock in the morning. It was much too early for social calls. When Mrs. Gerstner barged into Esme's bedroom, saying she had an unexpected guest, Esme had kept her face sheltered in the sheets when she asked who it was. She hadn't yet felt ready to face the daylight. The housekeeper told Esme the woman hadn't presented a calling card.

"Said she was an old friend and wanted to surprise you. She has an accent—English, I think."

The lack of information was irritating, but also effective. It was two weeks since Charlie had died, one week since his funeral. Esme had avoided seeing anyone by playing the grieving widow, which was close to the truth. She was grieving, for so much more than Charlie.

Curiosity, however, was enough to overpower her lethargy, and Esme managed to pull herself up and out of bed.

She washed up in the bathroom, her head throbbing each time she leaned over the basin. Then she took her time deciding what to wear. Esme's vanity was a form of self-preservation, and she couldn't abandon her fastidiousness simply because Charlie was gone. She had turned forty a few months before the accident, and though it wasn't a milestone she wanted to acknowledge openly, Charlie had brought her flowers and taken her out to dinner. If she wanted, Esme could choose to remember the evening as a happy one. She had tried very hard to have fun, and Charlie seemed grateful for the effort, even if he spent half the meal hopping to other tables to say hello. When Esme caught a glimpse of herself in the powder-room mirror, she'd been pleasantly surprised. Thanks to the fortune she'd spent on face cream and hair dye, she still looked attractive. For a woman of her age—the inevitable modifier.

Esme decided on a dress of dark-green silk, appropriate for a widow but not too gloomy. She could remember, vaguely, the mourning dresses she'd been forced to wear when her mother died. Thank God that tradition had gone out with the Victorians, because black wasn't at all flattering to Esme's complexion. She settled at her dressing table, her fingers moving confidently among the cosmetic bottles and brushes. Her lack of sleep was soon concealed with powder and eye pencil, and a swab of lipstick brought her mouth to life. Her cheek bore almost no trace of the gash she'd suffered in the lifeboat, though she'd feared it would be disfiguring at the time. There was only so much she could do with her hair, but she smoothed it as best she could. Her hairdresser, Mrs. Volensky, usually came every other day, but Esme had given her the week off.

Esme knew the alligator shoes might not be the wisest choice. They were higher and tighter than her other pairs, and she had had a close call when she turned out of her dressing room and nearly fell. But they were the best match for her dress, and Esme refused to cut corners when it came to fashion. She'd just have to be careful. She had an anxious moment at the top of the stairs, when her head went all dizzy and she swayed against the banister. But she managed to stay upright, despite the stabs of pain skittering inside her skull. Esme wrapped her fingers around the wood and stiffened her arm. A confident inner version of herself guided the struggling outer one: *Shoulders up, back straight, left foot, right foot.* With determined concentration, she made it to the bottom of the stairs and walked with smooth, even steps to the front parlor. It was only when she saw the woman standing by the fireplace that Esme's composure faltered. Despite the angled hat that covered half the visitor's face, Esme knew instantly who it was.

"Charlotte Evers," the woman said, holding out her hand.

"I remember," Esme said, not taking it.

Charlotte dipped her face toward the floor. At least she had the decency to be embarrassed. Esme's first impulse was to call for Mrs. Gerstner and have Charlotte escorted out. How dare she show up like this, with no warning? But that initial flash of anger quickly gave way to the disheartening realization that Charlotte's visit was the most interesting thing that was likely to happen today, or any other day in the foreseeable future. If Charlotte left now, Esme would always wonder why she'd come.

"Please sit," Esme said, curt but not quite rude. "I'll send for coffee."

Mrs. Gerstner wasn't hovering in the hallway, as she was supposed to when the Van Hausens had company, so Esme excused herself. In the minute it took Esme to track her housekeeper to the kitchen, Esme debated offering pastries as well, then decided against it. No need to encourage a drawn-out visit until she found out what Charlotte had to say. Wound up with anticipation, Esme nearly collided with a doorjamb on her way back to the parlor, and she forced herself to stop and slow her breathing. Charlotte mustn't see how close she was to losing control.

"I hope I didn't put you to any trouble," Charlotte said when Esme returned.

"No trouble," Esme said. "We so rarely receive visitors these days—the cook is beside herself with boredom."

She'd meant to lighten the mood, but Charlotte didn't look amused. Esme had to admit that Charlotte had held up well, though time had hardened her, too. There was a directness to her gaze that Esme found daunting. She seemed to see past Esme's gracious-hostess manners to the humiliating way she'd been coping with Charlie's loss.

"I heard about your husband," Charlotte said, formally polite. "I'm terribly sorry."

"Thank you." Esme could never find a suitable response to such well-meant expressions of sympathy. Was she supposed to smile bravely or weep genteel tears? She'd lost her instinct for what was appropriate. "It's very kind of you, to come in person," she said. "I didn't realize you lived in New York."

"I don't. I went back to London soon after the sinking."

Then why are you here? Esme wondered. She told herself to be patient and wait for Charlotte to reveal her hand.

"We all rather scattered, didn't we?" Charlotte asked, as if they were discussing old school friends. "Did you see anyone from the boat, afterward?"

"Well, Charlie, of course . . ."

Esme saw Charlotte brace herself for a show of grief. No. She mustn't talk about Charlie.

"And Sabine, my maid."

Charlotte nodded.

"She was with me for years," Esme said. "She turned out to be quite a good seamstress, and she began making dresses for me, and then my friends wanted her to make things for them, and it all progressed from there. She has her own boutique, now, on Madison Avenue."

"Well done," Charlotte said, "though I am surprised. She seemed such a meek little thing."

"She still is, in some ways," Esme said. "I don't think I've ever heard her raise her voice. She has a quiet kind of strength, though. I depended on her a great deal, in those months afterward, and she was so loyal. That meant a lot. I was sad to lose her as a maid, of course, but I did all I could to help her get started with the shop. I'm very proud of her." What would Esme have been, without Sabine? Sabine was the one who had comforted Esme when she cried for Hiram, the night before she married Charlie. Sabine had always listened; she had always understood.

"And you remember Mrs. McBride and her sisters?" Esme continued. "They used to call on me, when they were visiting New York. She passed away ten years ago or so, and Mrs. Westleigh just last year. I don't think the youngest one is up to traveling anymore."

"I wonder what happened to the little Swedish girl," Charlotte said.

"Anna," Esme said. She wondered, too. She remembered the young woman hunched in the middle of the boat, shivering, her face blank with shock.

"I haven't been able to travel by ship since then," Esme said. "It drove Charlie crazy, because he always wanted to spend a summer in France or Italy. He said money was no fun if you weren't spending it, and I know thousands of people make the crossing every year with no danger whatsoever, but I just can't seem to get myself on a boat. You may be one of the only people who understands why."

"I do," Charlotte said. "The White Star Line arranged for my passage home, and I was terrified the entire time. I didn't set foot on a boat again until this week."

It made no sense. Charlotte was so broken up over Charlie's death that she'd gotten over her fear of sailing, jumped on a ship, and rushed to see Esme, a woman she hadn't spoken to in twenty years?

"I'm honored you made such an effort on my behalf," Esme said.

That hit a nerve, because Charlotte looked away. She was definitely up to something. Mrs. Gerstner came in with a tray, and the conversation paused as coffee was poured and passed. When Mrs. Gerstner left,

Esme kept her cup by her lips, sipping slowly. She'd force Charlotte to talk first.

"Mr. Van Hausen's death made all the papers in England," Charlotte said.

"Goodness." Esme wasn't sure whether to be pleased or dismayed. "I didn't realize he was so well known there."

"Your marriage was one of the few happy stories to come from the whole *Titanic* catastrophe," Charlotte said. "You gave people hope when there wasn't much to be found."

Esme had a scrapbook in her room, filled with clippings from the week of her marriage. She could still recite the headlines: "The Triumph of Love over Loss." "An Unlikely *Titanic* Romance." "*Titanic* Widow Weds Her Rescuer." It had seemed as if the whole world were rooting for her and Charlie to be happy.

There'd been other kinds of stories, too, but those she hadn't cut out.

"There are many people, in England and America, who still think of you quite fondly," Charlotte said, so kindly that Esme might have mistaken her for a friend if she hadn't already been on guard.

"I've been amazed at the number of condolence letters I've received, from perfect strangers," Esme said. "It's quite overwhelming."

"People feel as if they know you, even if you've never met. They worry how you're coping. You must know that."

Charlotte was leaning forward, and her voice had softened into that of a sideshow hypnotist. She hadn't been so cunning in the lifeboat, Esme remembered. She'd thought shouting and haranguing would bring others to her side. Which it hadn't, of course.

"I'm a reporter for the *London Record*," Charlotte said. "I'd like to tell your story, yours and Mr. Van Hausen's."

Esme shrank back, repulsed. Charlotte had swanned into her home with sympathetic murmurs and put-on concern, thinking she'd trick Esme into doing what she wanted. Esme dropped her cup in its saucer with a clatter and stood up. Insults and questions swirled in her head, but all she managed to say was, "Get out."

Charlotte rose cautiously, a mouse placating a territorial cat. "I'm sorry if I've upset you. I'm sure you've been approached by all sorts of papers and magazines, and I thought you might agree to an interview with someone you knew, so as to stop all the bother."

"Why would I trust you?" Esme cried. She wanted to shriek loud enough to rattle the chandeliers. To launch into a rage that would hurtle her out of the onslaught of memories. She turned away, too quickly, and her knee slammed against a side table, knocking her off balance. Nauseous, swaying, she heard Charlotte apologize and say she could be reached at the Metropolitan Hotel if Esme changed her mind. Esme didn't turn around. She didn't look back as she teetered out of the room and up the stairs, making her faltering way to the bedroom. Back to the nightstand and the bottle that brought a sour but dependable relief.

So much for the triumph of love over loss.

The gin coated the back of her mouth like a medicinal penance. Now that Esme was safe in her second-story refuge, the blinds drawn against the accusing sunlight, she felt a resentful admiration for Charlotte's nerve. There was a time when Esme would have courted such attention, a time when she saw newspapers as allies instead of enemies. She hadn't minded playing the role of a sad-eyed young lover, one whose happiness was all the more precious for being tinged with heartbreak. Everyone, it seemed, had wanted her and Charlie to live happily ever after.

No one would thank her for admitting they hadn't.

Damp-eyed, embracing her self-indulgent sorrow, Esme grabbed the silver-framed wedding photo on her bureau and lay it beside her as she burrowed under the covers. Charlie had loved her, in the beginning at least; she was sure of that. But he loved her in the carefree way he was capable of, not with the dogged devotion that weathers the boredom of daily routines. Esme had spent years wondering what she'd done wrong, then years after that shoveling the blame on Charlie. It was only recently that she'd come to believe they were doomed from the start, long before the gushing headlines. The moment she'd pulled Charlie into the lifeboat—without even thinking, simply reaching out in need—was the moment she'd lost him.

How could they have foreseen the repercussions of that one action? Esme had been so grateful to have Charlie with her, to know he was alive. And saving him hadn't been wholly selfish, either. They all might have drowned if Charlie hadn't been there, keeping a cool head and rowing until his hands cramped in pain. On that night, it was impossible to imagine that each small decision might later be magnified beyond reason, or that one spontaneous gesture could be held up as evidence in the court of public opinion. Esme knew she hadn't been as careful as she should have been, but she'd been young and frightened and confused, and the only thing that made her feel better was Charlie. She could still remember how Charlie smelled when she leaned her face into his neck. So heady, so much hers. His warmth had seeped into Esme like a sedative, and she'd slipped her hand into his coat pocket, where his fingers clutched hers with forceful need. Charlie had been her anchor, holding her still.

They'd both been more mindful of propriety in the days following their rescue. Charlie was solicitous on the *Carpathia*, asking after Esme's health and joining her at meals, but they never spoke in private; Esme was taken into the care of the same Philadelphia society women she'd once regarded with bored contempt. Mrs. Thayer and Mrs. Widener were also recent widows—Mrs. Widener, appallingly, had lost her son as well—and Esme was soothed by their quiet camaraderie. In their presence, she wasn't expected to talk or be charming. She could simply savor her relief at having survived.

Esme grieved for Hiram in an obligated, perfunctory way. She didn't really miss him until she was back in Philadelphia, wandering through their sprawling home, feeling like a child playing house. The chair at the head of the dining table would always be his, just as the large armchair in the sitting room was still molded to the shape of his body. She might as well have been living with a ghost. But Esme didn't cry until his sister came to visit, her face splotchy and wan. As Esme's sister-in-law spoke haltingly of the brother she'd lost, Esme felt the full enormity of Hiram's absence. She'd dismissed him as plodding and dull, but he'd been a good man at heart. He'd deserved better.

Esme's guilt over Hiram in no way lessened her desire for Charlie. There was an inevitability to their marriage, a recognition among both their families that Charlie had taken on the role of Esme's guardian, but mourning etiquette still had to be observed. For Esme, that meant months of condolence calls and meals eaten alone. Her correspondence with Charlie was a lifeline, for it was only in her letters that Esme was able to reveal her true self: hungry for Charlie and their future. Though she thought of Charlie's body often, in her lonely bed, social niceties prevented her from even touching him. When Charlie called on Esme in Philadelphia, she received him with her father and the ever-obliging Mrs. Ayres as chaperones. When Esme spent a few days in Boston at the invitation of his mother, she stayed in a guest suite at the opposite side of the house from Charlie's room and felt as if she were being constantly watched and critiqued. But Esme was Charlie's choice, and his mother wouldn't deny anything to her adored youngest child who'd miraculously survived the *Titanic*. If Charlie wanted to marry Esme, he could.

When the engagement was announced, six months after the sinking, Charlie and Esme had already settled the terms of their married life. They would start fresh in New York, where Charlie's Harvard connections had already found him a job in banking, and his parents would buy them a suitably distinguished house. Esme took care to be circumspect with Hiram's family and friends, describing the upcoming union in practical rather than emotional terms, but she saw how much the news wounded Hiram's sister. It couldn't be easy to see her brother so quickly replaced. But Hiram's sister was gracious and gave Esme her blessing.

"Hiram wouldn't have wanted you to be alone," she said. "You're so young. You have a whole life ahead of you."

Queasy with guilt, Esme remembered her last glimpse of Hiram on deck, as he stoically watched her leave. Had he thought her a loyal wife, in those final moments? The thought that he'd gone to his death knowing about Charlie felt suddenly like a greater betrayal than her unfaithfulness, for it was a wrong she could never set right. In the bleak early morning hours before her wedding, as Esme paced and fretted over her red-rimmed, bloodshot eyes, she even blurted out her regrets to Sabine, who shook her head when Esme asked if Hiram had ever questioned Esme's nighttime absences. Sabine was too naïve to lie, but Esme wasn't comforted by her assurances. If Hiram had doubted Esme's fidelity, he wouldn't have confided his fears to a maid.

It was lack of sleep, Esme told herself, that made her so lackluster at the moment she should have been happiest. The wedding was appropriate to their circumstances: a simple ceremony performed at Charlie's family home, with only immediate family in attendance. When Esme said her vows, it felt as if she were acting out an elaborate fantasy: *This is what it would be like to marry Charlie Van Hausen*. And if their wedding night was a disappointment, with none of the passion of their shipboard couplings, Esme wouldn't allow herself to dwell on it. They needed time to rediscover each other, that was all.

It wasn't until the following day, when Charlie and Esme left for the train station, that they learned how much their lives had changed. A gauntlet of reporters and photographers extended along the sidewalk in front of the house, and Charlie and Esme had to jostle through them to get to the car. There were more newspapermen waiting for them in New York. Esme pretended to find it a bother, but secretly she was pleased. She'd always known that she and Charlie belonged together; now, it seemed as if the world agreed.

But true love only sells papers for so long. Within a few days, there were other stories, raising questions about Charlie and how he'd managed to live, when so many other first-class gentlemen had died. The old rumor that a man had snuck into a lifeboat dressed as a woman—which Esme thought had been put to rest at the Senate hearings—was exhumed and reexamined. Charlie's payment to the crewmen was once again questioned, his generosity twisted into something shameful. What made it worse was Charlie's unwillingness to fight back. The more Esme defended him, the more he retreated.

And now here was Charlotte, popping up like a ghost from Esme's haunted past. Older, of course, less histrionic, but still unmistakably herself. Charlotte was one of those lucky women whose allure wasn't solely dependent on youth. It was amazing, really, that Esme had remembered her so quickly, when they'd been together only a few hours, such a long time ago. Then again, those hours had dragged like years. Thinking of the lifeboat made Esme physically ache for the Charlie he'd once been, the man who'd grabbed her hand when she pulled. During all the rituals of loss she'd endured since Charlie's death, Esme had struggled to talk about her husband without hinting at her disappointment or their unhappiness. Now, she felt a shuddering longing for the Charlie who'd died long before. She still loved that man—she always would—and that realization released the tears she hadn't even known were there.

Esme and Charlie had never talked about the boat; she'd followed his example and tried to forget. But in an echo of her younger, lovestruck self, Esme wanted to talk about the object of her adoration, to relive every touch and feeling. Charlotte had been there. She might understand.

Esme wiped her face with her sleeve and dragged herself up from the bed. From the hallway telephone, she called the Metropolitan Hotel and left a message for Mrs. Evers, asking if they could meet. Then she took a bath and a nap. When she woke up, refreshed and nearly sober, a note in Mrs. Gerstner's neat handwriting was waiting on the bedside table: *Mrs. Evers invites you to dinner as her guest at the Metropolitan Hotel. 8:00 p.m.* It was the first time, Esme realized, that she'd be leaving the house since Charlie's funeral.

The Metropolitan was one of those genteelly shabby hotels that stays in business thanks to below-market prices and word of mouth. Just the sort of place that appealed to penny-pinching English travelers, Esme thought as she stepped out of the taxi. The doorman was slow-moving and seemingly mute, but Esme was relieved to be spared the fawning that would have awaited her at the Ritz or the Waldorf. How heavenly it was to be anonymous.

Charlotte was waiting in the cramped, ill-lit lobby, and she led the way into the equally glum dining room. The maître d' escorted them to a table by the front window, well away from the few other diners. Esme ordered soup, as per usual; in her efforts to remain slim, she'd grown accustomed to picking at meals rather than eating them. Saving her conversational strength for what was to come, she agreed with Charlotte that the weather had been lovely, and it was a shame to see all those hobos camped out in Central Park. Charlotte asked about Esme's children, and Esme felt a nourishing flush of pride. She'd made a success of that part of her life, at least.

"Robbie's at Harvard. We're so proud of him . . ." Esme stumbled and paused. "That is—I'm so proud. He's smart and he's kind, and you should see him on the football field! No one can keep up with him."

Charlotte smiled with what looked like genuine pleasure, but she couldn't know how extraordinary Robbie really was. He'd inherited Charlie's exuberance and Esme's bubbly laugh, but his good nature was underpinned by a wary protectiveness of those he loved. Esme never could have gotten through the funeral without Robbie beside her, slipping his hand in the crook of her elbow so she wouldn't stumble. Even as a child, he'd been the one to coax her out of her room when all she wanted to do was sob her way through a bottle. He'd had a way of calling out "Mother?" with a catch in his voice that she couldn't resist.

"Rosie—Rosalind—is thirteen. She's staying with Charlie's mother right now, in Boston. Mrs. Van Hausen was quite cut up, as you can imagine."

Mrs. Van Hausen had always been dour, and Charlie's death had sunk her into full-blown despair. Esme couldn't bear to be around her. Mrs. Van Hausen openly blamed Esme for Charlie's unhappiness, forgetting that a failed marriage was a joint accomplishment, and Charlie hadn't exactly held up his side of the bargain.

"Do you have children?" Esme asked.

Charlotte shook her head. "No, I never married." Then, almost as an afterthought, she said, "After Mr. Evers."

Esme was about to be polite and ask how long they'd been married, but Charlotte seemed intent on moving the conversation away from herself.

"I'm awfully glad you agreed to see me," Charlotte said. She reached into the handbag that sat on the floor by her chair. "I'll take a few notes now, if you don't mind, then we can do the official interview afterward."

Esme shook her head. "I came to tell you I won't do an interview. You can put that away."

She looked pointedly at the pen in Charlotte's hand. There was a pause while Charlotte seemed to consider whether it was worth arguing. Then she put the pen back.

"All right."

There was no reason for Esme to linger in a room where spilled sauce streaked the shabby carpets and the half-hearted lighting made everyone look sick. Esme could summon enough superficial conversation to get through the meal and leave before she said things she'd later regret. But what did she have to go back to? An empty house. Her bed. The bottle. It wouldn't be long before the last of the liquor was gone, and Esme didn't have the faintest idea how to find a bootlegger; Charlie had taken care of those arrangements. Dragging out this meeting would help her to ration what she had left.

But that wasn't the main reason Esme chose to stay. Charlotte was the last person she should confide in—a journalist, of all people!—yet Esme trusted her all the same. She realized, with a jolt, that Charlotte was watching her the way Charlie used to, back in England, before they'd ever kissed. It was the kind of look that draws one person to another: *I want to know you. Tell me who you are.*

And so Esme took a chance, just as she had with Charlie.

"Would you like to hear the real story of my marriage?" she asked Charlotte.

Charlotte looked wary.

"You can't write anything down, and you can't print anything I say. I have some very good lawyers at my disposal if you choose to break those terms."

"There's no need for lawyers," Charlotte said. "I'll keep whatever you tell me in confidence."

Perhaps she'd be content to simply listen, after all. There were so many things Esme wanted to say, confessions she could never make to her children or the lunch companions she referred to as friends. The truth was bubbling up, after decades of suppression, and Esme no longer felt sturdy enough to contain it. Charlotte suddenly seemed the only person who mattered. The only person who might give absolution.

"My grand *Titanic* romance," Esme intoned dramatically. "I believed in it as much as anyone. I was desperately in love with Charlie. Even before the lifeboat. We'd met in England, you see, and I thought he was the most handsome, perfect man I'd ever met. I was married, and I know it was wrong, but I simply couldn't resist him. You had to have suspected . . ." Esme shot Charlotte a glance, but Charlotte's face remained perfectly composed. Either she genuinely didn't know, or she was a masterful liar. "I'm afraid I wasn't very discreet," Esme said. "You must have noticed how I clung on to him."

"I didn't notice much about you or Mr. Van Hausen," Charlotte said. "I was more concerned with other matters."

His death is on your hands! Charlotte had screamed. She'd sounded deranged, which made it easier to brush off. Esme wondered if Charlotte still believed it. She was afraid to ask.

"I felt very bad about Mr. Harper," Esme said. "My husband was a good man. But I was never in love with him, not like I was with Charlie. I hadn't been very happy with Hiram—I guess that's obvious, given my behavior—but I thought things would be different with Charlie. We were starting out wildly in love, so of course we'd have a successful marriage. That's how it's supposed to work, isn't it?"

"I'd like to believe so."

"Were you very much in love when you married Mr. Evers?" Esme asked.

The question obviously took Charlotte by surprise. Her eyes roamed the restaurant, as if she'd find the right words in a far-off corner. In the end, all she said was, "Yes."

"You must think I'm a terrible person."

"No." Charlotte's hand reached impulsively across the table in a gesture of reassurance. "Reginald and I were hardly a perfect match. There were times I hated him, too."

Esme was unexpectedly touched by the confession. She might have even asked a few questions about Reginald Evers if the waiter hadn't returned with their food. Esme swirled the dollop of cream that bulged from the center of her soup and watched the tendrils of white expand. The smell made her queasy. Charlotte dug into her roast, leaving Esme to talk.

"It's awful to admit, but I saw the sinking as a sign that Charlie and I were meant to be together. If everything had gone as planned, we would have said goodbye in New York, and I'd have gone back to my boring life with Hiram, and Charlie would have been matched up with some heiress or another. We'd never have seen each other again. When Charlie appeared at that window—when he helped you into the boat—it felt like fate. Hiram wasn't even dead yet, but I felt like my true husband had been saved."

Esme was startled to feel her eyes tingle with tears. Whatever her private heartaches, Mrs. Esme Van Hausen never made a spectacle of herself in public. She forced down a spoonful of soup, steadying her breathing.

"And then we were rescued, and you can guess the rest. Charlie and I corresponded, and it wasn't long before we were talking about marriage, and I know some people said we moved too fast, but I didn't care." Esme tried to block out an image of Hiram's sister, her face rigid with a forced smile. "The sinking made both of us determined to follow our hearts. If you could die tomorrow, why not live today?"

It was one of Charlie's favorite sayings, one Esme had been happy to live by in the early years. It hadn't been quite so inspiring later, when Esme was pregnant and exhausted and Charlie announced he was taking flying lessons or going on a weeklong hunting expedition with friends. As if he'd had a premonition of early death, Charlie had packed more than his share of adventure into his forty-three years.

"All the papers in England ran stories about your wedding," Charlotte said. "Seemed your picture was everywhere."

"Did you write about it?"

"'My Night with the *Titanic* Sweethearts'?" Charlotte said scornfully. "No, I didn't tell anyone I'd met you. Hardly anyone I work with knows I was on the *Titanic*, to this day."

"It was sort of fun to be famous." Until the gossip started and Charlie began ripping up the papers whenever a new story appeared. Charlotte didn't need to hear about all that. "I enjoyed setting up house, talking to Charlie over dinner each night—we were always laughing, not quite believing it was true. It seemed like I'd finally gotten everything I ever wanted."

That first year had been magical, every day beginning and ending with kisses. The excitement of throwing their first parties, Charlie's delighted surprise when Esme told him she was expecting. It felt like a very long time ago, so long that all the emotion had seeped out from her memories. Esme could see their faces, their gestures, their affectionate looks. But they were frozen images, nothing more.

"I couldn't expect things to stay magical forever, of course. Charlie was so impulsive—it was one of the things I loved about him—but it was hard on me, sometimes. He hated his job, so he was grumpy when he came home, and he'd want a distraction, but I'd be tired after a day with the children . . ."

Having felt the loss of her own mother so keenly, Esme was determined to be an active, visible presence in Robbie and Rosie's lives. They had a nanny, as did every other family they knew, but Esme was the one who woke up with the children and fed them breakfast. She was the one who sang them to sleep. She'd never have dreamed, back then, of locking herself away from them, as had become an all-too-frequent habit. Off Charlie would go to Long Island for the weekend, or his cousin's house in Boston, leaving Esme on her own, a young mother for whom the 1920s never roared. She wasn't sure when Charlie started cheating on her, only that he grew less inclined to hide it. Maybe he thought she wouldn't care, after what she'd done to Hiram. But it hurt, far more than he knew.

"I got to feeling pretty sorry for myself," Esme told Charlotte. "I'd wonder where we'd gone wrong, and I started to think I was being punished, for how I'd treated my first husband. That made me think about Hiram, and I realized I'd never really given him a fair shake. We were so different, and I thought he was such an old fogey, but he never would have treated me the way Charlie did. He'd never have gone off to Florida on a whim and forgotten to tell me for three days. He wouldn't have left me alone when Rosie had a fever and I was scared sick. He had a steadiness I used to find boring, until I was living with the opposite. It's kind of funny, isn't it? There I was, finally married to the man I thought was the love of my life. And I'd never been so unhappy."

Charlotte's sympathetic silence encouraged Esme to go on.

"Once I accepted my misery, things got easier." Esme attempted a laugh, but it came out wrong. More like a cough. "I put my energy into the children and charity work. Entire days would pass when Charlie and I were both at home but didn't speak. And it wasn't entirely his fault. I'd known what he was like from the very beginning—the kind of man who makes a pass at another man's wife. Why should I have been surprised that marriage bored him?"

In a perverse twist of their earlier romance, Esme found the best way to capture Charlie's attention was by hurling insults and wine glasses across the dining room. Dramatic scenes were the only way they ever ended up together in bed. As the children grew older and Esme grew wearier, she began sleeping in one of the guest rooms. It was potently satisfying to slam the door and shout "I hate you!" without having to look at Charlie's face. Wouldn't that make a swell story for the papers?

"It's natural to have regrets," Charlotte said. "Especially when you're still grieving."

"I failed him, in the end." Esme nearly whispered the words, not sure she was going to say them until they were out. "He had a tough time, recently. Wall Street bankers aren't very popular these days."

There'd been angry letters and threats of a lawsuit. A furious woman pounding on the front door, accusing Charlie of stealing her life savings. Esme hadn't known how to get rid of her without calling the police, which only brought more attention to the whole sordid matter. She'd ignored the late-night phone calls, the headlines that said Charlie's bank was on the brink of collapse. Charlie had laughed it all off, seemingly as indestructible as ever. Esme hadn't realized how much the years had weakened him, too.

"Charlie died in a car crash, as you've probably heard. I had to identify his body."

Esme paused, remembering the splotch of blood on the coroner's otherwise pristine white coat. It had been all she could look at as the man explained what had happened to Charlie's face. He had taken pains to be thorough, telling Esme which part of the car hit which part of the tree, and how that particular angle and force tossed Charlie's body through the windshield. It was quick, he reassured her; Charlie didn't suffer. Or was that what he told every grieving family member who visited his dismal workroom? He told Esme about the whiskey stains on Charlie's shirt and the bottle in the car, thinking she'd be relieved to know how it happened: *Had a few too many, lost control, an unfortunate accident.*

But there were a few relevant facts the coroner hadn't known. Charlie had the constitution of an ox and never got stumbling drunk, no matter how many whiskey and sodas he downed. Esme had driven that same stretch of road with him countless times to the country house they rented each summer, and she'd never seen him so much as skid. He knew every curve, every hill, every potential danger. If his car careened into a tree hard enough to crush his cheekbones and shatter his skull, it was because he'd wanted it to. He'd wanted to die.

No point in being coy, Esme decided. "Charlie killed himself," she told Charlotte.

Charlotte's lips parted, just a bit. "Are you sure?"

"Sure enough. It's so silly, but I'm madder at him for not leaving a note than for doing it. I could forgive him if he'd only explained."

But what could she expect from a man like Charlie? Once he'd made the decision to end his life, he'd want to get on with it. Still, he'd owed Esme a goodbye. She'd have managed to write something, if it had been her.

I loved you. I'm sorry.

"I don't think he ever forgave me for saving him," Esme said. "He wouldn't have made it into the lifeboat if it weren't for me. I pulled him in. And he carried that guilt ever since."

Esme, sheltered in her widow's mourning in Philadelphia, hadn't seen the looks Charlie endured those first weeks in Boston, when he was sneeringly referred to as the "luckiest man alive." Charlie had joked about the rumors, which made her think he didn't care. But every glare added to the weight that eventually crushed him. Never again was he the eager boy who'd kissed Esme in that leaky shed. Her happy ending had dissolved into a fog of disappointment and liquor, her emotions permanently dulled.

But maybe Esme's heart hadn't stopped working altogether, because it twisted in her chest as her face crumpled, and tears spilled down her cheeks. She was dimly aware of Charlotte rising from the table and pressing her arm around Esme's shoulders. Eyes closed, Esme slumped against Charlotte, the sobs shaking them both. There were voices, crisp and quick, but Esme couldn't understand what they said. She didn't try to. She stood, obedient as a rag doll, when Charlotte pulled her up and walked her out of the room, through the lobby, to the elevator. The operator, little more than a boy, gave Esme a chagrined stare under his jaunty red cap, so Esme turned into the corner to cry. She cried as the elevator rumbled to the tenth floor, and she cried as they entered Charlotte's room. When Charlotte gently lowered Esme onto the bed, Esme wrapped her arms around her chest, shoring up her ruined self. Charlotte sat silently beside her, wise enough to know there was nothing to be said.

Later, when Esme's cries had softened to hiccupping breaths, there was a doctor, who talked to Charlotte, not Esme. He gave Esme something to sleep, and it was glorious: an elixir that eased down her throat and knit together the broken pieces. The medicine transported her from the dingy hotel room into memories that were more vivid than the moments they recaptured. Charlie was there, carrying baby Rosie, singing a song about an owl and a pussycat. Esme could feel the downy tenderness of Rosie's head and the confident strength of Charlie's hands. She saw Charlie on their wedding day, looking at her with a nervous half grin, and elation swept through her like a fever: *At last, he's mine.*

She was with Charlie in the *Titanic* library, when a single furtive touch could drive her half crazy with longing.

The library. There was something Esme needed to remember about the library. She tried to envision the chairs and the bookshelves, but the more she tried to summon them, the more the images faded. A voice was calling her name, pulling her away.

Esme opened her eyes and saw Charlotte sitting on the edge of the bed. Though the curtains were open, only a sickly hint of daylight brightened the window. It must be one of the cheaper rooms overlooking an air shaft.

"What time is it?" Esme asked. Her tongue felt puffy and dry.

"Ten o'clock," Charlotte said. "I sent a note to your house, saying you were ill."

Esme sat up. She was still in her cocktail dress from the night before; only her shoes had been removed. "I'm sorry to have inconvenienced you."

"How are you feeling?" Charlotte asked.

"Much better, thank you." Esme shifted her feet from the bed and smoothed her skirt. She could see a toilet through a narrow door in the corner—the room had a private bath, thank God. "May I freshen up?"

"Of course." Charlotte seemed to find the whole situation as uncomfortable as Esme. "I'll ring for some coffee, shall I?"

Esme retreated to the bathroom and warily approached the mirror. It wasn't as bad as she'd feared: her hair had for the most part kept its waves, and her face was pale but resolute. At least she'd gotten a good night's sleep. More than a good night; she'd been out for more than twelve hours. She couldn't remember ever having slept that long.

After gulping three glasses of water and washing her face, Esme felt anxious to leave. She remembered, with a sense of unease, how honest she'd been at dinner. What had made her talk that way? And then to break down completely, in the middle of a restaurant . . . she'd put herself in a very awkward position. Best to do what she always did when she woke up with vague but discomforting flashbacks of the night before: pretend it never happened.

When Esme stepped back into the bedroom, Charlotte was fiddling with two china cups on a silver tray, looking exhausted. Anyone would think she was the one who'd needed a doctor the night before. Esme saw a bottle of pills on the nightstand and slipped it into her handbag.

"Sugar? Cream?" Charlotte asked.

"I really should be going."

There was nothing on Esme's social schedule, but she felt a growing distaste for Charlotte's company. Last night, Charlotte had come across as sincere and sympathetic; Esme had thought of her as a friend. But she wasn't, was she? Charlotte was a journalist, for God's sake. Even now, she might be planning her next story: "*Titanic* Widow Spills All!" If so, her paper would soon receive a visit from the Van Hausen family lawyers.

"Oh, I thought . . . ," Charlotte began.

"Enjoy the rest of your visit," Esme said. Best make it clear that she had no intention of seeing Charlotte again. "Are you staying in town long?"

"I'm leaving for California soon," Charlotte said.

"Surprising another old friend?"

Charlotte gave Esme a nod of acknowledgment: *Point made.* "You could say so."

She was being deliberately coy, daring Esme to ask. Who from the lifeboat might be living in California? One of those Trelawny children, maybe? Esme picked up her bag and hat, the familiar motions boosting her confidence. Last night's breakdown was only a temporary lapse.

Esme faced Charlotte head-on. "Everything I told you was said in the strictest confidence."

"I know."

"You can't tell anyone. Or write about it."

"I already promised I wouldn't. You have my word."

Esme pulled on her hat in an emphatic gesture of dismissal and walked out. She felt surprisingly hopeful as she stepped into the elevator. Telling the truth might not have been such a mistake. It left her feeling lighter, less beholden to the past. Invigorated by the bustle of Park Avenue, Esme decided to walk home. She wanted to recapture the lovely feeling she'd had when she first woke up, when she'd still been basking in Charlie's adoring smile.

Esme paused at the front window of a stationery shop, bright with an array of pastel-hued paper flowers. She'd come here many times, to order invitations for New Year's Eve dinners and charity teas. This was where she'd picked up a box of notecards a few weeks after her wedding and smiled gleefully when she saw "Mrs. Charles Van Hausen" engraved in gold. Charlie's name had become Esme's, and it would always be. Charlie was her greatest love and her greatest disappointment, the person she'd revolved around for half her life.

The truth hit Esme like an errant wave: *I'll never see him again.*

The hours stretched out before her, a bleak expanse of empty days leading to empty years. Yet for the first time since Charlie died, she didn't feel drawn to the cushioned shelter of her bed. She wanted to be swept up in the flurry of the city: the nannies and their charges, the businessmen and the newspaper sellers, the wealthy housewives flaunting new hats, the delivery boys scurrying in jagged trails around anyone who dawdled. She wanted to move through them without speaking or touching, like a ghost, experiencing their humanity from a slight remove. New York wasn't always the easiest place to live, even when you had money. But it was her home. She belonged here.

Esme considered a detour through Central Park. Walking through the zoo would remind her of the many times she'd taken Rosie and Robbie there when they were little. She glanced at her watch and realized it was nearly eleven o'clock. Sabine would be opening her shop, only a few blocks away. Esme had a sudden urge to see her. Unlike so many other of Esme's so-called friends, Sabine didn't wear her out. She was quiet and deferential, never interrupting, always happy to listen. You could tell Esme's kindness meant a great deal to her, given their gap in social status. Esme quickened her pace. Wouldn't Sabine be surprised to hear about Charlotte! Esme wouldn't tell Sabine everything, of course; there was no reason to get into Esme's suspicions about Charlie's death. Her job, as Charlie's widow, was to protect his memory, for the sake of their children. Besides, she didn't know what really happened. For all she knew, it was an accident after all.

Esme had once heard something about confession being good for the soul. Dreary old Catholic nonsense, she'd thought at the time. Now it struck her as profound: she'd confessed to Charlotte and felt her sins wiped clean. This born-again version of Esme wanted to shower others with kindness. Sabine, to a certain set of New York society, embodied European elegance, but Esme had known her when she was a hotel maid with no style at all. It was Esme's trust that had allowed Sabine to flourish.

Amid the honk of taxis and jumble of bodies, Esme felt a spark of joy that took her by surprise. For so long, she'd thought of happiness as her right. When it slipped from her hands, she looked for someone to blame. But what if she'd been wrong? What if true happiness came only in these small moments, whose very humility ensured they'd be overlooked? She'd looked to marriage to fulfill her, but it never would have, no matter what. If the *Titanic* hadn't sunk, and Hiram and Esme had gone back to Philadelphia, she would have pined over Charlie the rest of her life. He'd always have been the perfect man, held up as an impossible ideal against Hiram. The funny part was that Charlie hadn't lived up to that ideal, either. But Esme never would have known that if she hadn't married him.

Esme clutched her handbag closer, hearing the clatter of the bottle inside. Ever since Charlie's death, the nights had seemed endless. She'd toss and turn, or sink reluctantly into troubled dreams that left her shaken. Thinking of the pills gave her a marvelous sense of calm. Sleep was no longer something to fear, because it would bring a reunion with her most cherished memories. There were only about a dozen pills in the bottle, but Esme knew she could always get more. She had access to the very best doctors, didn't she? She would take as many as she needed to banish the visions that haunted her on the very worst nights. The nights she saw Hiram bobbing in the water, staring at her in eternal anguish.

ANNA

Anna never read American magazines. But Mrs. Wickstrom at the Farmers Cooperative store did, and there was one open on the counter when Anna came in. Anna glanced at the pages while she was waiting for Mrs. Wickstrom to fetch more yeast from the storeroom. Upside down, the words were a jumble of black squiggles, but one of the pictures caught her attention: a close-up portrait of a man with dark hair and a jutting chin. There was a smaller photograph next to it, showing a couple in wedding clothes.

Anna reached out and turned the magazine to face her. The man seemed to be staring out from the page, directly at Anna. Older, but instantly recognizable. The caption underneath read "Charles Van Hausen, dead at 43."

"Good-looking, isn't he?"

Mrs. Wickstrom had a disconcerting way of appearing out of nowhere; Anna hadn't heard her come back in.

"Mr. Wickstrom says I'm a fool to care what rich families get up to, but I can't help myself. I love to look at the pictures of all the parties and clothes." She pushed the magazine closer to Anna. "You can take it, if you like." Then, briskly, "Five cents."

Anna slipped the magazine into her basket and watched Mrs. Wickstrom add the amount in her ledger. The transaction made Anna feel sordid, and she rushed through her goodbyes, not bothering to double-check her shopping list as she usually would. She was sure she'd forgotten something, but it wasn't worth the embarrassment of staying.

Anna had walked to the store; it was still warm enough, in late September, and she hadn't needed many things. But as she made her way down the street, nodding to a few acquaintances but not slowing to talk, she wished she'd taken the cart. It would take her half an hour to get back to the house, and she wanted to be there already, in the quiet refuge where she could make sense of her rising distress. Charles Van Hausen was dead, and it shouldn't matter. She hadn't known him; she had no reason to be upset. Still, she could feel his eyes boring into her.

The caption under the wedding picture had confused her, for she'd thought he and the lady in the lifeboat were already married. They'd had a great affection for each other; that was certain, because Anna could remember her clinging to his side and clutching at his arm for reassurance. She was the most dazzling woman Anna had ever seen, with jewels that sparkled in her hair. Anna hadn't known until today that her name was Esme.

Silently, Anna tried out possible pronunciations: *Ehs-mee? Ess-may?* The sounds were mysteriously exotic, like the woman herself. For a fleeting moment, Anna thought of sending a letter of condolence, but she rejected the idea almost as soon as it occurred to her. She rarely wrote letters in English, unsure as she was of proper grammar and spelling, and even if she did write, what good would it do? Esme probably didn't even remember Anna, other than as an anonymous, weeping girl. If they passed on the street, Esme would never recognize the person Anna had become: a housewife and mother whose downcast eyes and simple clothing deflected attention. Despite her many blessings, Anna still shrank from notice. Her atonement for living a life she didn't deserve.

Anna decided to put the magazine in the wood pile. She had no patience for self-indulgent melancholy, especially in herself, and there was nothing to be gained by mooning over what couldn't be changed. Yet as soon as she returned home, Anna dropped the basket in the front hall and went upstairs. She pulled open the trunk at the foot of her bed and sorted through the quilts and embroidered blankets, all hand-sewn by the fireplace on winter evenings when the darkness set in quickly. At the very bottom was a black wool overcoat, wrinkled and reeking of mothballs but otherwise unchanged.

Impulsively, Anna put it on, feeling the shoulders' weight settle over her own. Its size overwhelmed her slight figure, and the sleeves hung past her fingers. It felt like an extension of herself, in a way she couldn't explain but went deeper than reason. It would always be a reminder of that night and the sinful choice she had made later. But she knew that given the chance to go back, she would do everything exactly the same.

The coat belonged to the English woman, the one who'd taken charge of Anna when she was pulled into the lifeboat. The woman was strikingly pretty—like an angel, Anna thought—and talked in a steady, reassuring voice, though Anna couldn't understand most of what she was saying. As the others around them chattered in a confusing mumble of barks and hisses, the woman wrapped her coat around Anna with motherly briskness. It was a man's coat, far too big for Anna, and she burrowed into the wool, her hands and feet throbbing from the cold. Her relief had been so overpowering, and her mind so scattered by the disaster she'd escaped, that it was some time before she remembered Sonja and Emil were still in the water. The English woman was the only person who was kind to Anna when she cried.

The woman had introduced herself as Charlotte, a name that sounded to Anna as delicate as fine lace. Years later, Anna had wanted to name her first daughter Charlotte, but Josef had talked her out of it; he thought their children should have simple American names. Anna never told Josef why she had suggested it. She didn't talk to him about the lifeboat.

Anna had made a half-hearted attempt to return the coat to Charlotte after they were rescued. Aboard the *Carpathia*, the *Titanic* survivors were sorted as efficiently as products on a factory line, with each passenger shunted off to the appropriate class, and Anna tried to catch Charlotte's attention as they were led in different directions. Charlotte, shaking her head, waved off Anna's attempts to pass her the coat as they were sent their separate ways. Anna joined a line of bedraggled immigrants in the third-class dining hall, a procession of the near-dead, shuffling toward their own nautical version of Saint Peter's pearly gates. Anna was given a blanket and a pillow and directed to the third-class lounge. She was relieved to find Bridget and Mary there, weepy but unharmed. With tears more than words, they told Anna the Brians were lost, but when they asked after Sonja, Anna could only shake her head. Opening her mouth would allow the sorrow to escape, and Papa had always said wailing and carrying on was no way to honor the dead. Like the *Titanic* itself, her grief must be buried at sea.

By the following day, the third-class passengers had further sorted themselves by language and nationality. Anna hovered near a group of Swedish girls, grateful for the familiarity of their conversation but unable to make an effort at friendship. The Swedish American steward who had become their unofficial guardian said they could send telegrams to their families, and the others eagerly scribbled messages on the notepad he provided. But Anna couldn't find the right words. How could she tell her parents that Sonja and Emil were dead? And who would tell Josef?

In the end, Anna took the coward's way out. She wrote down her father's name and her hometown, then the words, *I am safe*. She did not send a telegram to Josef. She told herself she would write from New York, when she'd had time to order her thoughts.

But her thoughts were no less muddled when the *Carpathia* arrived in New York. The other Swedish girls had friends or relatives meeting them; Anna had no one. The mass of people she saw gathered at the pier shocked and alarmed her; how would she possibly get through? The steward told her that due to the special circumstances of their arrival and the outcry of public sympathy, the third-class passengers would be spared the usual processing at Ellis Island.

"Were you planning to travel on from New York?" he asked.

Anna said nothing. If she kept to her original plans and went to Minnesota, she would have to tell Josef his brother and future wife were both dead. She would always be a reminder of his terrible loss.

"The Swedish Immigrant Aid Society can help with arrangements," the steward told her. "They'll pay your train fare and give you food and new clothes. They might even be able to book your passage back to Sweden, if that's what you prefer."

Anna wished the man would simply tell her what to do, rather than give her the burden of deciding. He frowned, concerned, as the silence between them lengthened.

"I'll stay," Anna finally said. The choice was made as much from fatigue as anything else; Anna simply couldn't face another sea voyage. But the image of Josef, grieving, exerted its own pull. Much as Anna dreaded telling him, it would be a kindness if he heard the news from a friend rather than a stranger. Just because she went to Minnesota didn't mean she was going to settle there; she could always go home.

But even then, Anna's hopes were scattering down paths of possibility she'd never admit to following. Josef, whom she still loved beyond all reason, wanted to be married. And now he had no wife.

In the chaos of unloading, Anna had lost track of Bridget and Mary, and she made her way alone to a pair of women holding signs in Swedish. Both had come from Sweden themselves, more than twenty years before. In America, they told her, new immigrants were taken under the wing of those who'd preceded them, each past generation lifting up the next.

One of the women took Anna to her apartment in a taxi; it was the first time Anna had ever ridden in a car. In the kitchen, a trio of girls stared at Anna wide-eyed, and the oldest asked bluntly if she'd been on the ship that sank. Their mother, thankfully, shooed them away and gave Anna their bedroom for the night. Sleep came blessedly quickly, though Anna wouldn't have thought it possible. Perhaps it was the lingering smell of cabbage rolls, which reminded Anna of home.

After a breakfast of rye bread and cheese, Anna's benefactor gave her the supplies for the next stage in her journey: train tickets to Chicago and Saint Paul, and a bag containing two dresses, undergarments, and a new pair of shoes. The woman's daughters added a few of their hair ribbons. Anna tried to protest—it was far more than she deserved—until she was told the aid society had been inundated with donations for *Titanic* survivors. Everyone wanted to help in whatever way they could.

The train station was overwhelming, with crowds of people swarming in every direction. To Anna, it was a monstrous maze, where she might be propelled off course and herded onto the wrong track before she knew it. Hugging her bag in front of her with both arms, she found a porter and showed him her ticket. He looked her over, finding the result disappointing—there'd be no tip as a reward for this good deed— but grudgingly led her to the right platform. The train to Chicago wasn't very crowded, and the only other travelers in Anna's compartment were an older American couple, who were content to read once they learned she didn't speak English. The husband nodded Anna toward a window seat, and it was there that she began her journey across America.

She thought of the other survivors, scattering in different directions like dragonflies creating whirling trails across a lake. The grief was still there, an eternal, unwelcome companion, but it no longer dragged at her heart. For the first time in days, she felt something close to contentment. She stared out the window, knowing she'd be expected to write Mama and Papa about her impressions of this new country. But all through Ohio and Indiana and Wisconsin, she saw only isolated images: red barns, smokestacks, fields reaching to the horizon. She couldn't fit what she saw into a neat description.

Josef lived on his uncle Tomas's farm outside Saint Paul, and in his last letter to Sweden before Anna sailed, Josef wrote that he had arranged rooms at a boarding house run by a Mrs. Norling, where he would meet them when they arrived. The Saint Paul train station was almost as busy as New York's, but more welcoming to a girl who spoke little English. A ticket agent answered her hesitant questions in a flood of fluent Swedish; his mother, he told her, had emigrated from Halland thirty years before. The agent directed Anna to the streetcar stop out front and told her Mrs. Norling's house was on Payne Avenue. It wouldn't take long.

Anna took in the new city with nervous wariness, but her fear eased somewhat as she approached her destination. Payne Avenue was lined with Swedish businesses, from bakeries to dance halls, and though the buildings looked nothing like the village where she'd grown up, it felt like a homecoming. Here, she could read all the signs and ask for help without being stared at in confusion. She was no longer a stranger.

Mrs. Norling's house was shabby compared to its neighbors, with peeling white paint that revealed strips of bare wood. The front steps tilted to one side, and the narrow front yard had more weeds than flowers. Still, it was palatial compared to Anna's home in Sweden. She counted eight windows, up and down, and the front porch looked big enough to seat a dozen people.

Mrs. Norling opened the door and grimaced at Anna. It wasn't what Anna expected from a woman who sold hospitality for a living, and she nervously explained who she was. Mrs. Norling sprang immediately to life, waving Anna inside as her head nodded up and down like a parrot's.

"Oh yes, of course, come in," Mrs. Norling said, leading Anna into the front parlor. "You poor little thing. And poor Josef. It's been very difficult for him."

Anna felt her chest tighten. Was Josef here?

"There's been nothing but the *Titanic* in the papers for days! It's all anyone's talking about." Mrs. Norling motioned toward an end table that was barely visible under a pile of newspapers. "I've saved them all, if you want to look?"

Anna saw a photograph of the ship on the top page; she nearly shuddered with revulsion. "No, thank you," she managed, glancing away.

"Ah well, here you are, safe and sound. What a blessing."

"Josef knows about his brother, then?"

Mrs. Norling nodded. So Anna needn't worry about telling him the news. The clicking of the *Carpathia*'s wireless—all those lists of lost and saved—had traveled all the way to a Minnesota farm.

"Josef came here, soon after he'd heard about the sinking," Mrs. Norling continued. "His uncle's wife, Agneta, is my niece—I've known Josef since he came from Sweden. Such a fine young man, as I'm sure you know yourself. They said there was a great loss of life, but we had no way of knowing who'd lived and who'd died. It was awful to see Josef so worried, pacing back and forth, but all we could do was wait. Finally—a few days later—the newspaper printed an official list of survivors. He read it right here. He found your name, but not the others."

Oh, Josef. He must have gone over that list again and again, hoping there'd been a mistake. He would have been brave, Anna knew. He wouldn't have cried.

"He'd been so happy, when he made the arrangements for you to stay," Mrs. Norling said. "It breaks my heart to think of it. He was eager to see the young lady he was going to marry, of course, but he told me all about you, too. Said you'd grown up together, like a sister and brother. I said the girls can stay as long as they need while the wedding plans are made, and he told me he hoped it wouldn't be long. You could see he was nervous—as most men are, beforehand—but I knew he'd make a good husband. He'd started building his own house, you know. Couldn't wait to show it off to his new bride . . ."

It hurt, more than it should have, to hear how anxious Josef had been for Sonja to arrive. How much he had been looking forward to their shared future.

Mrs. Norling's voice trailed off, and she looked down at her hands, which finally lay at rest in her lap. The silence lingered in recognition of Josef's grief. Finally, Anna had to ask the question that had been in her mind since she walked in the door.

"Is Josef still here?"

"No, he went home a few days ago. I don't think he expected you to come all this way—we both thought you'd go back to your parents in Sweden. He'll be so pleased to see you. Shall I telephone him?"

Anna had traveled more than a thousand miles to see Josef. But now that the reunion was imminent, she felt more nervous than ever. She didn't want their first contact to be over the phone, exchanging sympathy in stilted voices. She didn't even know if she'd be able to speak.

Anna was shaking her head, trying to think how she'd explain, but Mrs. Norling was already standing. "He doesn't have a telephone at his new house, of course, but I'll talk to Agneta. She'll know where to find him."

Anna waited in the parlor while Mrs. Norling made her call in the front hall. All Anna could hear were occasional murmured phrases: *Can you believe it?* and *Poor dear.* Anna tried to distract herself by looking at the framed embroidery scenes on the wall, but they kept reminding her of Sonja's trousseau. All those beautifully sewn linens, lying at the bottom of the ocean.

Mrs. Norling marched back in, looking pleased. She launched into a complicated story about car trouble and train schedules, almost none of which Anna paid attention to, because all she wanted to know was the story's resolution: when she would see Josef.

Not for some time, apparently, because he couldn't get to town until later that evening.

"However, if you're willing," Mrs. Norling offered, "Agneta says the milk truck from Gollman's Dairy comes by every day at five o'clock. It's not far from here—I'm sure they'd give you a ride, and Agneta would be happy to have you stay the night."

Reuniting with Josef in the country—his natural element—seemed more fitting than inside Mrs. Norling's formal parlor. So Anna made the hour-long drive in a milk truck, and she would always associate her first sight of her new home with the clanking of metal jugs and the driver's cheerful whistles. Sounds that testified to the resilience of daily routines.

The dairyman left Anna at the end of a rutted dirt drive, which led to a modest barn. A plow and cart, unhitched from the horses that brought them to life, lay forlornly in the distance. To her left, marked by a narrow gravel path, was a small house, perched on the top of a rise not quite high enough to be a hill. It was simple and neat, like a Swedish country cottage, and Anna could already picture the inside: a cupboard bed and a ceramic-tiled stove—all the furnishings that would remind her of home. Not allowing herself the indulgence of hesitation, Anna walked to the front door and knocked.

There was no answer.

Of course not, Anna chided herself. Josef would be outside, working. Farmers didn't have time to sit and mope, and from what Anna remembered of Josef, a death in the family was no excuse. He would scrub down stalls and move bales of hay until his muscles screamed for relief, for Josef never allowed himself rest until a job was done.

Anna turned to the barn. She could hear horses stamping and whinnying inside, and when she grew closer, she could also hear a man's voice, talking in a low, soothing tone. The barn doors were open, and

Anna saw Josef inside, rubbing down a horse with a brush. She allowed herself the pleasure of watching him before he knew she was there.

"Good girl," he was saying. "There you go, my lovely. Good girl." Words whose meaning didn't matter as much as their sound.

After years of recalling Josef's image, Anna couldn't help but notice the details that jarred with her memories. His hair was darker, for one, and cut shorter; his chin and jaw had hardened, losing any trace of boyish roundness. But his movements were startlingly familiar: the way his arm reached wide with each stroke, the way he carried his weight on one leg so the opposite foot could tap against the floor. She would have known it was Josef even if she hadn't seen his face.

Anna could have stood there, watching him, forever. But the only thing worse than breaking the spell of this moment would be if he turned around and saw her gawking.

"Josef."

She said his name forcefully, with a confidence she did not feel. Josef jerked around and dropped the brush, leaving it to clatter against the floorboards. He rushed toward Anna, and she saw he was smiling, a smile that encompassed both joy and relief. And Josef, who had only held Anna once—a brief hug at the train station when he left for America—was wrapping his arms around her, and pulling her against him, into him, as if her body could meld into his and in doing so, heal him.

In that moment, Anna realized she hadn't left home. She had found it.

—

Anna wanted to stay, but her future beyond the next few days wasn't up to her. She would do whatever Josef wanted. They spent that first evening at Tomas and Agneta's house, silently agreeing that this supper would be treated as a social visit, unmarred by tragedy. Josef's three school-age cousins were well mannered enough not to ask questions—though they snuck curious glances at Anna—and Tomas asked after old acquaintances back home. Small-town gossip, no matter how mundane, can always be stretched to create a meal's worth of conversation.

After dinner, Agneta and her daughter cleared the table, and Agneta shooed Anna away from the kitchen. No need to help, she said, and why didn't she join Josef in the sitting room? Tomas had already excused himself, saying he'd read upstairs after he got the boys to bed. Clearly, there was a family conspiracy to give Anna and Josef some time alone.

That night, Anna told Josef what had happened on the ship—as much as she felt able. She tried to make it sound as if Emil and Sonja had died painlessly, and if her evasions covered up her own guilt, that wasn't her primary purpose. They were hit by pieces of the ship, Anna told him. It was quick; they didn't suffer. Once the first lie was uttered, it was easier to tell the others that grew from it.

Anna didn't say anything about the man she'd seen from the lifeboat.

She knew words were inadequate next to the depth of her remorse, but she tried. "I'm so sorry. I'm sorry I couldn't save them."

Josef, his elbows on his knees, brought his face closer to Anna's. "You saved yourself, and I thank God for that."

It was enthralling, to be the focus of Josef's attention.

"About Sonja," Josef began, and Anna braced herself. Jealousy was a sin, and she must act like the sister Josef thought her to be. "I know she was your friend," Josef said. "It's terrible that she died. But I haven't been able to mourn her. I feel sad, of course, when I think of her, but we hardly knew each other." Josef gave Anna an embarrassed half smile. "I don't know why I'm even telling you this—it sounds so cruel."

He trusts me, Anna thought with a faint but passionate hope. *I must prove myself worthy.*

"I understand," Anna said. "There's no fault in speaking honestly."

"Emil, though . . ." Josef let the name linger, a specter in the darkened room. "Ever since I came to America, I'd been planning to bring him over. As I was plowing the fields or building the house, I thought of how he'd be here, one day, working alongside me. Perhaps we'd go into business together, make something of ourselves. What will I do without him? I still can't believe he's really gone."

"I know," Anna said faintly. All she could think of was Emil's face, rigid with cold. Or was it horror? That face would follow her for the rest of her life.

"I don't envy your suffering," Josef said. "But you were there when it happened. It's real, for you, in a way it isn't for me. I keep thinking Emil and Sonja are back in Sweden, and your papa will share news of them in his next letter. In my mind, they're still alive."

Anna never would have expected Josef to harbor such wistful fantasies. He had always been so practical, accepting his life as it was rather than mooning over how it could be different. Then she remembered the way he used to look at her when she examined a cobweb's intricate patterns. He'd never made fun of her or chided her for daydreaming. Perhaps Josef had a richer imagination than she'd supposed, for he was one of the few people who didn't consider her thoughtfulness a flaw.

"I'm grateful you came," Josef said. "It helps to know what happened."

And now her duty was done. What next? Anna's apprehension must have shown despite her purposefully blank expression, because Josef smiled at her.

"Do you want to stay? In America?"

That question, at least, had an easy answer. "Yes. I was told Agneta had arranged a job, as a housecleaner."

"We'll talk to her tomorrow." Josef's face relaxed as he sat back in his chair. "Good. I'm glad."

"I'll have to see about lodgings . . ."

"Oh, don't worry about that. Agneta and Tomas will be happy to have you, for as long as you like. We are as good as family, aren't we?"

So Mrs. Norling had been right. Josef thought of Anna as a younger sister. Which meant she would never be anything else.

"Do you know, it's made me feel better, talking about Emil," Josef said. "Like he's here with us."

To Anna, it was horrible to think of Emil's restless spirit clinging to her, refusing to be set free. But if talking about his brother gave Josef even a minute of happiness, then Anna would do it. She would join Josef in reminiscences of Emil as he used to be, when they were boys back in Sweden. She would help him escape to a time when everyone he loved was alive—his parents and Sonja and Emil—and the berries were ripe and the harvest was in and there was enough to eat for everyone. That was the Emil Anna must choose to remember. Not the Emil who'd wanted to marry her, or the one who'd called out from the sea.

The next morning, Agneta told Anna the job was still hers if she wanted it, but there was no rush to start. Anna was welcome to stay at the farm as their guest for a few days first. Anna helped with the children and the cooking and fed the chickens and other livestock. In the late afternoons, she went to Josef's barn and watched him feed and groom the horses. The familiarity of the routine seemed to lull Josef into a confessional mood, and Anna nodded admiringly as he talked of his plans for the house and the new farming methods he hoped to try out. He spread out his life before Anna like a jeweler lays out his wares, hoping she'd be dazzled.

Anna didn't know why her approval gave him particular pleasure, but he seemed to crave it. For every quiet compliment she gave—"I like the red you chose for the shutters"—Josef grinned and tilted his head in a way that was meant to deflect her praise even as he savored it. It required no deception on Anna's part; she was genuinely astonished by what he'd achieved in only a few years. He was already well on his way to running his own farm, and in the winter, he'd earn good money doing carpentry in town. Josef had always been a hard worker, and here in America, he was rewarded for it.

A week after Anna arrived, Agneta arranged a visit with Anna's new employer. The woman was elderly and being looked after by a housekeeper who was nearly as ancient; Anna would be doing the heavy cleaning. The house was quiet and orderly, and the pay—in Anna's eyes—was extravagant given the relative ease of her duties. She agreed to start the next day.

She told Josef early that evening when she went to fetch him for dinner. Spring in Minnesota was no match for its lingering winter, and the air was sharp with cold. Still, Josef appeared in no hurry to arrive at Tomas's house. He slowed his pace when they reached the top of the rise by his house and pointed to the fallow fields.

"None of this is mine, you know."

"But it's your farm."

"It's my uncle's land. He doesn't charge me to use it, and whatever I grow is mine to keep, which is more than fair. But I came to America so I could own something of my own. Not work another man's property."

Josef stopped walking. He seemed to have decided that being on time for dinner wasn't as important as what he wanted to say.

"When I first came to Minneapolis, I worked at a lumber mill six days a week. Twelve hours a day. On Sundays, after church, I came out here and cleared fields and planted crops. I started collecting scraps from the lumberyard—planks that had flaws or had been cut the wrong size—and I started designing this house. I've always been a farmer, and maybe I always will be. But building is more satisfying. With a farm, you grow crops, and you harvest them, and then you start over. When you build something, it lasts."

How lucky Josef was, to have such clear ambitions. Anna couldn't think of anything she was particularly good at. Or anything she could do that would leave a lasting mark.

"I like living on a farm—growing my own food, having fresh milk and eggs. But farming's no way to rise up in the world. I've met men from Sweden and Norway and Finland who came here with nothing, and now they're living in big houses and driving new cars. America changes your thinking, Anna. It makes you believe anything's possible."

And it was, for people like Josef. People who were willing to take risks. But Anna no longer thought much further than her next meal. As she'd learned when Josef left Sweden, it was foolish to set your sights on a future that might never be yours.

"I had plans of starting my own business. Andersson Construction, with Emil as my partner. But with him gone . . ."

Josef took a deep breath, and Anna sensed his determination to keep steady, to fight back the temptation of tears.

"This was the year I was going to be married." Josef spoke softly, without self-pity. "The year Emil and I set up shop. To have it all taken away, in an instant—it doesn't seem possible."

"I know." The familiar whisper of guilt sidled up to her, like a persistent beggar who won't be ignored. *Why did you let go of Emil's hand? You could have saved him . . .*

"You must be wondering why I'm telling you all this." Josef turned to Anna, and she felt a familiar surge of gratitude. Josef was the only person who ever really looked at her. "It's because I wanted you to know everything. You'll be earning your own money soon, and you'll be able to do whatever you like. But before you leave, I wonder if you'd consider marrying me."

It felt as if Anna's body had suddenly filled with air, and she might float off into the sky. She kept her face expressionless, an outer fortress protecting the weakness within.

"We'd make a good match, don't you think? We know each other's families, we get along, and we're both hard workers. What do you think?"

It was the offer she'd hoped for, wasn't it? The offer that had crossed her mind like a whisper from the devil, when she knew Sonja was dead. She had no right to feel disappointed.

"We're family already," Anna murmured.

"Exactly," Josef said. He looked somber, not at all like an eager soon-to-be groom. "I mean no disrespect to Sonja. We'll have to wait a while—Agneta will know what's proper."

Anna tried to summon an appropriately pleased expression, but she'd always been a terrible liar. And Josef had known her long enough to see through her deception.

"Please don't agree out of kindness," Josef said quietly. "Do you want to marry me?"

"Yes." *But not like this,* Anna thought. *Never like this.*

"Then what's wrong?"

"Emil and Sonja," she blurted out. "It's not fair." She couldn't tell him what she really meant, that she'd never intended her wish to come true through another's death.

"Don't you see?" Josef asked. "They're the reason we should marry. We must live and have children and build this house. Do all the things they were never able to."

Josef believed Sonja and Emil's spirits were still with them, and in that moment, Anna had a vision of Sonja's face when they'd spoken after Josef had sent his proposal of marriage. Sonja had apologized and begged forgiveness; she'd promised not to accept if it would cause Anna distress. Anna knew, as surely as if Sonja had confessed it herself, that Sonja would be pleased to see Anna take her place as Josef's wife.

And Emil? She could almost hear his voice on that moonlit deck, the first time she'd seen him as a man rather than a boy. Emil hadn't blamed Anna for loving Josef, and he wouldn't want his beloved older brother to be alone. He would tell Anna to say yes.

If the dead did send their blessings, they came in chilly waves that made Anna shudder. She leaned into Josef, and his arm reached out, around her shoulders. Anna thought of her father, a man who never spoke of love but showed it in a hundred silent ways. She could not expect romantic speeches from a man like Josef, but he would be a good husband. Reliable and kind.

"I'll tell you one thing," Josef said, his voice nearly a whisper in the dark. "Mrs. Josef Andersson won't go around town in a charity coat, and a man's one at that."

Anna glanced down at the hem grazing her ankles, the rolled-up sleeves. Protectively, she pulled it tighter around her body.

"It's good quality wool," Anna said. "I can restyle it to suit me."

"That's my girl," Josef said, and patted her on the cheek. Not a kiss, but the next best thing, and enough to nudge Anna into a slow, shy smile. "Resourceful and frugal. I knew we'd make a good match."

Anna saw then how it would be: she and Josef hitched together like oxen, working side by side. A marriage built on shared labor and the satisfaction of a job well done. Until the donation from the Immigrant Aid Society, Anna had never had new clothes of her own; she had always worn her sisters' castoffs. Now, she would have a hand-me-down husband. Perhaps that was the best she could hope for.

Anna was nineteen when she married Josef in the Lake Crossing Lutheran Church six months later. She suffered none of the stereotypical mishaps of a young bride; there were no burnt breakfasts or shrunken socks to serve as holiday-dinner fodder in years to come. From the very beginning, she was a diligent housekeeper and cook, and Josef said his shirts had never been so well ironed. They were, as Josef had said, a good match, each politely considerate, each helping the other without needing to be asked. They ended most evenings yawning in the bed Tomas and Agneta had given them as a wedding present. Josef would kiss Anna on the forehead and say good night; Anna would curl up, her knees to her chest, to give Josef the space he needed to stretch out. On Sunday evenings, Josef would shift closer and wrap his arms around her waist; Anna would place her hands around his back and squeeze. Their marital relations proceeded with a solemnity appropriate to the Lord's day, and Anna submitted to her wifely duty with neither dread nor anticipation. A woman wasn't meant to enjoy it, she thought, but she always smiled when Josef had satisfied himself, the same way she smiled at the barn cat when he caught a mouse: *Good job. Well done.*

When the weather made its definitive shift into winter, Anna pulled out the black coat from her storage trunk. She decided where to cut and where to sew new seams and marked the measurements with pins. Then she began ripping out the lining, only to discover its secret. Behind the thick tailor's label—"Haviland & Sons"—she found three banknotes, each for ten British pounds. There were two more folded lengthwise into the collar. Anna had no idea how much fifty pounds might be in dollars, but the bills were smooth and crisp, fresh from a bank. Anna thought with a pang of the English woman, Charlotte. The coat must have belonged to her husband or father, a man who was most likely dead. Had Charlotte known about the money? She couldn't have, if she had given the coat so freely to Anna.

Anna allowed herself a few minutes to admire the money, shuffling it back and forth in her hands. Then she gathered it into a neat pile and hid it in the top drawer of her dresser, beneath her undergarments, while she worked out what to do next.

Anna fully intended to return the money to Charlotte. The problem was that she didn't even know Charlotte's last name, let alone where she lived. The problem nagged at Anna for the rest of the day, but she said nothing when Josef came in to wash up nor when they sat down to supper. She told herself that it wasn't worth worrying him with the problem until she'd decided on a solution. The shameful truth was that even then, Anna was wondering if there was a way she might keep it.

She didn't give in to temptation right away. The next time she was in Saint Paul, she paid a visit to Mrs. Norling and asked if she still had the newspapers from the days after the *Titanic* sank. Mrs. Norling did indeed; she had put them in a box of collectibles that she was convinced would be quite valuable one day.

Even with Anna's limited English, it was upsetting to see page after page devoted to the sinking. She understood only a few of the words: "lost" and "saved" and "tragedy." Eventually, she found a list of survivors, arranged by class. Anna wasn't used to analyzing the subtle differences in status that showed themselves in hats and shoes, but she knew Charlotte had been too well dressed for third class. Anna saw no one named Charlotte in first or second class. Then she realized only unmarried ladies were listed with their given names. If Charlotte was married, she'd be listed under her husband's name. And Anna had no idea what that might be.

Goaded by frustration, Anna scanned every page, her eyes running through line after line of stories. There were names everywhere; it seemed everyone who'd gotten off the ship had given a reporter their tale of woe. Anna couldn't imagine telling a stranger what had happened—it had been difficult enough telling Josef. But others had reveled in the attention. Charlotte, however, did not appear to be among them.

Anna closed the last of the papers, her eyes itchy and her shoulders sore. She realized to her dismay that she'd spent an hour on this fruitless search, reliving a night she'd vowed to put behind her. And she still wasn't any closer to finding Charlotte.

Anna did consider other possibilities. She could write to the White Star Line office in New York, which would have passenger records. She could ask the Swedish Immigrant Aid Society for help. Somehow, Anna never got around to writing those letters. She kept intending to, every time she opened her top drawer and pulled out a clean pair of stockings. It was one of those important but nonurgent chores that never seemed to get done.

And the longer the money stayed in the house, the more Anna came to think of it as hers. Josef worked from sunup to past dark, running the farm while also hiring himself out on building sites. Anna never coveted Charlotte's money for herself, only for how it might help Josef. What if they could afford a hired hand? What if Josef bought one of those new electric drills? The more Anna considered the possibilities, the easier they became to justify: Josef needed the money more than Charlotte, who most likely didn't even know it was hidden in the coat. Charlotte would never miss what she didn't know she had.

And if Anna hadn't been meant to keep the money, would a perfect excuse have come so easily? A year into her marriage, Anna received word from Papa that her great-uncle in Stockholm had died. He was a bachelor, a loner, and a bit of an eccentric, whom she barely remembered from a long-ago visit. But his death felt like a sign. A few weeks later, Anna told Josef she'd inherited some money, which would soon be wired to a bank in Minneapolis.

Josef never thought to question her story. He didn't ask to see proof of her inheritance or the bank transfer; he didn't ask why a man Anna never spoke of had left her a legacy. Anna took the pounds to the downtown branch of the Minnesota Bank & Trust, where she exchanged them for $250.

That night, mimicking the clerk who'd handed her the pristine, crisp currency, Anna laid the dollars out on the dining-room table as Josef watched, astounded. When he'd added up how much it was, he pulled Anna into his arms, pressing his face into her hair.

"Our luck's turned at last!" he marveled.

They laughed and kissed and laughed as they kissed, both of them surrendering to joy they'd never been carefree enough to embrace. In that euphoric moment, Anna knew she'd made the right decision. She'd given Josef the gift of freedom.

With the money for new tools and hired labor, Andersson Construction finished its first house ahead of schedule, and Josef soon signed contracts for three more. By the time Anna was expecting her first child, they had two farmhands and Josef was spending most of his days in town. When Sarah was learning to walk, they added a second floor to their house, and Anna spent the summer clearing stray nails away from her curious daughter. When Sarah was four and John a gurgling baby, Tomas sold Josef his portion of the farm, and they were landowners at last. Anna's children were never true farmers' offspring, not like she and Josef had been. They regarded the horses as playmates rather than work machines and the barn as their playground. They had daily chores, but they never knew what it meant to live solely off the food you grow. By the time Susan was born, the fields were no longer being cultivated, and all but two horses had been sold to pay for a new Oldsmobile.

If Anna came face-to-face with her past self, she had no doubt the girl in the lifeboat would be astonished by all she'd accomplished. She'd had a good life. A happy life. Sarah was now the same age Anna had been when she married, but her daughter had greater ambitions; she was at a secretarial college in Saint Paul. John, though only fourteen, was already learning about the family business; he had a quiet depth that reminded Anna of Emil. John could achieve great things, she believed, if he ever came out of his shell. Susan was still a work in progress, an eight-year-old who shifted moods as quickly as a clotheshorse sorts through new gowns. Spoiled, as the youngest often is. Anna knew her children thought her dowdy and old-fashioned, that they rolled their eyes at her broken English when they thought she wouldn't see. She couldn't fault them for favoring Josef over her. Anna would have done the same, in their place.

Anna was sitting on the bed, the coat wrapped around her like a blanket, when she heard footsteps coming up the stairs. It must be Susan, home from school. Anna knew she should get up but couldn't quite muster her arms and legs to obey. The steps came closer, and Anna looked up and saw Josef in the doorway, looking at her, surprised.

"Are you all right?" he asked.

Anna's only response was to reflect Josef's own confusion back at him.

"I'm meeting Mr. Wilton at the factory at four o'clock. I was going over the plans last night and left them on my desk."

Josef walked over to the bed and put a hand on Anna's cheek. She was moved by the gesture, until he slid his hand to her forehead: he was checking for fever. Josef looked down at the coat, and his lips dipped into a frown.

"What's wrong?" he asked.

A simple enough question. A question she felt too overwhelmed to answer. Seeing the picture of Mr. Van Hausen had brought it all back: the men at the oars, Charlotte's arm around her shoulders, her own pleading sobs. Time and age had distanced Anna from that bewildered, half-frozen girl, so much that she might as well be another person. Yet Anna was still carrying the guilt of that previous self. Why? She'd been so young, so frightened. Wasn't it time that poor girl was forgiven?

Speaking softly, looking at her pillow rather than Josef, Anna tried to make her husband understand. "An Englishwoman gave me this coat, when I was pulled into the lifeboat. I was so cold—I could hardly breathe. She wrapped it around me, and it felt like she'd brought me back to life. Her name was Charlotte."

Josef listened, impassive. He never spoke solely for the purpose of filling a silence.

"Emil was behind me. If he'd been only a few feet closer, they would have pulled him in, too. I saw him in the water—he was calling out . . ."

Anna began to cry, silent tears that solemnly rolled down her cheeks. She cried for Emil, who'd come so close to being saved, and for herself, who'd failed him. Anna knew she should have told Josef everything long ago or never at all. Bringing it all up now served no purpose other than to make Josef upset. Whenever he spoke about Emil with the children, he always told happy stories, his memories of his brother softening with time. Forcing Josef to confront the reality of his brother's death was no kindness. But hadn't Anna always known she would disappoint him, in the end?

Josef reached out, then stopped his hand in midair, as if her tears might burn. Josef, so handy when it came to the chores of daily life, didn't have the tools to fix her. Quietly, Anna told him what had happened in the lifeboat. The fights, the screams, the threats. How she'd tried to make herself understood; how futile her efforts had proved. Josef simply listened. When Anna saw the gleam of tears in his eyes, she knew she must be strong, for his sake. She wiped her face and managed to steady her breathing.

"Emil asked me to marry him," she whispered. "On the ship."

"Did he?" Josef's lips curled into a reticent smile. "I didn't think he'd have the nerve."

It was clear the revelation hadn't come as a shock. "You knew?" Anna asked.

"He was in love with you," Josef said. "Wasn't it obvious? Even before I left for America, he was saying you'd be married one day."

So Josef had known, long before Anna did.

He waited for her to continue, and when she didn't, he prodded, "What answer did you give him?"

"None. I said I wasn't sure. But I would have said yes, in time. I wanted us all to be together. I loved you so much—for as long as I can remember. Marrying Emil was the next best thing to marrying you." Anna knew she should end her revelations there, but she was too curious—or too weak—to resist. "That's why I understand. How you felt about me and Sonja."

"Sonja?" Josef's face shifted, and the muscles in his cheeks tightened.

"She was your first choice. And I was the next best thing."

"Do you think I'm still pining away for Sonja?"

Anna shook her head and came perilously close to crying again. She didn't know how to speak of such matters; she and Josef had never tried. Josef sighed, and though he sat perfectly still, Anna could see the mental effort he was making to sort out his thoughts before speaking.

"It was a mistake, asking Sonja to marry me," he said at last. "I was lonely, and I wanted a wife who'd remind me of home. In my mind, you were spoken for, by Emil . . ."

"And you thought of me as a sister. I know."

"I did, yes. Until you came to see me. That afternoon in the barn."

The scene was still vividly real to Anna. Josef's arms clutching at her back, his relief flooding through her like a tonic.

"If you had drowned, and Sonja had been the one to survive, I would not have felt the same joy. I knew, right then."

Josef reached for Anna's hand and gave it a gentle squeeze. With those few words, he told Anna all she needed to know. He had never regretted their marriage or wondered what his life would have been like with Sonja. Once Josef set himself to a task, he saw it through faithfully, and the duties of a husband were no different than any other job.

Downstairs, the front door opened with a clatter; Susan was home. Anna pushed the coat off to the side of the bed. She sat up, neatening her hair, as Josef stood and adjusted his belt. Anna was already embarrassed by her outburst. She'd had a moment of uncharacteristic self-pity, but now it was time to see to Susan and get started on dinner. Had she really left the groceries sitting at the bottom of the stairs?

Josef patted Anna on the shoulder. A fatherly pat, the kind of touch that pledges enduring, unquestioning love.

"Do you feel better?" he asked.

Surprisingly, she did. For years, Anna had locked away her guilt and fear, but like mice behind the walls, they'd been scratching to get out, tormenting her with their muffled protests. Now they'd been released, and she was free. But if she truly wanted to set the past to rest, she had to tell him everything.

"There's one more thing," she said. "There were banknotes—British pounds—hidden inside the coat. I tried to find Charlotte to give them back, but I couldn't. So I kept the money and pretended it came from my great-uncle."

Of all the things Anna had told Josef that day, it was this revelation that most shocked him. "Your inheritance? You lied?"

Anna nodded, her face reddening. "I'm sorry."

But Josef didn't seem angry. If anything, he looked impressed.

"Well, it turned out for the best, wouldn't you say? I might never have started the business otherwise. Any other crimes you care to confess?"

"No," Anna mumbled, looking down at the floor. She heard Josef laugh and felt his hands wrap around her arms and pull her forward.

When Susan Andersson ran up the stairs a few seconds later, she was greeted by an astonishing sight: Mama and Papa hugging, right in the middle of their bedroom. Mama's cheek was resting against Papa's chest, and Susan thought she was crying, but no, she wasn't; she was smiling, and Papa was looking down at her like he was the luckiest man in the world.

CHARLOTTE

Los Angeles felt like another country. It might well be, given the time it had taken to get there. It was the air, Charlotte thought: dusty and dry, the warmth lulling you into immobility. The town itself wasn't much, to her jaded eyes, but everywhere she saw signs that its ambitions were growing: construction crews and scaffolding, motorcars spiffy enough for Mayfair. A sense of promise that lured dreamy-eyed wanderers into believing they could make a fresh start.

Dreamy-eyed wanderers . . . Charlotte jotted the phrase in her notebook for future use. Even with the windows open, the taxi was stuffy, and she pulled off her jacket and loosened her damp blouse from her chest. None of the clothes she'd packed were appropriate for the California climate, and she felt out of place in her brown tweed suit, a dowdy wren in a land of butterflies and parrots. But this was where her search for Reginald Evers had led, and thanks to the *Record*'s generous expense account, this was where it would end.

Charlotte could have neglected her promise to Lady Upton. It would have been easier, in many ways, if she had. But curiosity had won out over apprehension. There was no Reginald Evers listed in the New York City telephone directory, but Charlotte found two mentions of him in the archives of the *New York Express*, both reviews of plays in which he'd appeared in secondary roles. That sent her on a round of visits to theaters, where a manager at the Palace told her, sure, he knew Reggie Evers. He was a director out in California now, making movies. That's where the money was, these days.

Charlotte delayed her return to London, sold Teddy on her plan to write a series of columns from Hollywood, and bought a cross-country train ticket. (First class, of course, since the *Record* was paying.) First, however, she had to file her story on Charles Van Hausen. Charlotte's visit to Esme's house had gone about as disastrously as it could have. Charlotte had been genuinely surprised when Esme agreed to meet her at the hotel later, and even more shocked when Esme launched into her maudlin confessions. At first, Charlotte's journalistic instincts had prickled to life: *What a story this would make! Teddy will be over the moon!* But she'd quickly realized she would never write about Esme. Esme was like a fine piece of china: daintily pretty from afar, dangerously fragile up close. Convinced her husband had committed suicide, rattling around in that ostentatious mansion, so terribly, terribly sad. Charlotte had always remembered Esme as spoiled and overdramatic, and perhaps she still was. But that night, in the hotel room, Charlotte had also felt sorry for her. They would never be friends, yet Charlotte felt a duty to protect Esme all the same.

The following day, Charlotte sent Teddy a gushing profile of Charles Van Hausen, "an adventurer whose appetite for life was only outdone by his appetite for love." She described him as a devoted husband and father, and sent along a picture of the oldest Van Hausen boy, who was gorgeous enough to warrant a quarter page at least. She wrote that Esme was "living in seclusion, laid low by grief." Which was true.

Now, Charlotte was on the brink of another momentous reunion. Her taxi pulled up at the Sultan's Palace Hotel, which looked to Charlotte like an opium addict's vision of a mythical Arabian stronghold. Teddy had recommended the place the last time they spoke.

"Plum Wodehouse stayed there—said it's full of soused writers who've got all the gossip." Teddy spoke hurriedly, cramming as much as he could into the extravagantly expensive transatlantic phone call. "I'll expect daily reports. Get me something on Charlie Chaplain—he's English, he'll talk to you. And pictures of starlets. If they're British, all the better . . ."

Dual minarets stood sentry on either side of the hotel's entrance, and the windows were framed with bright green and blue tiles. Charlotte walked through the arched front doors into a courtyard centered around a mosaic-lined swimming pool. A woman was floating serenely in the middle of the water, her hair splayed out around her in rays like a child's drawing of the sun. The woman—who barely reacted to Charlotte's arrival and questions—said lazily that the office was the front door on the right. But there was no one inside. Charlotte waited on the nearest lounge chair, feeling prim and self-conscious as people drifted past, calling out to each other and trading affectionate insults. The Sultan's Palace felt more like a boarding school than a hotel.

The manager, as it turned out, was making a repair in Charlotte's room. When he finally returned to the office, and then showed her up the stairs to the second floor, he pointed out the patch where the plaster was still wet. Charlotte wondered who or what had made such a big hole in the wall but was too tired to bother asking. Her room lacked the rest of the building's exuberance: there was a bed, a small table, a chair, and not much else. Its monastic simplicity was the ideal setting for serious writing—no distractions—but after a few minutes in that bleak space, Charlotte understood why everyone gathered around the pool instead.

It wasn't long before Charlotte drifted back down to the water, drawn by what appeared to be a nightly cocktail party. At first, she felt uncharacteristically ill at ease; she was one of only a few women staying at the hotel, and the oldest one by miles. The others were actresses and models and dancers, each more gorgeous than the last. The men ranged from earnest youngsters who believed films could be Great Art and cynical theatrical types who believed in nothing more than a steady studio paycheck. When Charlotte began introducing herself, she was welcomed at first with flattering enthusiasm. A lady reporter! From London! But the novelty wore off after a few desultory conversations. She wasn't working on a film, and she didn't know anyone working on a film. Therefore, her appeal was limited.

Charlotte did find out enough to get her bearings. She gathered business cards and arranged visits to sound stages, sweet-talked her way into dressing rooms, and scribbled in her notebook as publicity-department minders doled out studio-approved stories about the stars. (Why yes, Joan Crawford and Douglas Fairbanks Jr. were deliriously happy, their marriage a real-life love story.) Charlotte found herself unexpectedly charmed by the brazen artificiality of a motion-picture set: castles built of plywood, temples of cardboard. None of it real, and defiantly so. Here, a Kansas farm girl could reinvent herself as a Polish princess, and the shy son of Italian immigrants could be transformed into a romantic hero. In a town with no history, you could be whomever you wanted.

It was the perfect place for a man like Reg.

Charlotte found out Mr. Evers was under contract to Paramount, and by sweet-talking a studio secretary, she got his home address. It was in what the hotel's manager simply described as "the Hills," not far from the hotel. There were no convenient excuses of distance or difficulty to put her off.

Charlotte put on her best day dress, one she'd bought for a country weekend when she'd wanted to impress a certain gentleman with a scar and a limp, who hadn't turned out to be quite the war hero he had implied. The long sleeves and relatively high neckline looked matronly compared to the scraps of sheer fabric the other women at the Sultan's Palace paraded around in, but it gave Charlotte a severe elegance that felt appropriate to the occasion. She walked through the hotel's courtyard and was gratified to see that she could still turn a few heads.

As Charlotte's taxi passed from apartment buildings and bungalows to orange groves and barren hillsides, her nerve began to falter. Would it be better to send a letter instead? The driver stopped at the bottom of a narrow, steep driveway and gave her a questioning look. Charlotte couldn't see where the drive ended, but she decided to have mercy on the car's brakes and paid her fare. Gathering her courage as she stepped out of the car, she began trudging upward. There were voices calling out somewhere behind the hedges on her right, interspersed with rhythmic thumps. After a few more steps, she was high enough up to see a tennis court. Two men were skittering back and forth on either side, their shirts a brilliant white in contrast to their tanned faces and arms. To her left was the house, a saffron-yellow Spanish-style villa with a red tile roof. A half dozen cars were parked along the circular driveway, and Charlotte hesitated. She'd no intention of crashing a party.

As she stood there, wavering, a young man with ruddy cheeks and smooth dark hair came bounding out the front door, like a puppy let off his leash. He drew up short when he saw Charlotte.

"Hello!"

Americans had an unnerving habit of greeting Charlotte with such warmth that she always wondered if they'd met before. As he approached, she felt sure they hadn't, though he had the kind of face that looked familiar. His sculpted cheekbones and soulful eyes were those of a matinee idol, the kind whose picture gets clipped from magazines and pinned up in wistful girls' bedrooms.

"Here to see Reggie?" the man asked.

"Yes." The word was out before she'd officially decided to stay.

He held out his hand. "I'm Percy."

Casually informal—so very American. "Charlotte."

Percy shook her hand decisively, and Charlotte knew she was staring, but he didn't seem to mind. He really was quite attractive, and the fact that he knew it didn't detract from his charm. Then Charlotte realized where she'd seen him. "Were you in a film with Ramon Novarro?" she asked. "Something about pirates?"

Percy's smile widened, which made his face glow all the more. "*A Rogue at Sea*. Don't tell me you saw it? Not my best work, I'm afraid."

"Oh, I liked it very much."

Charlotte hadn't liked it at all—what passed for the plot was sentimental nonsense—but she'd spent enough time around theater people to know that self-disparaging comments must always be countered with compliments.

"You're English, huh?" Percy asked. "You know Reggie from back home?"

Charlotte nodded. "I happened to be in town and thought I'd surprise him. It might not be the best time, if he's got visitors . . ."

"Oh, it's just the usual gang. Reggie opens the house to everyone on the weekend. I'm running home to pick up some new records, but you can go on in. Reggie was by the pool, last I saw him."

The interior of the house was a sprawling, open space, its dark wood furniture and terra-cotta floor tiles a somber contrast to the California sunshine. Charlotte walked through the central seating area—all oversized sofas and thronelike chairs—toward a set of open French doors. She peered out onto a patio and swimming pool; beyond, the sloping grounds had been carved into a series of terraces, one with a putting green, others with fruit trees and flowers. The pool was vast and blindingly white, with umbrella-topped tables at either end. Visitors were huddled in groups of two and three, some on lounge chairs, others with their legs in the water. Charlotte hovered in the doorway, watching the tableau as if it were a film scene. Waiting for the leading man to arrive.

And then she saw him, wrapped in a navy-blue dressing gown, one hand holding a pipe, his thumb caressing the stem. Charlotte stepped forward, pushing one of the doors wider as she stepped through, and his attention was drawn by the movement. He looked at her first with blank politeness and offered a tentative smile. Then she came closer, and his hand dropped. The pipe dangled from his fingers, forgotten.

"Charlotte?" said the man everyone knew as Reggie Evers, but who to Charlotte would always be Georgie.

As if in a dream, she tried to speak but couldn't. It seemed impossible that the two of them should be here, on this sunny California afternoon, when they'd last seen each other on the rain-soaked deck of the *Carpathia*. One impulsive decision had led to two utterly different lives. His golden hair was darker now, and his jawline was more prominent. He'd aged, yes, but was still entirely, recognizably Georgie.

He walked over, his mouth twisted in a rigid smile. "I think this calls for a drink."

Georgie ushered Charlotte toward a cart crammed with cut-glass decanters. So much for Prohibition. Georgie poured them both a scotch and soda, then held up his glass. Charlotte raised hers in response.

"To old friends," Georgie said.

We were never friends, Charlotte thought. "Not too old, I hope," she said instead.

It was enough to break the tension, and Georgie laughed. Charlotte took a sip of her drink; he'd mixed it strong. The two men in tennis whites came jogging over with their rackets, and one called out, "Reggie! You're taking me on next!"

Georgie waved him away. "I am otherwise occupied." Very upper-crust posh, as if he'd just come from the House of Lords. "Try Dunkie instead. Five dollars he beats you in straight sets."

There was a round of laughter, a sense of Georgie as the indulgent father amused by the youngsters' antics.

"Let's go inside," Georgie suggested, and Charlotte followed him back to the house.

He led her down a hallway to his office, where the first thing she noticed was a massive wood desk and the second thing she noticed was the photograph on top, of Georgie with Mary Pickford. If the goal was to impress visitors, it worked.

"Where do we start?" Georgie asked, his bemusement barely masking his nervousness. "How long has it been?"

"Twenty years," said Charlotte. And then, because she already felt bad for catching him off guard, "Georgie, I'm sorry . . ."

"Georgie. I can't remember the last time someone called me that. Well—I suppose I can. It must have been you."

Those terrible, bewildering days aboard the *Carpathia*. Charlotte remembered, viscerally, the first hours after the lifeboat, as she had wandered the decks, searching each knot of survivors for Reg's face. The smell of the blanket flung over her shoulders, wooly and damp. Some men had made it into the final lifeboats; others had been pulled from the water. If there was anyone who knew how to wriggle out of a seemingly doomed situation, it was Reg.

Instead, she found Georgie, huddled in a deck chair, his face drawn and pale. Georgie, whose suffering only enhanced his good looks, like a boyish saint in a Renaissance painting. Charlotte's heart lurched, and she ran to the chair, her face etched with a silent question.

Georgie shook his head. "Reg didn't make it."

"How do you know?" she demanded.

"I saw him die."

In a dull monotone, Georgie told Charlotte what had happened. They'd been near the stern, unsure what to do as the deck continued to tilt, and then there'd been an enormous roar. Some sort of explosion that toppled one of the smokestacks. A twisted piece of metal crashed into Reg's face—it must have killed him instantly—and Georgie had barely enough time to register the horror of it before a force pushed him backward, over the rails. Disoriented and desperate, he'd splashed and shouted until he reached an overturned lifeboat that had been swept off the ship. For hours, he and twenty others had stood on its sloped keel, clinging to each other to keep upright, leaning to keep their balance with each swell of the sea.

Georgie told the story in a flat, detached voice, as if none of it mattered, and Charlotte churned with rage. How could a useless idiot like Georgie be alive when Reg was dead?

Two officers were working their way along the deck, writing down messages from the *Titanic* survivors to be wired to their relatives. The men spoke in hushed voices, deferential in the face of suffering.

"What am I to do?" Georgie mumbled, eyes cast downward, fingers picking at the edge of his coat.

I couldn't care less what you do, Charlotte thought. *I never want to see you again.*

"Tell your parents you're all right," she said, trying to keep her voice level. Georgie looked ready to cry, and she hadn't the patience for a scene. "They'll wire money to you in New York, won't they? Then you can go home."

"I can't go back!" Georgie's eyes pleaded with hers, frantic. "My father disowned me. He said he'd rather I was dead than disgrace the family." To Charlotte's disgust, tears began trickling down his cheeks. "Now he's got his wish. There's nothing left for me, with Reg gone. I should have died, too."

Charlotte almost said it: *I wish you had.* Georgie's whiny self-pity was more than she could take.

"What shall we do?" he asked.

We? Charlotte hadn't any intention of linking her future with Georgie's. But the very last remnants of her loyalty to Reg stopped her from walking away. A wisp of an idea took hold, solidifying as she examined it from all angles. It could work.

"What if you were dead?" she asked.

Georgie stared at her, wide-eyed.

"We could tell the officer making up the passenger list that you're Reginald Evers. And you saw George St. Vaughn die."

His head tilted to the side, and his lower lip drooped, like a half-wit child's.

"You'd have a fresh start. I'll vouch for you as my husband until we reach New York. After that, you're on your own."

Georgie was slow to understand—no surprise—so Charlotte sat beside him and explained how it would work. And it was their closeness and complicity that made an approaching steward assume they were husband and wife before they said a word. The steward asked if they would like one of the staterooms set aside for married couples. Georgie glanced at Charlotte, and she glared back: *Be a man for once. Make up your mind.*

"Yes," Georgie said, with a quick nod. "Very well."

Charlotte never would have suggested the name switch if she'd thought through its implications: the days she was forced to hover beside Georgie, the nights they shared a cramped second-class cabin. Luckily, the subdued mood of their fellow passengers made the deception easier. They didn't have to fake cheerfulness when they sat side by side on deck chairs or summon conversation over dinner. The weight of shared grief hung over them like a fog, and they climbed into their berths each night fully dressed, exhausted yet sleepless. The first evening, Charlotte heard Georgie crying, though he tried to muffle the sound with his pillow. She pretended she was asleep. If he cried the following nights, she didn't hear it. Perhaps, like Charlotte, he'd learned to do so silently.

They never talked about Reg.

The last time they'd seen each other was in New York Harbor, as black rain lashed down like a curse from God, and they'd gone their separate ways at the Cunard pier. Georgie put on a brave face, but Charlotte was convinced he wouldn't last a week. He'd get by all right for a time—she'd seen the money in the inner pocket of his coat, her pickpocket's eye still sharp. He could afford a week or two in a nice hotel; he could buy a new wardrobe. But he was young and sheltered and out of his depth. Sooner or later, he'd get frightened; then he'd wire his mother and beg forgiveness. Before long, he'd be back on his posh estate in England, doing his duty. For months after the sinking, Charlotte expected to see the story splashed across the papers: "A Miraculous Return" or "Lord Upton's Son Survives!"

But George St. Vaughn never came home. And eventually he'd disappeared from Charlotte's consciousness, too.

Those first weeks had been difficult, Georgie now admitted. "I felt quite abandoned," he told Charlotte, and she could hear reproof in the slight pause that followed. Faint, but still there. "Then I met a chap at a . . . a sort of drinking establishment, who fancied himself an impresario and asked if I'd ever considered the stage."

Charlotte could imagine the sort of seedy "establishment" where the conversation had taken place. A young man like Georgie—gorgeous, innocent, British—must have been a veritable beacon for lechers. But Georgie, improbably, had used his looks to his advantage. He'd begun with bit parts in dance-hall and variety shows and moved up to leading roles, though he was refreshingly candid about his lack of talent.

"If you're the least bit good-looking and speak as if you're just down from Oxford, it's not hard to get cast," he told Charlotte. "I always knew my main job was to stand in front of the lights and smolder. Acting didn't really come into it."

Theater reviewers seemed to agree, from what Charlotte had read in the *Express*. Perhaps that was what pushed Georgie to move behind the scenes, though he told Charlotte he'd simply gotten bored reciting lines and wanted to do something more challenging. He'd started as a set decorator, then moved to California in 1923, just in time to take advantage of the moving-picture boom. They were so desperate for directors back then, he said, that they'd give a one-reeler to anyone who knew how to operate a camera.

Charlotte asked if she might have seen any of his films.

"Not unless you're a glutton for punishment!" Georgie laughed. He waved a hand at the wall behind her. It was covered with garish posters of pouting women and scowling men, the titles in great white swaths along the top: *She Done Him Wrong. The Devil Is a Dame.*

"My speciality is 'good girls gone bad,'" he said. "A sweet young thing is seduced and led into a life of crime. Sometimes she's saved by the love of a good man; otherwise she goes down in a hail of gunfire. Very tawdry, and usually third-billed. It's good fun, though. And as you can see, it pays well."

He seemed eager to impress her, though Charlotte couldn't think why. Everything about Georgie's new life was a reproof to hers: the magnificent house, the crowd of friends gathered around the swimming pool, the pile of money that made it all possible. When Georgie asked what she'd been up to, Charlotte felt the luster leak out of her life. The flat she was so proud of now struck her as cramped and gloomy, her glamorous job a rote exercise in forced jollity. She had friends, yes, but dinner-party friends, and going-to-the-theater friends. Hardly anyone she'd invite over on a Sunday afternoon, and almost no one she trusted enough to confide in. She'd left Georgie to fend for himself, and he'd done it. He'd proved her wrong.

When Georgie offered a tour of the house, Charlotte didn't have to fake her awe. His bedroom was massive but tranquil, with all-white linens and windows overlooking the mountains. Waking up there, she thought, must feel like you'd made it halfway to heaven. Charlotte followed Georgie out onto the balcony, where she could see the full sweep of the property. More people had gathered by the pool, and the sounds of clinking glasses and determinedly jolly laughter drifted upward. Again, Charlotte felt as if she were watching a film. The guests were all so lovely, walking with the easy grace of dancers. Their animated faces made every conversation look fascinating, tempting Charlotte to eavesdrop.

But there was something odd about the scene, too, something Charlotte couldn't put her finger on until she'd watched for a few minutes, half listening to Georgie drone on about landscaping. Slowly, eyes darting back and forth, she realized that it was mostly men at the party, and that one was grabbing another possessively by the arm, and others were whispering close up against necks and ears, exchanging complicit smiles. Charlotte was more worldly than she'd been aboard the *Titanic*; she'd been to theater gatherings where costume designers and male dancers linked hands in back corners. She knew such things went on, but they occurred in a shadowy, alternate world. She'd never seen such behavior indulged in so openly.

If Georgie's open house was turning into *that* sort of party, it would be best if Charlotte made her excuses and left. And yet she couldn't quite pull away. She looked at all those lovely young actors and singers, so alive they were practically shining, and she felt an unbearable sadness that the person who most deserved to be here wasn't standing next to her.

"How Reg would have loved this," Charlotte murmured.

She could picture him so clearly: giving her a devilish smirk, pulling her by the hand. *Come on, Lottie, time to join in the fun,* he'd say, and she'd go, because following Reg was like leaping onto a carousel. She'd never met anyone who inspired her to be so freely herself.

"Do you think of him much?" Georgie asked quietly.

"No, not really," Charlotte said, ashamed of her disloyalty. "You?"

Georgie only mumbled, a sound that could have meant "All the time" or "Now and then." Charlotte kept looking at the party, unsure how far this conversation should go.

"It was easier not to look back," she said, explaining to herself as much as Georgie. "I was so angry at him, those days before . . . before he died. It made the grief that much worse, knowing we'd parted on bad terms."

Georgie had to know what she meant, though she couldn't bear to face him and see it confirmed. He'd been there, after all. He'd heard Charlotte sputter out her refusal when Reg begged her to help disguise Georgie in her clothes. He'd seen Charlotte turn away, bristling with rage; he'd watched her ignore Reg even as he pounded on the window and stopped the lifeboat that saved her life. If Charlotte had known those would be her last moments with Reg, would she have behaved differently? Would she have thanked him as she stepped through the opening in the shattered glass? Charlotte hadn't said a word; she hadn't even looked back. Her pride had meant more than the kindness of a final goodbye.

"You needn't feel bad," Georgie said, and at first Charlotte didn't understand what he meant, because she'd always feel bad, for the rest of her life, for how she'd treated Reg. "Reg's ludicrous plan to dress me up as your sister," he explained. "I'd never have done it, even if you agreed. I wouldn't have left him."

But I did, Charlotte thought, and she stared very fixedly at the dip of the land in the distance and the shadows of the trees stretching across the grass. She mustn't start blubbering in front of Georgie.

"I saw your mother," Charlotte blurted out. "Two weeks ago."

Georgie looked perplexed, as if Charlotte had spoken in a foreign language.

"It's the reason I came to see you—I'm sorry I didn't tell you right from the start. She thinks you're dead, of course, and all this time, she's wondered what happened. Whether you suffered at the end. She knew about you and Reg, and she'd seen his name on the survivor lists afterward, and she'd always wanted to find him and ask him, but she didn't dare do it while your father was alive."

Charlotte knew she was speaking too quickly, like a child defending herself against a punishment, but she wanted to be finished and on her way.

"My father's dead?" It was impossible to tell what Georgie was thinking. His face was utterly still.

"Oh dear, I wasn't thinking . . . yes, last year, I believe. Your brother as well. In the war."

It felt wrong to be telling him these cold truths in this setting, with their faces lit by the amber glow of the late-afternoon sun. A house like Georgie's was meant for dancing and champagne toasts at dawn.

"I heard about Tom," Georgie said. "I've made discreet inquiries about my family from time to time. Anonymously, of course." He sighed, gathering his thoughts. "Tom bullied me horribly when we were children, but other than that, he wasn't a bad chap. Just the sort to throw himself against the German front line for the sake of his country. It must have torn Father up, though. Tom was always the favorite, for obvious reasons."

"It tore up your mother as well. But she told me it was much harder on her when you died."

"Did she?" Georgie seemed genuinely surprised.

"Her solicitor wrote to me, at the paper. There are still some places—legal forms, that sort of thing—where I'm listed as Mrs. Reginald Evers, and I suppose that's how he found me. Your mother asked me to visit, and I put her off forever, but eventually I felt guilty about ignoring her and arranged a visit to The Oaks. She's practically a recluse—never goes out, hardly sees anyone. She's got photos of you and Tom all over the sitting room, and she kept wanting to tell me about her 'darling boys.' I felt quite sorry for her."

Georgie abruptly turned and walked back into the bedroom. Charlotte hovered in the doorway, worried she'd offended him. Georgie opened a drawer in a bedside table and pulled out a metallic strand with a circular gold object swinging from it like a pendulum. A pocket watch. Georgie handed it to Charlotte.

"A present from dear Pater on my eighteenth birthday."

Charlotte looked at the cover, which was etched with a family crest. She popped it open and saw the initials "GSV" in elaborate Gothic script.

"I nearly sold it," Georgie said. "During those first years, in New York. God knows I needed the money. Yet I kept it, like a sentimental fool. I kept it because it was all I had left of my parents, even though every time I looked at it, I remembered how much they hated me.

"When the porter at college found me and Reg . . ." Georgie paused and looked at Charlotte, as if deciding how much to tell.

There were two tufted chairs in front of a large picture window, and Charlotte sat in one, telling him with her eyes that she would listen. Georgie took the watch back and sat opposite her, sliding his fingertips along and around the chain. He smiled gently, a gentleman's assurance that he was perfectly all right and wouldn't make a fuss.

"Well, there was no mistaking what we were up to," Georgie said. "You can imagine the uproar. I was sent home in disgrace, with the understanding that I could plead youth and ignorance and pin the blame on Reg. If I was suitably repentant, I'd be allowed back next term. But Father wouldn't play along. He was livid, as angry as I'd ever seen him. Howling that no son of his would perform such deviant acts. He put on quite a show."

Georgie was making light of it, pretending time had drained the story of its sting. But Charlotte saw the wounds that had never healed. The pain that made Georgie hate himself, even now.

"I thought Mother would take my side," Georgie continued. "She'd always spoiled me. Called me her baby long after I was out of the nursery, I'm ashamed to say. The whole time my father was berating me, my mother didn't say a word. Finally, to my utter shock, Father banished me from the house. Quite medieval, don't you think? I was sent away with only the clothes I was wearing—luckily I'd a few pounds in my pocket and a line of credit at the bank in Oxford, or who knows what I'd have done. As Father was ordering me out, I kept waiting for Mother to rein him in. To say he'd done enough, or we'd talk it over in the morning. She never did. She stood there, watching, as I walked away crying like a schoolboy. It was like she'd turned to ice.

"I phoned the house the next day, from the inn where I'd spent the night in town. The housekeeper answered, and I said, 'It's me, Master George, please let me speak to my mother,' and she said she'd been told Lady Upton wasn't taking any calls. I said, 'Not even from her own son?' and she said those were her orders, and I promptly broke into tears—proving my father right, I suppose. I still remember the click when the phone was put down. It was the sound that severed me from my family forever."

Georgie was still a performer; his glance drifted mournfully downward as he sighed. But that didn't mean his emotions weren't real.

"Reg saved me," he said. "That sounds foolish, doesn't it, given what happened? But he took me in when I had no one else. I wrote to Mother a few times—when I told her I was leaving the country, I felt sure she'd write back, to say goodbye, at least. She never did.

"I don't know if Reg intended to take me, when he first planned his trip to America. We hadn't talked much about the future—we hadn't talked about it at all, to be honest. But when he asked me along and talked about all the adventures we'd have together, it felt like I'd been given a second chance at life. When he was lost"—Georgie took a momentary pause, swallowing down the pain—"I was shattered. But I couldn't go back. I owed it to Reg to live a life of truth, the sort of life he'd have had if he survived. Begging my parents for forgiveness would have been a betrayal of Reg, and it would have been useless, besides. I'd no doubt my parents preferred to see me dead than a nancy boy."

"I think your mother would give anything to know you were alive," Charlotte said.

Georgie shrugged and looked down at the watch. "Six o'clock," he said. "Julio will be serving the canapes."

"Julio?"

Georgie grinned. "My butler."

"Good gracious. Does he serve in full livery?"

"Poor chap, he'd roast." Georgie stood and offered his hand.

Below, by the pool, someone had turned on a gramophone, and voices were singing, "It don't mean a thing! If it ain't got that swing!"

"I should be going," Charlotte said.

"Oh, please stay. I'd like you to."

"Are you sure? I don't know"—how to put it delicately?—"I don't know if it's my sort of crowd."

"Afraid you'll be corrupted?" Georgie laughed, amused by Charlotte's reticence. "No orgies, I promise. Just dinner. I'd love everyone to meet you."

She'd assumed it was the other way around: *I want to impress you by showing off all my dazzling friends.* Charlotte was unexpectedly touched by the sincerity of Georgie's invitation. It gave her a warm quiver of pleasure, followed quickly by thirst for another drink.

"That's very kind of you," she said. "I accept."

They walked from the bedroom, Georgie leading the way. At the top of the stairs, he paused and asked, "You still go by Mrs. Evers?"

"Yes," Charlotte said, "I never remarried. Well, I wasn't married in the first place, but no one needs to know that."

"It's just occurred to me that it makes for rather awkward introductions. Hello, everyone, I'd like you to meet . . . Mrs. Reginald Evers!"

They both laughed, and Charlotte was struck by how quickly her earlier reservations had faded. At eighteen years old, Georgie had been like a castle on a movie set: a fine-looking façade with nothing behind it. Now, in his late thirties, he'd grown into himself, and Charlotte was genuinely enjoying his company. Perhaps she had changed as well.

"You could introduce me simply as Charlotte—one of those exotic adventuresses with no surname."

"No, no. You have to be Russian or Italian for that. You're much too British. Charlotte Evers will do. I'll say you're my cousin."

"We used to spend summers together, in the country," Charlotte suggested.

"And Nanny was always scolding us for running about and making a mess at tea."

"She was a wet blanket, wasn't she?"

How easily the imagined vignettes shook shape: Charlotte and Georgie as children, their clothes muddied, eating toast in front of a nursery fire. The two of them older, shoes flung aside, exchanging insults and giggles over a game of croquet. The invented memories came to Charlotte in such detail that they might as well have been real.

Drinks and nibbles extended into a five-course dinner. Georgie seated Charlotte at his right, and the conversation was lively and loud. Everyone wanted to talk to Georgie's surprise visitor, and Charlotte was gratified by the attention. More than once, she was reminded of her escapades with Reg, as she and Georgie traded made-up stories of their childhood, playing off each other with the ease of experienced performers. After dessert, the gramophone was wheeled into the sitting room for dancing, and Charlotte never lacked for partners. In London, the onslaught of all that beauty and talent might have irritated her or made her sarcastically dismissive. That night, she felt more generous. Most of the people there were so young and eager for approval. It was the easiest sort of kindness to say something nice and watch them bloom, as if compliments were currency and Charlotte a benevolent ruler tossing out coins from her carriage.

It was only at the end of the night—after the guests had made their way home in huddles of two and three, saying goodbye with elaborate European kisses on the cheek—that Georgie and Charlotte found themselves alone again. He insisted on driving her rather than ringing for a taxi and teased her about staying at the Sultan's Palace, while she protested that she found it marvelously bohemian. The night had turned cool, and Georgie urged Charlotte to borrow one of his jackets. They paused by the front door as Georgie placed it over her shoulders, and Charlotte was suddenly overcome by a visceral memory of Reg. He'd stood behind her in just the same way, wrapping his coat around her and pulling it taut around her life belt. Putting her survival above his own.

"I miss Reg so much," Charlotte said. "I hadn't realized, until tonight." She felt the same looming dread she felt when on deadline, the urgency of putting words in the right order as the seconds ticked past. "I was beastly to him. And to you."

Georgie reached out a hand, and Charlotte stretched out her fingers to hold on. But no, he was only adjusting the back of the jacket. His eyes were turned away.

"The situation, with me and Reg," he said quietly. "It wasn't tawdry. I was in love with him."

Charlotte wanted to tell Georgie she understood, but she hadn't, not at all. When she met Georgie, her notions about sex were vague and based mostly on rumor; she'd never even seen a naked man. But she'd known with self-righteous certainty that what he was doing with Reg was wrong. She'd never allowed herself to believe that Georgie and Reg had real affection for each other, or considered how her constant disapproval might have hurt them. Charlotte had told herself no decent person would condone such behavior. But she was hardly an exemplar of virtue herself, given the things she'd done.

No, Charlotte realized, it went deeper than that. She'd tried to deny Reg the happiness he deserved because she was jealous. Because he hadn't chosen her.

"Reg loved you, too, you know," Georgie said.

"Please," Charlotte protested. "You mustn't worry about sparing my feelings."

"I told you, didn't I, that he thought of you as a sister? It was the truth. He never talked about his parents or where he'd come from; he said you were the nearest he had to family. That he'd even come close to marrying you."

"I wanted to marry him, very much," Charlotte said. "He turned me down." Ridiculous, really, how much that rejection still hurt.

"Most men of our kind do marry," Georgie said, "if they want a normal life. Things are a little freer here in Los Angeles, if you're discreet about it, but I was married for a time myself, in New York. Sadie, a lovely little dancer. Very young, very naïve. It only lasted a year. Luckily for me, you're not anyone in Hollywood until you've had at least two divorces."

Charlotte wondered if Sadie blamed herself for the marriage falling apart. She hoped Georgie had been brave enough to tell her the truth.

"Reg was more honorable than me," Georgie said. "I know that's a strange thing to say, given his past. He could have married you, and you'd have done his cooking and washing and raised children while he went off and enjoyed his little dalliances. In many ways, marrying you would have been the easy choice. He didn't do it because he was too fond of you. He was afraid you'd find out who he was and hate him for it. Better to break your heart straight off, when you were young enough to recover. He hoped you would understand, in time. That you wouldn't cut him out of your life."

"I didn't know." Charlotte's chest pulsed with remembered pain. "I thought you'd come in and pushed me aside . . . oh, it all sounds so silly now."

"We were put in an impossible situation, weren't we? Both in love with the same man, like a cheap melodrama! And Reg felt terrible. It's a vile feeling, to know you've hurt someone you care for."

It shouldn't matter, after all this time. But it made Charlotte's heart swell. She thought of Reg as she'd first known him: bursting with life, always game for a laugh. The man who had changed her life. That Reg had been overshadowed by the man who drowned, the end darkening what had come before. None of that seemed to matter anymore. It was enough to know Reg had loved her. He always had.

"Reg told me to be patient, that you'd come around in time," Georgie was saying. "I was mad for Reg, so I did my duty and fawned all over you. No wonder you couldn't stand me."

"I was wretched to you!" Charlotte managed a rueful laugh.

"I made the same mistake actors do at auditions, when they're desperate for a part. They talk too much and blast these enormous smiles, begging you to like them. It's exhausting. Those are the ones who never get the roles."

How much of Charlotte's cruelty had been driven by ignorance? *I didn't think it was possible for one man to love another,* she wanted to tell Georgie. Or, *I didn't believe your feelings were real.* Instead, she simply said, "I am sorry."

"Apology not necessary, but gratefully accepted," Georgie said.

"I've no doubt your mother would apologize as well, if you saw her." Georgie shook his head quickly, rejecting this turn in the conversation, but Charlotte kept going. "It seemed to me she was very much under your father's thumb. When he cut you off, she felt she had no choice but to go along."

"She was quite Victorian that way. In thrall to her lord and master."

"She regrets what happened, deeply," Charlotte said. "I didn't promise her anything; I only told her I'd try to find Reg when I came to America. If you could have seen her face . . . it's as if that small hope is the only thing keeping her alive. I hope you'll write to her, at least, but it's entirely your decision."

"Is it?" Georgie asked with an amused scowl.

"One letter. You could make an old woman happy, and no one else need ever know."

"And if I don't write, you'll be back on my doorstep, asking why I haven't."

"I've train and boat tickets booked—I'll be back in London next week. I won't bother you again."

"Hmmph." Georgie's response was noncommittal. He held up his car keys. "Shall we?"

They drove the ten minutes in silence, snaking first down an empty hillside road, then blending into the stream of cars traveling through Beverly Hills. Charlotte felt peacefully empty, cleansed of the anger and guilt that had always obscured her thoughts of Reg. Now, only the deepest, truest layer remained: affection, and gratitude, and a bittersweet tang of remorse.

Georgie pulled up in front of the Sultan's Palace and turned off the car. He turned to Charlotte and said, "I'll do it. I'll write."

She gave him a look of exaggerated, wide-eyed surprise.

"I'd be a monster if I didn't," he said.

Charlotte smiled, thinking how thrilled Lady Upton would be—if her heart didn't stop from the shock.

"Thank you," Charlotte said. "I don't think you'll regret it."

"Ever since the sinking, I've been determined to have as few regrets as possible," Georgie said. "I've made mistakes, more than my fair share, but I will never lie on my deathbed and think, 'I wish I'd done that.' I've done everything I wanted."

"Then you're a lucky man," Charlotte said.

She wished she could say the same. There were dozens of things she'd meant to do or say but never gotten around to. She thought of Mr. Healy, and the letter she'd always intended to write. What a coward she'd been.

"You know," Georgie said, "they're desperate for voice teachers here. The studios pay very well if you've got a posh accent and can teach farm boys how to talk *proper*." He dragged the word out, in an overstated twang. "It's not a bad place to live, Los Angeles. Sunshine year-round, fresh oranges every morning for breakfast."

Charlotte could envision it, briefly, but that future was a mirage. The girl who'd stepped off the *Carpathia* might have made a go of it. She was too far along to start over.

"I'm afraid I've developed a taste for fog and rain," she said lightly. "Awfully kind of you to suggest it, though."

"If I do come back to England—not that I plan to—but if I do, may I call on you?"

"Of course," Charlotte said. Then, more warmly, "I do hope you will."

They smiled at each other, and Charlotte felt Reg's spirit with them, nudging them closer together. *He'd rest in peace,* Charlotte thought with uncharacteristic sentimentality, *if he knew we were friends.*

Georgie's voice and bearing were still British, but he'd adopted an American forthrightness that Charlotte admired. He openly admitted his faults and wasn't afraid to speak honestly about the past. If he'd stayed in England, the dutiful son of Lord Upton, he'd never have become the man sitting next to her, a man at ease with himself and proud of the life he'd created. Charlotte handed Georgie one of her cards. She didn't know if he'd make the effort to correspond, or if they'd ever see one another again. If not, she'd understand. London and The Oaks would feel very far away tomorrow, when he woke up and looked out at the mountains from his mammoth bed.

But Charlotte hoped this wasn't the end. Georgie, she realized, had reawakened a long-buried part of herself. He'd given her back Reg.

"I never asked you," Charlotte said, tentatively. "Were you near the ship when it went down?"

Georgie nodded.

"It must have been awful."

Georgie immediately understood what Charlotte meant by "awful." "We had to push a few men away from our lifeboat," he said. "We'd have tipped over otherwise."

Charlotte put all her effort into breathing steadily. There was no reason to get into all that, not now.

"I imagine you had an easier time of it," Georgie said. "You took a seat and rowed away, eh? Any millionaires in your boat?"

"Charles Van Hausen. And Mrs. Harper. They married afterward, as you might have heard." Charlotte intended the words to be carelessly amused, but they came out wrong. There was some sort of catch in her throat. "And Mrs. Dunning, and Mrs. McBride. There was a Swedish girl, absolutely drenched . . ."

She needed to be clearer. To explain what happened in a logical way. Charlotte remembered the hotel manager giving her a mischievous smile and telling her he had bottles of whiskey in the back, available for the right price.

"There was a man, in the water," Charlotte declared, reckless with the elation of honesty. "Would you like to come up for a drink? You're the only person I know who might understand."

PART THREE:
THE LIFEBOAT

APRIL 15, 1912

1:55 a.m.

The sailor grabs the top of Anna's life belt and pulls. The shift in weight tilts the boat, and the old woman's cane slips from her fingers, landing with a clatter at her feet. The woman across from her gasps and clutches the boy and girl at her side. Anna kicks her legs wildly, uselessly, as the edge of the boat presses against her chest. Every breath is a struggle.

There are fifteen people in this lifeboat built to hold sixty-five. They sit on four wood benches, in emotional states that range from nervous distress to uncomprehending shock. The passengers are American, British, and French; eleven adults and two children. The two crewmen are English and not accustomed to maneuvering on the open sea. They have no training in sailing or navigation, and a lifeboat drill scheduled for that morning was cancelled; they owe their survival to the unknown officer who added their names to the emergency muster list. Slightly more than two hours have passed since the iceberg scraped the *Titanic*'s hull, and it has been one hour since the first lifeboat was lowered. Lifeboat 21, one of the last to leave the ship, has been in the water for five minutes.

The sailor shifts his grip to Anna's waist, tipping the boat farther to the side. Esme braces herself against the bench where she sits between Charlie and Sabine. The maid's face is pinched tight with fear. In the back of the boat, a trio of middle-aged women unleash a Greek chorus of protests as the feathers on their hats swirl. Esme is pressing Charlie's handkerchief to her face to staunch the bleeding from her cut cheek. It's not painful; the cold air has numbed her skin. But she wonders if it will cause a scar and if she is a terrible person for worrying about her looks at such a time.

The *Titanic* is sinking. The tip of the bow is already submerged, and the water continues to progress inexorably upward, leaving a scatter of flotsam in its wake. The passengers of Lifeboat 21 watch the tiny, distant figures still aboard attempt to stave off the inevitable, scurrying upward as the tilt of the deck grows ever steeper. Even as they see it happen, it seems impossible.

Grunting, the sailor drags Anna inside. Water streams from the hem of her dress, and she collapses into a self-protective huddle at Charlotte's feet. The boat settles into an even sway. Charlotte looks down at the bedraggled creature below her, whose face is hidden beneath a tangle of brown hair. Indistinguishable shapes churn in the surrounding sea. Charlotte keeps her eyes on the girl instead.

Esme sees someone bobbing in the water, a few yards off. The face is a blurry flash of white amid a tangle of deck chairs and wreckage, and Esme can't tell if it's a man or a woman, dead or alive. Charlie and the sailor look at each other, silently conferring. Already, Charlie has assumed a certain authority, which Esme thinks no less than his due. It's only natural that the crewmen would look to a first-class gentleman for leadership. She places the handkerchief on the bench between them, hoping Charlie might use it as an excuse to touch her, if only for a moment, but he doesn't seem to notice.

"We should go," Charlie says.

His decisiveness spurs the sailor into action. He and Charlie had both taken up oars to row free of the ship, but they'd made little progress and stopped completely when they saw the girl in their path. Now, the sailor cuts the rope binding the rest of the oars and hands one to the bearded, sour-faced crewman in the back, whose clothes are grimy with soot from the engine rooms.

"Mr. Wells, is it?" Mr. Healy asks.

The fireman nods.

"Able Seaman Edmund Healy. We'll turn her around at the bow."

Mr. Wells takes the oar and dangles it from his hands, testing out its weight. He points the paddle away from the boat and down, and it splashes ineffectually at the surface of the water.

"What are you doing?" one of the three matrons snaps.

"Saving our lives," Mr. Wells shoots back.

"Have you ever rowed before?" Her voice is a mix of sharp British consonants and broad American vowels, an accent widespread among well-traveled, well-funded society women. "You must put it in the oarlock, to hold it in place."

With a gruff exhale, Mr. Wells slides the handle into position. "Never held an oar before in my life," he says, boastful of his inexperience, and the matron gives her companions a pursed-lipped look of disapproval. He doesn't notice, or pretends not to.

"We'll need someone to steer," Mr. Healy says, looking doubtfully at his prospects. The old woman will be no use; neither will the fretful mother. The pretty young woman in the middle might do—she'd impressed him with her steely self-assurance when she stepped into the boat—but she's busy tending to the girl they've just rescued. Mr. Healy's eyes meet those of a middle-aged woman with broad shoulders and the unruffled composure of a longtime headmistress.

"I'm from Portsmouth," she says. "I know a bit about sailing."

Just as he'd hoped: no fuss and no dithering. Mr. Healy takes her hand and escorts her to the triangular bench that fills the rear tip of the boat. The woman grabs the wooden tiller and pushes it from side to side, testing the movement of the rudder below. When she nods in satisfaction, Mr. Healy gingerly winds his way back to the middle of the boat.

Sitting on the front bench of the boat, Charlie secures his oar, his movements forcing Esme to shift away. Her right arm and leg press against Sabine, and though it's awkward to be so close to one's maid, Esme pretends she doesn't mind. They're all in this together, and she must set a good example.

Behind Sabine, Mr. Healy begins rowing. The bow jerks unsteadily. Mr. Healy looks back toward the woman at the tiller—she gives him a "Don't blame me" shrug—then sees Mr. Wells's oar hanging limply from its lock, while Mr. Wells rubs his hands with exaggerated vigor. Two minutes in, and the man's already shirking his duty. Mr. Healy, flustered by the weight of command, says nothing. If all these lives are in his hands—an unbearable, unwanted responsibility—he can't afford to provoke the other men. He needs them too much.

A few feet from Mr. Healy, Charlotte is kneeling by Anna. Water has pooled from the girl's soaked dress, and Charlotte feels it sink into her skirt and chill her legs.

"Don't worry," Charlotte says. She reaches around Anna's back and pats her shoulder, tentatively at first, then more firmly when Anna doesn't resist. "You're safe."

Anna doesn't understand what Charlotte is saying, but she recognizes the voice as a kind one. She can't stop shivering. Even if Anna herself has lost the will to keep fighting, her muscles are determined to shake her back to life.

The girl must be freezing, Charlotte thinks, in such a thin dress. And only a shawl around her shoulders, thoroughly drenched and likely to freeze solid. Charlotte takes off Reg's coat and wraps it around Anna. Then she pulls Anna up onto the bench, rubbing her hands to warm them.

Anna is only dimly aware of Charlotte's efforts. Her mind is struggling to make sense of what has happened. She was on the deck with Emil and Sonja; then they were in the water. Is Sonja dead? Even thinking it feels like a sin, as if Anna were wishing it true. Emil was swimming right behind her, but he isn't here, which can only mean they will pull him in next. She can see the sailor, the one who appears to be in charge, looking out, searching.

Mr. Healy holds up his lantern. Its glow is stubbornly faint, despite his attempts to strengthen the flame, and the moonlight isn't strong enough to illuminate the turmoil around them. "Where's he gone?" he calls out.

"Who?" the old woman asks, bewildered.

"There was a man, near the girl we rescued," Esme tells the old woman. "We're trying to find him."

Charlie's expression is intent as his eyes survey the darkness. "He was close."

Mr. Wells thrusts his oar down with an angry shove, splashing the matrons in the back. They glare at him furiously, displaying the same expression in triplicate. Esme is pleased to see that the other passengers look to Charlie as much as Mr. Healy for guidance. As she shifts in her seat, she catches a glimpse of the *Titanic*'s back half, rising like an accusation from the sea. The monstrous image dominates the horizon, yet no one points or gasps or cries. The passengers sit straight-backed and silent, and many turn their faces away from the unfolding disaster. Anxious to show Charlie that she's as strong as the rest, Esme gulps down her dread.

"No use looking for 'im now," Mr. Wells says sharply. "If we stay here, we'll be caught in the suction."

The mother frowns. "What do you mean?"

"The ship's going down. Its weight will pull down everything around it."

Mr. Wells's pronouncement sends a ripple of alarm through the previously stoic passengers. Sabine drops her head and presses her hands together in prayer. Esme, touched, remembers Sabine's father and how Esme promised him she'd keep his daughter safe. Brimming with motherly protectiveness, Esme gives Sabine an approving pat, but the maid's eyes remain shut. She is praying fervently for Mr. Harper, the kindest man she knows.

"Is it true?" Esme asks Charlie in a whisper. "Will we be pulled down?"

"I don't know. It might be like a whirlpool, only a hell of a lot bigger."

It's the swearing that makes Esme realize Charlie is afraid, too.

"We must look to our own safety first, mustn't we?" Esme asks Mr. Healy tightly.

Mr. Healy speaks to her with the deference due a lady wearing a fur coat. "I will do everything I can." Turning to the back, he calls out to the woman steering, "We'll make a turn to port."

Behind him, Anna's muddled thoughts shift into place. They are leaving. They can't! Emil is there, in the water, and if they don't pull him in, he will die. She straightens up with a jolt, knocking Charlotte's arm away.

"Emil!" Anna cries. "We have to save my friend!"

Charlotte gives Anna a sympathetic but puzzled look. She doesn't understand Swedish, of course, and Anna tries to remember the dialogues in her English phrase book. She studied those pages for hours, but none of the suggested conversations have prepared her for this. All she can think of are childish, useless words: "Train." "Bread." "Please."

"My name is Anna Halversson," she blurts out. It's the only English sentence that comes to mind.

Charlotte smiles, a patient mother encouraging her baby's first steps. "My name is Charlotte Evers," she says slowly, pointing to her chest.

Anna struggles to make Charlotte understand. "Name Emil Andersson," she tries, pointing out toward the blackness. "Emil!"

Charlotte can only shake her head, helplessly apologetic. She'd thought, at first, that Anna spoke some English, but that doesn't appear to be the case. Poor thing—she must be shouting about someone she left behind on the boat. Her father, a brother. Charlotte thinks of Reg and her chest seizes with a sudden sharp pain. Where is he?

Anna looks frantically at the water. Emil can't be far away. She remembers the final kick she made to reach the boat, and how her left foot had hit something hard. Was it Emil's life belt? His face? She doesn't think she is strong enough to have hurt him, but he'd been weakened by the cold. She thinks of Emil, half frozen and suffering, and her heart pulses with panic. She has to find him. If he dies this close to rescue, she will never forgive herself. She will not deserve to live.

Anna tries to tell Charlotte all this, in a frenzy of words she knows Charlotte won't understand. She hopes the desperation in her voice will be explanation enough. She throws her hands out, toward the water, pointing blindly, until an English word pops into her mind, a word Sonja had told her would be useful during their travels.

"Help!" Anna shouts, pointing away from the boat. "Help!"

Charlotte grasps Anna's flittering hands, trying to calm her down.

"Yes," Charlotte says with exaggerated nods. "We're going for help." She says the last word slowly, emphasizing it for Anna's benefit.

Anna, despondent, breaks into ragged sobs. *Perhaps the girl simply needs a good cry,* Charlotte thinks. It's no wonder, with what she's been through.

"Make her stop," the mother mutters from the row behind. "She's going to upset the children." The boy and girl sitting on either side of her look more curious than upset. The mother nudges their faces away from the *Titanic,* but the boy keeps sneaking looks.

"The poor dear," the elderly woman says. Her hands, a lumpy mass of arthritic joints and swollen veins, rest on the top of her cane. "She's lost someone, I imagine."

Anger simmers beneath the mother's cool English restraint. "We've all lost someone."

Charlotte feels an overwhelming urge to slap the woman. How dare she talk as if everyone left on the *Titanic* were already dead! Reg is the cleverest person Charlotte knows, clever enough to find his way into another lifeboat or cling to the wreckage until the rescue boats arrive. Yet Charlotte sees no lights on the horizon. Not even the glow of another lifeboat's lantern. Where have they all gone?

The passengers sit at attention, like toy soldiers, as the lifeboat makes a slow, stiff turn. Charlie and Mr. Healy lean into their oars and pull back with broad, strong movements, but their efforts are barely enough to budge the boat. Mr. Wells lights up a pipe, to loud protests from the women in the back. "I will *not* be treated in this manner!" one of them pronounces, but Mr. Wells pretends not to hear. He continues to smoke, each exhale defiant.

Most people have turned their backs on the *Titanic*, shielding themselves from its destruction, but Esme can't look away. She hears a muffled rumble as the ship's bones twist and break, the engines and machinery and beams crashing downward. There is a hypnotic quality to the ship's leisurely descent. Esme imagines describing the scene to her friends, sometime in the future. The words "tragically magnificent" come to mind, and she is swept up in the self-important gratification that comes from witnessing history.

Esme feels the mood in the boat shift. The immigrant girl is the only one crying, but the other women are struggling to maintain their composure. The old woman is pale—like she might faint any moment—and the mother is looking around wildly, and the women in the back are squawking over the fireman's smoke, as if it matters at a time like this! They'll all be at each other's throats if someone doesn't impose order. Esme turns to the younger crewman, the one who appears to be in charge. He has an open, honest face, and a self-possession Esme admires.

"Mr. Healy, is it?" Esme asks. "You have command of the boat?"

"Yes, ma'am."

"We need a distraction. I thought I might make introductions."

Mr. Healy doesn't see the point of social niceties at a time like this, when it's taking all his strength to pull clear of the ship. But if the rich American woman keeps the passengers occupied, it will stop them pestering him, at least. He guesses they have ten minutes at most before the *Titanic* is gone. He pushes his oar up and down, back and forth, wondering why he can't see the light he'd been told to head for. One of the officers on deck told him the rescue ship was only a mile or so away, but Mr. Healy hasn't been able to find it. He mustn't let anyone else know; it would only start a panic. His only hope is to stay close to the other lifeboats, which are already worryingly far away.

Esme shifts her body around so she can make eye contact with the others. "We must work together," she says loudly, instantly drawing all eyes. "It's the only way we'll survive. So we might as well get acquainted. I'm Mrs. Hiram Harper, from Philadelphia."

For a moment, Esme sees the absurdity of her gesture. Here she is, in the middle of the open ocean, acting as if she's hosting a dinner party. But her fellow passengers don't seem put off by her presumption. They watch her intently, greedily, grateful to have their attention drawn away from the *Titanic*'s death throes.

Esme tilts her head slightly to the left, toward Charlie. "Charles Van Hausen," she says. "Of the Boston Van Hausens."

She is gratified by the reaction to his name: eyes widening in recognition, a few direct stares. She has placed a claim on Charlie by introducing him, but she can't imagine it's raised any suspicion: it must be obvious to all of them that she is a woman traveling without the protection of her husband, and he is a family friend acting as her escort. There were a dozen such pairings on the *Titanic*; it's perfectly respectable. The old lady gives Esme a puzzled look, but Esme barely notices. She is too preoccupied by the women in the back, who seem quite pleased to have a Van Hausen on board.

"My maid," Esme says, with a gesture toward Sabine.

The slight shift of her body brings the *Titanic* in view. The stern is still partially afloat, and Esme feels a bright, jumpy sort of panic. Why haven't they gotten farther away? It's all happening so fast, but she mustn't speak of it, mustn't acknowledge what is happening a quarter mile away. She turns and smiles encouragingly at the woman with two children.

"Mrs. David Trelawny," the woman says stiffly.

She is wearing a brown traveling coat and modest hat; her children are bundled up like Arctic explorers. Judging from the woman's voice, they are British, middle-class, and not accustomed to making conversation with strangers.

"My daughter's called Eva, and this is Tommy. He's six and Eva's nine." Mrs. Trelawny's voice has started to falter. "My brother-in-law's to be married on Sunday, in New Jersey."

Her arms are like wings encircling her chicks, and she flaps them from the children's heads to their shoulders and back. Everyone in the boat can sense her unspoken questions: *Will there be a wedding? Or a funeral instead?*

The old woman on the bench next to Mrs. Trelawny speaks up next. "Mrs. Abraham Dunning. I am returning to New York after a sojourn in southern France for my health." Her voice quavers with age, but she speaks confidently. "This is my tenth Atlantic crossing. All the others passed without incident, not even a rainstorm. I used to joke about my luck, didn't I, Braxton?" She twists her shoulders in a stiff half turn and looks at the woman holding the tiller. "My nurse."

"That you did, ma'am." Nurse Braxton's voice is deep, her demeanor humorless. Just the sort of person Esme can imagine bossing around her patients.

"I shall certainly have a story to tell now," Mrs. Dunning says. "Won't we all?"

Mrs. Dunning shakes her head wryly, and the amusement in her voice strikes Charlotte as unseemly. "Charlotte Evers," she says.

Charlotte thinks, fleetingly, that it's not her name at all. It has no meaning without Reg. She tips her head toward Anna. "She told me her name was Anna Halversson, but I haven't been able to understand anything else."

"Halversson?" Mrs. Dunning asks. "Norwegian, are you? Swedish?"

Anna nods. She knows what "Swedish" means, at least. Worry for Emil has settled into her bones, a leaden ache. What can she do, when she cannot make herself understood? He's gone now, taken by the waves or the cold, and she wishes she could crouch back in the bottom of the boat. If only she could block out all these people and voices and grieve in peace.

"You're good to look after her, Miss Evers," says one of the women in the back.

"Mrs. Evers," Charlotte corrects her.

"Beg your pardon." The woman takes a deep breath, the sort of ostentatious gesture one makes before delivering a speech at a charity luncheon or reproving a servant. "I am Mrs. William McBride. These are my sisters, Mrs. Westleigh and Miss Armstrong."

Charlotte judges them to be in their forties or fifties, their faces variations on a theme. Round cheeks, high foreheads, lips that curve naturally downward. All are stocky from years of easy living and the labor of good cooks.

"The Armstrongs of Baltimore?" Mrs. Dunning asks.

"Yes." Mrs. McBride nods with affable pride. "I don't believe we made your acquaintance on board?"

"The fault is mine," Mrs. Dunning says. "I took meals in my stateroom. I had the pleasure of meeting Porter Armstrong many years ago. Is he a relation?"

"Our father," Mrs. Westleigh says.

"Fancy that," says Mrs. Dunning. "We met at Westport, the summer I came out. He was one of the most dashing men of my season. Had no end of admirers."

The sisters titter like girls at a coming-out dance, and Anna doesn't understand why the ladies in the back of the boat are smiling. It's as if they don't realize the world is collapsing around them. Is that what it means to be rich? To never be afraid?

Esme has heard of the Armstrongs. Not quite high society, but gobs of money. Mrs. McBride, who has taken on the role of official mouthpiece, is explaining that the sisters travel abroad each spring. Last year it was Egypt; this year, they'd taken painting lessons in Florence.

"We end each holiday with a few days in London, at the Savoy," Mrs. McBride explains. "A welcome return to civilization. One can only take so much foreignness, don't you find?"

The boat makes a sudden shift to the right. Nurse Braxton has swung the tiller too hard, at the same moment that Mr. Healy has paused to stretch his cramped hands. The view has now shifted, and Sabine gasps. Mrs. Trelawny lets out a short, anguished cry, and Charlie's oar drops to his lap. The passengers of Lifeboat 21 watch in silent horror as the very tip of the *Titanic*'s stern shifts and settles and sinks, disappearing into the inky water.

"What time do you make it?" Mr. Wells calls out to Mr. Healy.

Mr. Healy holds his pocket watch next to the flickering lantern. "Two-twenty."

Mr. Wells exhales with a loud puff. "That's the last of our wages, then." In response to a stare from Mrs. McBride, he says, "They stop our pay as soon as the ship goes down."

There is no whirlpool, no suction. The ship is simply gone. Out of the darkness, a rumble gathers and grows, expanding into a monstrous roar of anguish and grief. Hundreds of desperate voices moan and scream, begging for salvation, and the passengers of Lifeboat 21 listen in silent shock. *Titanic* survivors will describe the sound differently in the coming days and weeks: one will compare it to locusts on a summer night, another to the cheers at a baseball field when the home team hits in a run. None of them will ever forget it.

It is impossible to see the people in the water. Mr. Healy relights the lantern, but the flame remains tentative. All Charlotte can make out are a few specks of white—life belts, she presumes—amid a jumble of wreckage. The nightmarish howling pummels her, each cry a blow directed at her chest and heart.

"What's going on?" Esme asks, even though she knows. She simply can't believe it's possible. There were no crowds on the deck when she boarded the lifeboat; she'd assumed most of the other passengers had already left. Where have all these people come from?

"The orders were quite clear," Mrs. McBride says. "We were all told to report to the boat deck." Implying that she'd done her duty, and the drowning have only themselves to blame for dawdling.

Mr. Healy holds up the lantern. To Charlotte, a few feet away, his face looks sickly. "There weren't enough lifeboats," he says.

"They said another ship was coming," Mrs. Trelawny says. "For the men."

Mr. Healy decides not to respond. She can see for herself that it never did.

Charlotte looks at Mrs. Trelawny's pale but stoic face. She is putting on a brave front for the children, Charlotte supposes, but she must be thinking of her husband. He could be out there right now, fighting for his life. Mrs. Harper's husband, as well, and Georgie and Reg. The captain and the officers and the stewards and engine-room laborers—all those men who did their duty and went down with the ship. It sounds like a noble sort of death, but it isn't: it's loud and painful and terrifying. No one surrenders to the water without a fight. Through the din, Charlotte hears a high-pitched shriek that she's convinced is female.

There are women out there, too. *Good God,* she thinks, *there might even be children.*

Charlotte turns to Mr. Healy, who is staring into the tumultuous void. The dim moonlight illuminates only the shapes and gestures of those still clinging to life. His quiet, dignified strength gives Charlotte hope. He is the consummate British sailor, the spiritual descendant of Sir Francis Drake and Lord Nelson, a man as much at ease on water as on land. He will know what to do.

"We must help them," he says.

Mr. Wells speaks up, adamant. "I'm not going back there."

"It's Mr. Healy's decision, isn't it?" Charlotte demands.

Mr. Healy puts down the lantern. "We will do what we can."

Mr. Healy picks up his oar, but everyone else looks around, as if waiting for countermanding orders. Charlotte can't understand why they're all acting so helpless. Every minute they spend debating is a human life potentially lost.

"Mrs. Trelawny," Charlotte urges. "Your husband may be there . . ."

Mrs. Trelawny hisses at Charlotte to be quiet. "Not in front of the children!" she says in an angry whisper. "I will not have them upset!"

They'll be far more upset if their father dies, Charlotte wants to retort, but she manages to hold back. They'll get nowhere if they descend into bickering. Tommy's eyes are clamped shut, but Charlotte gives Eva an encouraging smile.

"It will come out all right," Charlotte says, trying to be kind, but Eva is old enough to know she is lying. Mournful, she presses her face into her mother's shoulder.

"Do not speak to my children again," Mrs. Trelawny orders. Defiantly, she turns away, freezing Charlotte out.

Charlotte picks up an oar and settles on the opposite side of the bench from Mr. Healy. "I'll row," she offers. Then, to the boat at large, "Who else?"

Charlie is ready, though he looks more apprehensive than energized, gauging the prevailing mood. Esme takes advantage of his stillness to shift slightly closer. If she could only touch him. She lays one hand on the bench between them, hoping he'll notice. One squeeze is all she needs to settle her worries. If only that incessant wailing would stop. If only she weren't so afraid of all those desperate hands, grabbing at the boat, pulling and pushing, tipping them over.

The screams come at Anna like knives, cutting her with guilt. She hears Emil and Sonja, demanding to know why Anna has been saved and they have not. Had Papa not ignored Mama's objections and taught her to swim, she'd never have made it to the boat. It was only her ability to kick and push her body forward that brought her miraculous rescue. Anna is not sure what Charlotte is saying, but from the way she is gesturing at the water, it is clear she wants to go back. Anna points to Charlotte's oar and mimes that she will row, too. It will mean moving to a different part of the boat—she can't row while she's seated between Charlotte and Mr. Healy—and she tries to stand. But her shoeless feet have long since gone numb, and she staggers against Charlotte and falls back.

In the back of the boat, the Armstrong sisters have drawn into an even more tightly contained unit.

"I don't think that is the wisest course of action," Mrs. McBride says.

"We have space," Charlotte says, gesturing toward the wooden platforms that run along either side of the boat. Designed as seating, neither are being used. "We could easily take a dozen people. Perhaps more."

"It'd be risking all our lives," Mr. Wells objects. "We'll be swamped."

"Oh goodness," Mrs. Dunning says, and her breathing shifts.

Nurse Braxton climbs down from her position at the tiller and leans toward her employer. "You mustn't distress yourself, ma'am." To Mr. Wells, at her right, she says, "You think it's dangerous to go back?"

"It would be madness," he says.

He can't know, Charlotte thinks. He's a fireman, a job little removed from factory work. He's already admitted he knows nothing of boats or sailing. But she notes the way Mrs. McBride and her sisters are listening to him, as if he's some sort of oracle. Mrs. Trelawny has shifted her attention from her children and is listening, too. Mr. Wells, gratified by the attention, nods like a grizzled old sage of the sea. All pointedly ignore Mr. Healy's expectant stare.

"We'd set off a frenzy," says Mr. Wells. "Imagine, all those poor fellows, fighting to get in 'ere. Wouldn't be surprised if we capsized."

The Armstrong sisters produce a unified murmur of concern, and Mrs. Dunning frowns. Nurse Braxton takes a small package from her pocket and hands a pill to Mrs. Dunning.

"She mustn't be distressed," Nurse Braxton says, as if Mrs. Dunning were a child frightened by a ghost story. "She has a weak heart."

"Please . . . ," Mr. Healy urges, trying to maintain his authority, and Charlotte knows she is the only one who can sway the rest to his side.

"People are dying!" she shouts.

That's a bit much, Esme thinks, and she can tell from her shipmates' expressions that most agree. The sounds coming from the water are awful enough without Charlotte haranguing them, too. She's not the captain of their shaky little vessel; the sailors are the ones who know what's safe. And Charlie, of course. Esme knows he'll make the right choice.

"We don't have to go all the way back," Mr. Healy says. "Only a little farther, close enough to see if any swim to us."

An uneasy compromise, but it's the best he can do in the circumstances. Mr. Healy and Charlie and Charlotte dip their oars in the inky water; the boat slides forward. Mr. Wells might well be right. Returning to the scene of the sinking could put them all in danger, and Mr. Healy's first loyalty must be to those lives already in his hands. Still, it's likely they'll be able to rescue a few people. A bulky mass floats by their starboard side, some indistinguishable remains of what was once the finest ship he'd ever seen. Mr. Healy gives the signal to stop. He waits, still and tense, as pleas from the water wash over him like curses, impossible to track and impossible to ignore. They are ghosts that will haunt him for the rest of his life.

Anna cradles the oar in her lap, feeling helpless. She has always been proud of her ability to take on hard work without complaint; gifted with neither beauty nor charm, it is her only advantage. Now her stiff fingers cannot even grasp the handle. It doesn't matter anyway, because the others have put down their oars, and the boat bobs aimlessly. Anna tries to move her toes, but her extremities will not comply. She pulls her feet up and realizes they are still soaking wet. No wonder they haven't thawed: there is a layer of water at the bottom of the boat.

The Armstrong women look annoyed by the cries for help, as if they were a personal affront. Nurse Braxton hovers over Mrs. Dunning, her own patient's discomfort taking priority over the suffering of the nameless. Mrs. Trelawny's mouth has condensed into a thin, straight line, and she is holding her children tight. Eva's eyes wander, as she stealthily follows each observation and disagreement, but Tommy stares down at his lap, hands pressed over his ears. Charlie is on edge, a man of action frustrated at not being able to do anything. Esme tries to catch his attention, but he is preoccupied by the noise; like Mr. Healy, he stares out at the water. He's handsome even when he's sad, Esme thinks, and wishes she could kiss him. Blot out all this misery by burrowing into the one thing she's certain of: Charlie's love.

Charlotte and Mr. Healy exchange glances. She is not sure why—their Britishness, the working-class accents they both try so studiously to hide—but she feels a kinship with him. His steadiness reassures her, and though she hardly knows the man, she trusts him to do the right thing.

"Do you see anyone?" Charlotte asks.

"Not yet. It's hard to be sure, in the dark." Then, hesitantly, as if he already knows the answer but feels compelled to ask anyway, "Are you traveling with your husband, Mrs. Evers?"

"Yes." A lie. "He has business interests in America." Another lie. Charlotte has never been much concerned with telling the truth, but it feels wrong to mislead this decent man.

"I'm sorry," Mr. Healy says quietly, offering silent condolences.

He doesn't know Reg, Charlotte thinks, indignant. *Reg will find a way.*

The cries for help continue, but they have become distinct, separate sounds. Solos instead of a symphony.

"It's thinned out," Mr. Healy says.

Which Charlotte immediately understands to mean: *Enough people have died that we won't be overrun.* "What shall we do?" she asks.

"Our duty," Mr. Healy says. Then, to the boat, he announces, "I can hear voices, quite close. It won't take much effort to find them."

Charlotte takes up her oar and verifies that it's tucked in the oar-lock. Mr. Healy makes similar preparations. He looks to Charlie, who nods.

"Ready, Mr. Wells?" Mr. Healy asks.

The fireman drops his oar with a defiant clatter. "I'm not going in there."

"Do you think . . . ?" Mrs. McBride delicately allows the unspoken part of her question to linger. *Do you think there's any point?*

"It'd be going against Captain's orders," Mr. Wells says.

A deliberate provocation, intended to sow doubt in their commander's abilities. Mr. Healy tries to keep his voice level. "What do you mean?"

"We were told to row for the other ship."

No use hiding it from the passengers now. "I never saw lights," Mr. Healy says. "I don't think it ever turned up."

"Aren't we supposed to stay close to the other lifeboats, then?"

"Yes, and where are they? Will *you* chart a course for us to find them, Mr. Wells?"

Esme tries not to worry. She was certain when the lifeboat launched that they'd be rescued any minute, yet Mr. Healy is right. There's been no sign of another ship, and the other lifeboats have disappeared. They are drifting, alone, in the middle of the sea. The enormity of all that water terrifies her, and the boat suddenly seems horridly flimsy and open; one large wave could wash them all overboard. Esme pulls her coat more tightly around her chest, stroking the fur, telling herself she mustn't lose control in front of Charlie.

A strained cry hurtles through the dark. Charlotte feels the force of it, like a punch. It's a man's voice, deep. Could it be Reg? It's ridiculous to think that he of all people would make it to this particular boat, but the suspicion takes hold and digs in. He could have watched her lifeboat from the deck and swum toward it when the ship sank. Wouldn't that be just like him?

"Turn around!" Charlotte shouts. She twists back and forth, try-ing to grab everyone's attention, her body skittish with hope. "There's someone behind us!"

Anna scrambles to retrieve the oar tossed aside by Mr. Wells. She doesn't know how it's possible, but Emil is out there. She heard him, clearly, and that means she has been given a second chance to save him.

"*Vi kommer!*" she calls out.

The Armstrong sisters exchange perplexed looks, and even Charlotte is surprised by the girl's sudden outburst.

"What can she be saying?" Mrs. Dunning asks Nurse Braxton, as they watch Anna wrestle the oar into place. The sight would be comi-cal, in another setting: a skinny little thing battling a piece of wood that's nearly her height and not all that much thinner. Still, Esme feels a grudging admiration for her. Anna's efforts might not move the boat any faster, but at least she's willing to make an effort, unlike that lazy Mr. Wells. It's only a matter of time before he lights up his pipe and sets off another round of grumbling from Mrs. McBride.

Anna can row as well as any of them; she has gone out in Papa's boat hundreds of times. But she can't get a grip on the wood, not with her frozen, clawlike hands. She could cry with frustration, but she won't, because crying would only weaken her further. She must be strong, for Emil.

In the back of the boat, Mr. Wells is sulking, and the Armstrong women are murmuring to each other. They haven't shown much interest in a rescue mission, but they haven't spoken up against it, either. If Charlotte can convince Mrs. McBride to help, her sisters will fall in line.

"We need as many people rowing as possible," Charlotte says, working hard to moderate her voice. Polite subservience is the way to convince a woman like Mrs. McBride. "Please. We haven't much time."

"I don't know what good we'd do," Mrs. McBride says doubtfully. "I haven't rowed in years."

"I have rheumatism in my wrist," Mrs. Westleigh says, holding up one limp hand as evidence. "I wouldn't want to make it any worse."

Miss Armstrong offers only a startled look, which Charlotte takes to be answer enough. That ninny would do more harm than good messing about with an oar.

"You could work the tiller," Charlotte tells Mrs. McBride. "Help us turn around."

Mrs. McBride looks to her sisters for approval, and Charlotte wants to scream: *Get up, you stupid woman!* But she can't lose her composure, not now. Reg could be in the water at this very moment. She must find out if it's him.

Slowly, with the dramatic composure of someone who revels in attention, Mrs. McBride scoots to the back of the boat and grabs hold of the tiller. "Which way?" she asks.

"We'll turn her to port," Mr. Healy says. Then, when Mrs. McBride stares at him blankly, "Left!"

It can't be Hiram, Esme thinks. He's old and slow—she's not even sure if he knows how to swim. But she has an eerily clear vision of Hiram plodding toward her through the water, his arms moving in methodical strokes, his face set in that familiar expression of amused detachment: *You weren't really going to run off with Van Hausen, were you? Silly girl— I'm here to take you home.* As the boat slowly turns around, Esme feels a sudden urge to throw herself against Charlie's back and pull his hands off the oar. She's afraid of what they'll find.

Other cries occasionally pop out from the void, like frogs croaking in a country pond. But they are intermittent and tentative, coming from nowhere and disappearing into nothing. The person closest to the boat—whoever he might be—is louder and more forceful. Seeing the boat's movement, he urges them on with a desperate exclamation that is almost certainly the word "Help!"

Anna hears it clearly: *Hjälp.* She pulls the sleeves of the coat over her clumsy hands and tries to clutch the oar, but it slides out of her grasp. No matter—the boat is moving at last. Emil is close; she can feel it. They will pull him out of the water, and he will be so wet and so cold, and she will wrap him in Charlotte's coat and pull it tight around him. She will rub his frozen hands with hers, and she will bring him back to life.

All this time, Emil has been fighting. With every shout, every breath, he has been calling to Anna, telling her he hasn't given up. If God has indeed spared him, Anna must prove herself worthy of his devotion. When he is here, beside her, and his shivering has calmed and he is able to speak, she will tell Emil yes. She will marry him. That will be her offering.

They are so close. Charlotte can see a white blur: the life belt, bobbing in the water. She can't see the man's face, only a darkness that could be Reg's hair or could be an illusion of the moonlight. Soon, she will know for sure, but the boat keeps turning, and suddenly the bow is pointing away and Mr. Healy is crying out, "Stop!"

Charlie tips his oar up with an irritated sigh. He shoots Mr. Healy a look of commiseration: *We're the only ones here who know what we're doing.* Esme wants to tell Charlie what she suspects about the man in the water, but she can't catch his attention.

Mr. Healy stands and glares at Mrs. McBride.

"What is it?" she asks.

"You kept us turning when we were meant to go straight," Mr. Healy says, frustration evident in the tightness of his voice. "The man's right there—can't you see him?"

"It's difficult to see anything," Mrs. McBride says, all wounded pride.

"Turn us back to starboard. Right."

"Now you've got me all flustered," Mrs. McBride protests. She fiddles with the tiller. "This way?"

"Mr. Wells!" snaps Mr. Healy. "Will you lend a hand?"

Mr. Wells, legs stretched out leisurely before him, shakes his head. "Already told you, I don't know nothing about sailing."

Why aren't we moving? Anna's blood is pounding; she can't sit still. Why do they keep talking when every second is a matter of life or death? She is the only one who knows what it feels like to freeze. How the cold paralyzes from the outside in, so your body dies around you even as you still breathe. The man's face is hidden, but she no longer needs to see it; she is convinced, with blind certainty, that only someone as strong as Emil could have survived so long in this murderous northern sea. He's gone silent, and Anna mentally wills him to hold on. He can't give up, not when they're so close. Then she sees a flash of movement. The man is moving his arms. Waving, or swimming, or both.

Anna leaps up and shouts for everyone to look. She knows they won't understand what she's saying—"He's alive! My friend! Hurry!"— but her outburst catches the other passengers' attention, and they follow where she's pointing.

It's not Hiram, thinks Esme. But she can't be absolutely sure, because she can't bear to look at the figure in the water. She had managed to distance herself, somewhat, from all those upsetting screams when the ship sank. They had melded into an indecipherable wail that didn't even sound human. It's different, seeing an actual person out there, his arms flailing like a baby bird's wings. Dread sinks over Esme like a net, holding her tight. They must save the man, of course they must. But what will she do if it's Hiram? It can't be, can it?

If only the Swedish girl would stop shrieking.

Charlotte stamps her feet, from frustration as much as the cold. Her toes are stinging with pain, and when she looks down, she sees they are submerged in water. Her mind notes the sight as odd; surely it wasn't that wet when she crouched down to help Anna? But she is too preoccupied with the impending rescue to consider the implications.

Mr. Healy rummages around at the front of the boat. When he stands, he is holding the line of rope that lashed the oars together. He ties one end into a large loop and announces, "I'll pull him in."

Charlotte feels a surge of relief that her trust in him has been vindicated. Of all the people in this boat, he's the only one smart enough to know what needs to be done and brave enough to do it. The man is floating only a few yards away, and Mr. Healy throws out the line with a sharp flick of his wrist. It lands inches from the man, and the passengers watch as he laboriously slides a hand toward it.

For Anna, the scene unfolds with agonizing sluggishness. The man in the life belt manages to reach the rope, but his hands are so frozen as to be nearly useless. It takes three tries before he can keep hold of it, then countless stops and starts as he pulls it over his head, his arms rigid as a tin soldier's. By the time he shifts the loop around his chest, Anna has curled her hands into tight balls and pressed them into her thighs. Why won't he look up so she can see him? The man's hair is dark, darker than Emil's. But it is night, and she remembers Emil stepping out from the lake after an evening swim. His hair never looked blond when it was wet. There is still hope.

Mr. Healy tugs on the rope, and the boat jerks. An ominous swish of water cuts through the silence.

One of the Armstrong sisters lets out a gentle "Ooh!" Then all three of the sisters are shifting in their seats, making splashes with their boots. Mr. Healy pulls again, and the water in the bottom of the boat shifts from side to side in rippling waves.

"Hold on!" Mr. Wells shouts. The gruff command makes them all start, and Mr. Healy turns around. "We're taking in water!" Mr. Wells says. He has cast aside his previous indifference, and his face pulses with agitation. "There's a leak."

"Check the hull," Mr. Healy tells him, the rope still in his hand but hanging limply. He looks down toward his feet, then around the edges of the boat. To the passengers, he says, "Look around you. Tell me if you see water coming in."

The passengers lean over and begin searching. The boards are solid and tight-fitting; there are no cracks or holes, no trickles or sprays.

Mr. Healy would pace the whole boat if he could, inspecting every inch. But there's no time, and he has to move slowly, to keep her on an even keel. He is baffled, but can't let his worry show. Frantically, he tries to calculate how quickly the boat will fill up, given the time they've been in the water and how much has already seeped in. He has to know how many hours they have left, but he's so tired, and everyone is staring, and his muddled brain can't work out the numbers. He looks at the passengers, who wordlessly stare back, expecting him to deliver salvation.

Fools.

Then Mr. Healy remembers. Sharply, he asks, "The plug, Mr. Wells?"

"I put it in . . ."

"Check it."

Esme gives Charlie a questioning look.

"There's a hole in the bottom," Charlie explains. "For rainwater to drain out when the boat was stored on deck. That sailor put a plug in it as we were being lowered down."

"It's broken?"

"I don't know. But there shouldn't be this much water. Something's wrong."

Esme's own fear is fueled by Charlie's worry. There's a leak in their boat, and they're alone in the ocean. Hiram had told her, before they even left New York, that sailing was safer than ever, thanks to the wireless. Even if a ship did go down, there was plenty of time to radio others for help. She had put all her faith in a rescue ship that never arrived.

Or maybe it had. Maybe it found the other lifeboats and left without them.

Mr. Wells is kneeling at Mrs. Dunning's feet; she and Nurse Braxton have pressed against each other to make room. Mrs. Trelawny hasn't released her hold on Tommy and Eva, but the boy leans over his mother's arm to watch. Mr. Wells sticks his hand in the water, which comes halfway up his forearm. He prods around, his face a concentrated grimace, then stands.

"Must be a crack," he says. "Can't see any other way the water's getting in here."

"Or the plug was placed wrong." Mr. Healy's voice is frosty.

"I placed it just as I was supposed to."

"If it's the least bit crooked, it won't be watertight . . ."

"Come see for yourself!"

Esme can see Charlie tensing as he considers whether to play peacemaker in what will soon be an all-out fight. Esme wishes he would. The two sailors obviously dislike each other, but they should know better than to bicker like children.

Why do they keep fighting? Anna wonders, appalled. Has everyone else forgotten the man they came to save? She reaches toward the rope, which still trails from Mr. Healy's hand. Charlotte grabs Mr. Healy's arm and points outside.

"Please," she urges.

Charlotte's touch sparks Mr. Healy into action. He starts to wind the rope around his hand, and Mr. Wells calls out, "Stop!"

"For heaven's sake . . . ," Charlie begins, but his is not the only voice. Mrs. Dunning is chattering to Nurse Braxton, and the Armstrong sisters are asking questions, and Tommy has started to cry. Mr. Healy ignores Charlie and is about to say something to Mrs. McBride when Mr. Wells steps between Charlotte and Anna, pushing them both roughly aside. He stands next to Mr. Healy, his very closeness a threat, and Charlotte thinks of tomcats behind the fishmonger's, hissing over scraps.

"We're not pulling no one in if she's taking water," Mr. Wells says. "No extra weight."

"One more person won't make a difference," Mr. Healy protests.

"A big fellow could tip us right over. Wasn't easy getting her in, was it?"

Mr. Wells points at Anna, who does not understand his words but recognizes the disdain in his brief glare. She does not know how she has made this man angry, and she slides closer to Charlotte, her only protector.

"Oh dear," Mrs. Dunning is saying. "It does sound dangerous."

Nurse Braxton purses her lips, mirroring her employer's disapproval. Miss Armstrong brings her hands to her mouth in a gesture of girlish dismay.

"And she's a little thing," Mrs. Westleigh says. "I don't see how we can pull a man in without upsetting the boat."

Mrs. McBride nods. Esme looks at the sides of the lifeboat. They are taller than a regular rowboat, intended to create the illusion of a safe enclosure. But Mr. Wells is right: the weight of a man will throw off their balance. It's a risk they can't afford to take.

Charlotte grabs the rope that hangs slack from Mr. Healy's hands. She tugs, and the figure at the end jerks, but he's no longer moving his arms. Is he conserving his strength or has he given up? She pulls again, frustrated at how slowly he moves forward, even though she is tugging so hard her shoulder muscles scream. And then, suddenly, she feels a heavy push against her back, and her body jerks away from the rope.

She trips over Anna's legs and falls into the water at the bottom of the boat, her hip landing with a thud against the wood. She looks up and sees Mr. Wells holding a knife, the same knife Mr. Healy used to cut loose the oars. Mr. Wells slices forcefully downward, cutting the lifeline.

Charlotte and Anna both cry out, Charlotte in bitter protest and Anna in horror. Charlotte winces as she tries to stand, but Anna is already up, leaning over the side of the boat, trying desperately to catch hold of the strand that is tied around the man in the water. But the end has already drifted away, out of her reach, and Mr. Healy grabs her by the arms and pulls her backward as she screams.

Mr. Wells, his work done, turns away and returns to his perch in the back of the boat. Mrs. Dunning, Nurse Braxton, and Mrs. Trelawny look down as he passes, relieved by what he's done but unwilling to openly condone it. Mrs. McBride and Mrs. Westleigh give each other approving nods, but they, too, ignore the fireman when he takes his place behind them. He's done the right thing, they believe, but that doesn't mean they'll engage him in conversation.

Mr. Healy points Anna toward Charlotte, silently pleading for her help. Anna stumbles into Charlotte's arms, and Charlotte presses Anna's head against her chest. The gesture muffles Anna's sobs, but her anguish ripples through the boat. Charlotte looks wildly around her, at the faces that show a mix of sadness and embarrassment and grim denial. Mr. Healy is turned away, fiddling with the rope, avoiding her.

"Please," Charlotte says, addressing her fellow passengers in a final appeal. "We can't leave him to die. Mrs. Trelawny . . ."

Mrs. Trelawny looks pointedly away. Her family is its own self-contained island, and Charlotte can tell by her expression that Mrs. Trelawny will not listen to anything she says. She has retreated inside herself.

Charlotte looks at Charlie, whose hands rest lightly around the oar in his lap. He gives her a rueful half smile, a look that acknowledges her plucky spirit while urging her to accept defeat. The betrayal stings. Charlotte has thought him an ally, one of the only ones who did his share and rowed without complaint. If he chose to rally the boat for a rescue, they'd all obey without question, because who would speak up against a dashing American millionaire? Charlotte sees, now, that Charlie's actions have been driven by pragmatism, not conviction. He doesn't care if the man in the water lives or dies; he cares about whether he's seen as doing the right thing. He rowed harder and faster than anyone when it suited him, but the mood in the boat has shifted, and he won't go against the popular will.

At least Charlotte can count on Mr. Healy to help. She eases a shaky Anna onto the bench and takes hold of an oar. Resolute, she looks to Mr. Healy for the signal to start. Slowly, he shakes his head.

"We must go," she urges.

"It's no use."

His voice is little more than a whisper; his shoulders are slumped in defeat. Charlotte can still hear occasional distant shouts, but so much fewer than before. So much fainter. Every voice is an accusation, and her own breath comes raggedly, as if she, too, were fighting to breathe.

"They're drowning!" Charlotte cries.

"They're not drowning. They're freezing to death."

And with that, a shocked silence settles over the boat.

Mr. Healy turns his back to Charlotte, and that is even worse than seeing his mournful face. Charlotte looks at the icicles that have formed in Anna's hair, and she feels a chill so deep that her bones seem to shiver. The oar slides from her hands into her lap, and then into the water at her feet.

When Anna sees Charlotte's surrender, she knows it is the end. There will be no more fighting, no more attempted rescues.

They'd come too late, in any case. When Anna made her futile grab for the rope, she'd seen how the man's head was slumped over his life belt. He hadn't called out or waved his hands; he hadn't moved at all. Though she couldn't see his face—she never did—Anna knows he is dead.

Please, let it not be Emil.

Anna shuts her eyes and prays. She can't bear to think of Emil in the water by himself, crying out for a rescue that never came. God would not be so cruel as to guide Emil to her lifeboat only to let him die.

Or was there a touch of mercy in such an ending? During those last moments of his life, Emil would have heard Anna's voice. He would have known she was coming. He wouldn't have been alone.

Rage surges through Charlotte, prodding her to keep fighting. She looks ahead, at the French maid who's been so quiet she might as well be invisible. Mr. Van Hausen and Mrs. Harper are paying no mind to anyone other than each other. They're talking in whispers, faces practically touching, and Charlotte feels a prickle of suspicion, her instincts for trouble well honed. Then she realizes Esme's hand is inside Charlie's coat pocket. The intimacy of the gesture is the final piece of a puzzle, and the truth takes shape. Mrs. Harper has not been faithful to her husband.

Esme swiftly turns around. She sensed someone staring, and it's that imperious Charlotte, hovering right behind them. Charlotte meets Esme's accusing look with a scowl, and Esme feels a flicker of unease. She hasn't seen anything, has she? Still, Esme pulls her hand out slowly from Charlie's pocket and leans away from him. Feeling his skin—the rub of his thumb against her fingers—has restored her.

The screams of the dying have weakened into sporadic pleas, the calls of seagulls at dusk. Mrs. McBride's face is set in an annoyed grimace, self-interest having twisted guilt into anger. *Hurry up and die,* she and her sisters seem to be thinking. *Get it over with, so we don't have to hear you anymore.*

And then, at last, there is nothing. No sound but the gentle slap of water against the lifeboat's hull. The passengers of Lifeboat 21 are alone in the vast open sea. Anna has been praying for an end to the suffering of the souls in the water, but their release brings no relief. She looks at the others in the boat, who seem equally unnerved by the eerie silence. The women in the back look angry; the sailor next to them is holding his pipe but hasn't yet decided whether to light it. The little boy is wriggling to escape his mother's tight grip, and his sister is watching the woman in the fur coat, who is absentmindedly stroking the cut on her cheek. The diamonds in her hair glimmer like stars.

Mr. Healy turns to Charlotte, the muscles in his face clenched tight. "We did what we could."

As if they were equally culpable. As if they'd both given up.

"Did we?" Charlotte asks sharply.

"My duty is to my passengers," he says. "I must put their safety above all other concerns."

"We let a man die, right in front of us." Charlotte doesn't bother to hide her bitterness; she no longer needs to charm anyone into taking her side. "We as good as murdered him."

"Murder?" Mrs. Dunning asks. "There's no call for that sort of language."

Mr. Wells lets out a disgusted snort, and Mr. Healy gives the fireman a reproving stare. If only Mr. Wells would stop provoking the rest of them. It's hard enough commanding this boat without a near mutiny on his hands.

Unfortunately, Charlotte has risen to the bait. "His death is on your hands!" she says, pointing at Mr. Wells. "We had him, and you cut him loose!"

"Aye, and I'd do it again."

"Stop it," Mrs. Trelawny snaps. Tommy's crying has settled into a steady whine.

"He was half dead already." Nurse Braxton speaks with the authority of a woman who is rarely contradicted. "Even if we'd been able to lift him into the boat, it's unlikely he would have survived."

"She did!" Charlotte gestures toward Anna. "She was in the water, and she survived!"

Anna wishes they would all stop looking at her. She is so tired. Tired of feeling helpless, tired of being overwhelmed by words she doesn't understand. All she wants is to go home. More than anything, she wants to hug Papa. He is the only one who could help lift the weight of her grief.

"Every one of you has that man's death on your conscience." The words spill out from Charlotte in a torrent of disgust. "We would have reached him in time, if you hadn't dithered about."

Mr. Healy tries to stop her. "Don't, please . . ."

"One man." A man who might have been Reg. *Forgive me, Reg. Forgive me for not saying goodbye.* "He was someone's son or brother or father. He meant nothing to you, but he may have meant the world to someone else."

Esme begins to weep. It wasn't Hiram in the water; she's almost completely sure. But she can't help thinking of him standing on the deck, ready to meet his fate without a word of complaint. Poor old loyal Hiram. She never loved him, not like she loves Charlie, but it seemed a sorry end for such a decent man. It's wrong to be thinking of the future already, when Hiram might possibly still be alive, but if he *is* dead, and she *does* end up marrying Charlie, Esme believes Hiram would understand. He always wanted her to be happy, didn't he? She likes to think of him watching over her, like a guardian angel.

"We'll be all right, won't we?" Esme whispers to Charlie.

He doesn't answer. At first, Esme feels slighted by his inattentiveness, until she realizes he is searching for signs of the other lifeboats. How like Charlie, to keep up hope when everyone else is sulking! Of course they'll be all right; she doesn't need to hear him say it. They're together, aren't they? Only a few hours ago, Esme was mourning their inevitable parting, convinced she was about to lose the love of her life. Yet here they are, side by side. Charlie followed her into the boat, and he has held her hand and kept her safe, just as she knew he would.

Charlotte stamps her feet. The water is up to her ankles, and she sees that Mr. Healy has noticed, too. *How much time do we have left?* she nearly asks, but she doesn't want to frighten the others. Neither does he, from the beseeching look he gives her. Their earlier rapport has been replaced by wary tension. Mr. Healy is watching her, afraid of what she might do or say. Charlotte has always been quick to act and speak her mind, qualities she used to think of as virtues. But her impulsiveness has pushed away the one person in this boat she has any respect for, and she doesn't know how to set it right.

"What provisions do we have?" Charlie asks.

The question is addressed to Mr. Healy, but Mr. Wells responds. "A barrel of water and a tin of hardtack."

"How long will that last us?"

"A day or two. No more."

With Mrs. McBride shocked into silence—for once—Mrs. Westleigh speaks on behalf of her sisters. "We'll be rescued before then, won't we?"

Mr. Wells shrugs. To Esme's irritation, he appears to be enjoying himself, frightening the passengers for his own amusement. She looks pointedly at Charlie, hoping to nudge him into speaking up. When he ignores her, she whispers, "You must make him stop."

"Why, if he's telling the truth?"

Charlie's curtness cuts into Esme, and her feigned bravery withers. So this is how it ends. Days and nights drifting in the north Atlantic, more than a dozen people without enough to eat. Or will the lifeboat sink before the food runs out? She looks around at the others: slumped-over Mrs. Dunning, sleepy Tommy Trelawny, glowering Mrs. McBride— and wonders what will happen when they're forced to start rationing. Esme trusts Charlie and Mr. Healy to be fair, but not Mr. Wells, and she wouldn't put it past those Armstrong sisters to cheat their way into an extra serving. Mrs. Trelawny will fight on behalf of her children, and Nurse Braxton on behalf of Mrs. Dunning, and before you know it, they'll be at each other's throats. Even the Swedish girl must be stronger than she looks if she swam through that deadly water. She's already proven that she doesn't give up easily.

If only Charlie didn't look so disheartened. Charlie's life force has always burned hotter and brighter than anyone else's—Esme has fed off it, craved it for herself—but the events of this night have extinguished it, leaving a glassy-eyed shell. In a moment of insight that upends her, Esme understands that this is Charlie, too. The part of him she was never allowed to see. Charlie will never be a true hero, because he always follows, never leads. In the boat, his eyes caught in the moonlight, he is a statue: beautiful but helpless.

Well, if it comes to it, Esme will fight for both of them. No one in this boat will dare go up against a Van Hausen and a Harper.

Charlotte can feel the miasma of despair move over and through her fellow passengers. The darkness is receding, but the approach of a new day offers none of the hoped-for consolations. They are still lost, still alone. Freed from the terror of the sinking and no longer distracted by the shrieks of the dying, they must face the sobering reality that there is no promise of salvation.

Mr. Healy is rummaging in the bottom of the boat, his hands splashing in the water. He hasn't given up, but the others watch him listlessly.

"Mr. Wells, have we any glasses?"

"I didn't see any."

"Did they give any thought to provisions?" Mr. Healy mutters, his voice strained, as he continues to search the flooded hull. Charlotte wonders if he's already planning to ration out the drinking water—they should wait a while longer, surely? Then she realizes he is looking for a spyglass, to spot another boat. Charlotte is moved by Mr. Healy's dogged persistence, and the last remnants of her determination urge her to help him. She should be searching alongside him, or seeing what can be done to make the plug more secure, or rallying the others to row—to warm up, if nothing more. But Charlotte is too exhausted, and she can no longer bear to be the object of angry stares. All she can do is drift, like the boat itself, and watch as Mr. Healy makes his lone and possibly futile attempt to save them.

And then Charlotte is aware of a gradual shift, as if everyone has taken a simultaneous breath. Faces turn; skirts and coats rustle. In the gray haze of sunrise, Charlotte sees a cavalcade of icy boulders jutting out from the sea. They are white and deep blue and all the shades in between, each angle distinct, a display of serene strength.

"What's that?" Tommy asks, his high-pitched voice breaking the silence.

"Icebergs," Mr. Healy says.

He looks so tired, Charlotte thinks, a wan facsimile of the efficient sailor who'd thrown out a line to a dying man. She hasn't thought until now that he must have lost friends, too. Loyal crewmen who did their duty and went down with the *Titanic.*

"There's a ship!" Charlie shouts out, and they all jostle to look, bodies twisting up and around. Esme can't be sure at first; it's impossible to see anything other than those glacial outcroppings. Then a distant shape resolves itself in her mind—*the bow, a smokestack; Charlie was right!*—and Esme lets out a yelp of joy. Elation floods her so completely that her body moves without thought. She reaches for Charlie and presses her forehead against his chest, and she feels the flutter of his fingers in the hair at the back of her neck. It's flagrant and reckless, and Esme doesn't care.

Mr. Healy barks out orders. "We must row for her. Row for our lives. Mr. Van Hausen, Mr. Wells . . ."

Charlie has already picked up his oar. Mr. Wells's mouth is half open, like a dog panting for his supper. He presses an oar into the lock and gives Mr. Healy a spritely salute.

"Aye, aye, Cap'n!"

Nurse Braxton scrambles back to the tiller as the men position their oars. Mrs. McBride reaches for an oar bobbing in the water at her feet.

"I will join you, gentlemen," she announces.

Mrs. Westleigh and Miss Armstrong look gleefully impressed by their older sister's pluck. It is impossible to tell what Mrs. Trelawny is feeling; her head is bent downward, and she is either crying or praying.

Charlotte picks up an oar and gives Anna an encouraging smile.

"A ship," she says. Does the girl understand? "We're saved."

She grabs hold of Anna's hand and squeezes; her skin is still so cold. Charlotte feels a fleeting pity for this poor, lost little thing, who doesn't look nearly old enough to be on her own. Then Charlotte's thoughts turn back to herself, and she wonders where this ship will take them. London? New York? She doesn't care, as long as Reg is on deck, waiting for her.

Anna looks at the ship in the distance and thinks only of blankets and soup and coffee. Her body is assaulted by shivers; she shakes and shakes and can't stop.

Mrs. McBride gloats about her prowess with the oar; her sisters offer delighted encouragement as Mr. Wells laughs. The boat barrels forward, propelled by rowers working in union, locked in the same rhythm.

Charlie is grinning, and his cheeks are flushed, and Esme thinks he has never looked so handsome.

"Mr. Healy and Mr. Wells, I've got ten dollars for each of you when we board," Charlie says, his breaths labored but steady. "I hope that's enough to replace what you've lost."

"Much obliged," Mr. Healy mutters, his eyes on their target, while Mr. Wells lets out a more delighted, "Thank you, sir!"

Relentlessly, Lifeboat 21 glides across the glassy sea, as its passengers move into their futures.

PART FOUR: AFTERMATH

ANNA

March 1933

To Mrs. Van Hausen, with most sincere greetings . . .

Anna tipped the pen sideways, tapping it with her thumb. Did that set the proper tone? She was still so uncertain of her written English. A woman like Mrs. Van Hausen would have all sorts of impressive correspondents, and Anna didn't want to come across as a country rube. She heard Josef stomping his boots outside the kitchen door and slid the letter under a stack of seed catalogs on the corner of the desk.

"Easier than I thought!" Josef called out.

He'd been working on the car, trying to discover the source of a rattling noise that had been irritating him for days. In a few hours, he would be driving to the Lake Crossing train station to pick up Sarah for her usual weekend visit. During the past few months of Saturday suppers and Sunday lunches, Anna had watched her children marvel at the change in their parents. She saw Sarah and John glance at each other when Josef reached for Anna's hand, perhaps wondering whether age had made them more sentimental. Susan simply beamed.

Anna heard water splashing in the kitchen sink, then Josef leaned around the doorframe of the front room. His cheerful, questioning expression made Anna ashamed of her secrecy. She ought to have told him what she was thinking weeks ago. After all, it would have to be a joint decision.

Anna waved Josef into the room and pulled out the letter she'd started. Her fingertips rubbed absently along the paper as she talked.

"You remember when I told you about Charlotte? From the lifeboat?"

Josef nodded.

"I've always felt bad about keeping her money."

Josef leaned against the doorjamb, bracing himself for more than a quick exchange.

"It's not your fault," he said. "You couldn't find her."

"I didn't try very hard. There was another woman in our boat, Mrs. Van Hausen, as she's now known. I saw an obituary for her husband, in a magazine, and it said she lives in New York. She's very rich—I'm sure I could find her address without much trouble. They have directories for all the big cities at the telephone company offices. Mrs. Van Hausen might know Charlotte's surname and where she lives—it's worth a try, at least. I could write to the White Star Line offices, too."

"Sounds like you've already put some thought into this," Josef observed.

"You know how many people are suffering since the stock market crash. Losing their jobs and their homes. I could tell by Charlotte's clothes that she wasn't rich, and I can't help wondering if that money might make a difference in her life. After all, we have been so blessed."

Josef folded his arms tight across his chest, his face impassive.

"If I can find her, I want to give the money back," Anna said. "Can we afford it?"

The Depression hadn't spared Andersson Construction. There were fewer houses being built and less money coming in. But people still needed roofs repaired and windows replaced. Josef kept busy, and Anna never had to worry about putting food on the table or buying new shoes for her children. The debt she owed Charlotte went so much deeper than money, but this would be the easiest way to show her gratitude.

Josef considered the consequences of Anna's request, in his usual thoughtful way. No one else would have noticed the flicker in his eyes when he made his decision, for no one else had spent as much time looking into them as Anna.

"It's the right thing to do," Josef said.

ESME

April 1933

"Hard to imagine, isn't it? That soaked little girl as the mother of three children?"

Sabine nodded, the pins in her mouth bobbing along with the movement of her head. Esme tried to keep still. With any other customer, the assistant seamstress would be doing the hemming, but Sabine always saw to Esme's clothes herself.

"She saw an article about Charlie in a magazine," Esme continued. "Imagine that! Even out there on the prairie, people know who he is."

Sabine deftly slid a pin through a length of shimmering silk. Navy blue, appropriate for a widow but not depressingly somber. Sabine had a talent for translating each woman's personal preferences into a tasteful public image.

"It's very nice she should write," Sabine said, pulling herself up from a crouched position. She surveyed the hem, which fell to mid-calf. Just right.

"Oh, I haven't gotten to the best part," Esme said. "Anna asked if I knew how to reach Charlotte."

Esme smiled, pleased by Sabine's surprised expression.

"The English woman?" Sabine asked. "The one who came to your house?"

"Can you believe it? Apparently, Anna has been wanting to write Charlotte for years, but she didn't remember Charlotte's last name. And now it turns out I not only know Charlotte's name, I have her calling card and can tell Anna exactly where she lives!"

"It is a sign from God," Sabine said.

Was it? Both Charlotte and Anna had sought out Esme after hearing about Charlie. How strange, that his death should bring them together again.

"Anyway, I wrote Anna back this morning. My good deed for the day." Esme twisted her hips from side to side, admiring herself in the mirror. "Oh, this is lovely."

Sabine smiled, in her typically modest way. How many times had Esme seen her look downward, deflecting praise with a twist of her chin? It struck Esme that she knew Sabine's expressions and gestures as well as those of her own children. Yet Sabine's thoughts—her soul—were as much a mystery as they'd ever been. Though they were both past forty and had spent half their lives together, Sabine was in many ways still a stranger.

Esme felt unusually clearheaded that morning; she'd been out late at a concert with Rosie the night before and hadn't taken her usual dose of medicine before bed. Yet she'd slept well, with no dreams. She'd forgotten how good it felt to sink into oblivion. To have her mind go blank, for eight blessed hours.

Sabine stretched out her hands as Esme slid the dress off her body. It was a natural reflex; Sabine was always ready to catch whatever Esme cast off. Only today, it felt different. Today, Esme looked over her shoulder as she shrugged away the silk and watched Sabine's hands flutter amid the fabric. She noticed a streak of gray colonizing Sabine's dark hair. It felt like Sabine had always been there, hovering behind Esme, picking up and carrying away and fetching whatever was needed. Her silent, self-effacing protector.

Esme pulled on her wool skirt and buttoned her blouse, waving away Sabine's offers of help. With modern fashions, even the most spoiled woman could dress herself. Who needed a ladies' maid? Then, with a clarity that caught her off balance, Esme remembered a moment from her wedding night with Hiram. How self-conscious she'd felt in her elaborate dress, until Hiram stepped up to unfasten the buttons, as if it were the most natural thing in the world. No fuss, no suggestive leer—just Hiram doing his best to put her at ease. She'd been so grateful, so relieved . . .

"Madame?"

Sabine was watching Esme, concerned, and Esme was surprised to feel her eyes sting with tears.

"I'm all right," Esme rushed to say, as she'd done a hundred times since Charlie's death. Then, looking at Sabine's dear, familiar face, "I was thinking of Mr. Harper."

Sabine looked sad, but also grateful, her pain mingled with relief. Esme never talked about Hiram, but she saw that Sabine still thought of him, too, and she realized their shared loss would forever knit them together. Whether Sabine felt the normal affection of an employee for a generous employer or something more intimate didn't matter. Sabine wouldn't mind Esme wallowing in the past. She might even welcome it.

"He was a good man," Esme said. "A kind man. I wish I'd been a better wife."

Sabine nodded, briefly and decisively. She'd never chide her former mistress, but her acknowledgment of Esme's sins marked a rare moment of honesty between them.

The bell over the shop's front door chimed, signaling the arrival of a new customer. Esme spoke quickly, knowing she hadn't much time.

"I've been talking to the children about our summer plans. Rosie's always going on that she's the only one of her friends who's never been to Europe, and I thought to myself, why not? It would be good to get away, after all that's happened. I never thought I'd get on a boat again, but Rosie begged and begged, and Robbie said an adventure would do us good . . ."

Esme's voice trailed off. She wasn't sure how to explain the next part. How to ask with the requisite nonchalance.

"Where will you go?" Sabine asked politely.

"Rosie wants to see London, and she says Nice has become quite fashionable."

Sabine had turned away, busy with Esme's dress. She pulled it onto a hanger while simultaneously craning her neck to see who'd come into the shop.

"Would you like to come?"

Esme knew she'd rushed the invitation; she should have built up to the offer before blurting it out. Sabine looked taken aback, and no wonder. It wasn't as if she and Esme were friends. They never met for lunch or gossiped over tea. Yet Esme felt herself straining against the constraints of their relationship.

"You could see your family," Esme said.

At first, she was hurt by Sabine's impassive silence. Then Esme realized Sabine had locked her face into that blank, stiff expression because she was trying not to cry. For the first time, Esme wondered what it had been like for Sabine to leave her parents, her friends, her country—everything she'd ever known. During all the years Sabine had served her so faithfully, it had never occurred to Esme that her maid might be homesick. She'd never thought of giving Sabine the time and money for a visit back to Paris.

"I'll pay for everything," Esme insisted. "I'm selling the house—I hardly need it since I never entertain. It will be a relief, actually, not having to manage that monstrosity." And the words Esme had said half-heartedly to her lawyer and Charlie's business associates when they discussed her finances suddenly felt true. Letting go of the house would lighten her spirits. She would be free.

"You are sure, madame?"

The fact that Sabine hadn't even bothered to protest was a sign of how much she wanted to go. Esme wanted to hug her as she would have hugged Rosie or Robbie. For years, she'd thought of Sabine as one of her children—someone she was responsible for, even though they were practically the same age. The passing of time had subtly reversed their roles: Esme remained childlike and dependent on others as Sabine matured into self-sufficiency. Sabine had never married, never been distracted by the demands of motherhood. She'd carved out her own destiny.

"Of course I'm sure," Esme said. "My French is atrocious. We'll be in dire straits without you."

Sabine shook her head, but she was smiling, and Esme smiled back and reached out. Their fingers intertwined and squeezed. *We used to laugh all the time,* Esme remembered. *We'd laugh and laugh, and Hiram would roll his eyes, pretending to disapprove.*

How had Esme never realized that Sabine was the truest friend she had? Sabine had known Esme as both Mrs. Harper and Mrs. Van Hausen; she'd seen Esme at her worst and never faltered in her allegiance. Esme had thought she'd never cross the Atlantic again. Worn down by Rosie's pleading, she'd tentatively agreed to make the journey, knowing she'd have to drug herself half senseless in order to board the ship.

Or maybe not, if Sabine was along. Sabine would understand why Esme was nervous about sailing; she might even share the same fear. They could confide in each other, take strength from each other. Esme might even be brave enough to leave her bottles at home.

CHARLOTTE

May 1933

Mr. Healy lived in a modest terraced house, indistinguishable from its neighbors on the quiet Southampton street. One large picture window downstairs, two smaller windows on top, the sort of stolidly respectable dwelling the poor aspire to and the rich dismiss. A house that didn't reveal anything about the people who lived inside.

Finding Mr. Healy had been easy enough. The White Star Line office had been very helpful, especially after Charlotte told them where she worked and said she might mention White Star's newest ship in her next column. A secretary told Charlotte that Mr. Healy had served on the *Olympic* in the years after the war and was now a captain with a commercial shipping line. She even gave Charlotte his address.

Ever since Charlotte had returned from America, the memories that had been stirred up by her conversations with Esme and Georgie had become clearer and more persistent. The past, at times, seemed more vibrant than the present. And every time Charlotte pictured the *Titanic* and what came after, her thoughts circled back to Mr. Healy. His steadfastness in the boat. His determination to save whomever he could. She still thought of him as one of the most decent men she'd ever met. Yet the last time she'd seen him, at the hearings, his entire body sagged with the burden of that poor man's death. Had his guilt eased with time? She hoped so; she liked to think he'd gone on to live a full, happy life.

It would take only a few minutes to dash off a note in a suitably breezy tone; Charlotte was an expert at fitting words together to achieve a desired effect. The difficulty was in explaining why she wanted to see him. Every reason that occurred to her sounded appallingly sentimental. Or half mad.

Do you still think about the lifeboat?

You'll never believe what happened to Charles Van Hausen!

I've never forgotten you.

Georgie had been urging her to do it for months. Georgie, who'd reconciled with his mother and become one of Charlotte's favorite correspondents, liked to tease her: *Have you tracked down the dreamy sailor you told me about? Does he have three chins and twelve children?* Georgie was coming to visit Lady Upton in a few weeks, and he threatened to confront Mr. Healy himself if Charlotte hadn't spoken to him by then. Charlotte didn't think he'd do it, but Georgie's pestering added a twist of guilt to her inaction.

Then came another letter from America, postmarked in Minneapolis. The news it contained was startling enough to jolt Charlotte into action. Mr. Healy had been there; he'd seen Anna wrapped in Reg's coat. She remembered the relief she'd felt when Mr. Healy passed out the oars: *He knows what he's about; we're in good hands.*

He'd know what to do.

Charlotte knocked on the door, two quick raps. She'd prepared herself for an aged version of the face that stalked her memories, so she wasn't taken aback by Mr. Healy's receding hairline or the crinkles around her eyes. What surprised Charlotte was how genuinely pleased she was to see this middle-aged man she barely knew.

Mr. Healy shook Charlotte's hand, polite but restrained, and invited her in. He looked much calmer than Charlotte felt, as if the potential awkwardness of this reunion had never crossed his mind, and Charlotte tried to mimic his composure. Her usual technique when meeting someone new was to unleash a barrage of cheery conversation, but she could tell he'd be put off by too much chatter.

"Thank you for coming," Mr. Healy said, taking Charlotte's hat. "I thought, at first, of suggesting a café—it would have been more proper, I suppose?"

Charlotte shook her head, as if it didn't matter to her one way or the other, though she had been surprised when he'd responded to her letter with an invitation to his home.

"My concern was that the conversation might turn to matters best discussed in private. I'm sure you understand." Mr. Healy showed Charlotte into the front parlor. "Please sit down; I'll fetch the tea."

The house had a somber aura of solitude. Charlotte glanced around for clues to his living arrangements. The parlor was cramped but pristine, with a dark-green sofa and matching armchair. Prints of nautical scenes hung in simple wood frames on the walls. There were no toys or photographs or any other evidence of family life, and Charlotte had seen only a single coat on the rack in the hall. But perhaps the parlor was kept neat for visitors, and the children's things were banished upstairs.

Mr. Healy returned with a tray and set it down on the side table next to Charlotte. A silver tea service was set crookedly in the center, with floral china cups on either side. An array of store-bought biscuits had been spread across a matching floral plate. Charlotte was rather touched by the haphazard arrangement. Mr. Healy had clearly prepared it all himself.

Charlotte nodded yes for both milk and sugar, then took an introductory sip. The tea was hotter than expected, making her wince before she set down her cup. Mr. Healy sat in the armchair opposite Charlotte, unruffled, waiting for her to speak first. It was rather exasperating to have no indication what he was thinking.

"I imagine my letter came as a surprise," Charlotte began.

"Indeed," Mr. Healy said. "But a pleasant one."

"Was it? I'm so glad."

Charlotte's nerves began to settle. Mr. Healy was too well mannered to ask directly why she'd come, but she caught a flicker of apprehension in his placid gaze.

"Do you ever talk about the *Titanic*?" she asked, hoping to catch him off guard.

Mr. Healy shook his head. "Best not to," he said.

"That's what I believed, for a very long time," Charlotte said. "I came back to London not long after. I started a new job, I made new friends, and I told no one. There didn't seem any point in reliving it or being part of all that gossip or recrimination. I thought I'd put it behind me, but it's the strangest thing . . ." Charlotte wondered if Mr. Healy would understand, but there was no point to coming if she wasn't going to be honest. "The more time has passed, the more I find myself thinking about what happened."

"Are you planning to write about it?" Mr. Healy asked.

"What do you mean?" Charlotte asked, surprised.

Mr. Healy looked momentarily abashed. "I know you work for one of the papers. I'm sorry, I can't remember which one."

"The *Record*," Charlotte said.

"That's it. My wife used to buy it from time to time."

So there was a Mrs. Healy. Charlotte wondered where she was and if she knew her husband had a visitor today. Perhaps Edmund had purposely asked Charlotte to come at a time when he knew his wife would be out.

"I remember seeing your name on a story," Mr. Healy said. "Something about a fox loose in a manor house."

"Oh yes! The indoor fox hunt Lady Darlington arranged for her husband's birthday." Charlotte was surprised he remembered; it had to be more than ten years ago. "Hounds careening up the stairs and knocking over the family china. It was utter madness."

"I was chuffed to think of you swanning around with all those peers," Mr. Healy said.

"I was only half a step up from the help," Charlotte said. "Lady Darlington always invites society columnists to her house parties. She's desperate to cultivate a reputation for outrageousness."

"Sounds entertaining."

Everyone thought it was. They saw Charlotte's life as a series of amusing escapades, not knowing the drudgery that each daily column required. For what felt like eons, Charlotte had faked friendliness and pretended to find insipid bores fascinating. She'd wasted years of her life—and much of her talent—chronicling the childish antics of the upper classes. Yet that work would be her legacy.

"I used to enjoy it," Charlotte said. Mr. Healy's curious look encouraged her to go on, to acknowledge the doubts she hadn't allowed herself to examine. "I like meeting new people, and I like telling stories. I'm good at it. But it feels as if I've been running toward a prize that was always just out of reach, and it's only recently I've realized there isn't one. There's no mountaintop to conquer. Simply more of the same."

The despondency of her admission struck Charlotte only once she'd said it aloud. It was certainly more than she'd meant to share.

"Your turn," she said brightly. "I ought to address you as Captain Healy, oughtn't I?"

Mr. Healy nodded, but with none of the roosterish pride Charlotte was accustomed to in military men.

"It was very brave of you to go back to sea afterward. I avoided sailing for years."

"My father was a sailor, and my grandfather before him," Mr. Healy said. "I had no choice."

Of course he didn't. Charlotte's social circle was filled with people who'd struck out on their own, reinventing themselves as poets or actors or aristocratic daredevils. She'd forgotten, momentarily, that most people didn't have the will or funds to defy family expectations.

"I was there for your testimony, at the American hearings," she said.

"Were you?" Mr. Healy's eyes crinkled in surprise. He hadn't seen her, then. She'd never been sure.

"It must have been difficult," Charlotte said.

"It was, rather." Mr. Healy's hands cradled his teacup, the fingers interlacing. "I hadn't a penny to my name, and there I was, in front of that crowd, in a charity suit from the Seamen's Friend Society."

Charlotte remembered how the too-large jacket made him look like a schoolboy playing dress-up in his father's clothes. How his voice shook when he tried to put the unexplainable into words.

"Seeing what they ran in the papers was worse," Mr. Healy said. "One minute I was the hero who'd pulled a drowning girl from the water, and the next I was the villain who'd left others to die."

Charlotte immediately understood what his eyes were asking. "I never wrote about you. Or anything to do with the lifeboat."

"The attention wore me down," Mr. Healy said. "I was sick for a time—needed a bit of rest, more than anything else. I stayed with my parents for a few months. Kept to myself. Then, when my pa was down to his last shillings—God bless him—I went back to the White Star Line. I was on the Atlantic crossing two days later."

"Oh my," Charlotte murmured sympathetically.

"There's no time for moping, if you're doing your job. I put my name in for extra watches or whatever needed doing. Then the war came, and I joined the navy and made supply runs to the Mediterranean. Thought I was missing out on all the glory, but it worked out for the best. And I was second officer on the *Olympic* afterward."

The *Titanic's* sister ship. How could he have borne it?

"Now you're a captain," Charlotte said, with a nod of respect.

"The *Meridian*. She sails twice a month to the Caribbean."

Mr. Healy leaned forward and offered more tea. He poured with deft confidence, but unease lingered in their shared silence. Charlotte found it odd that he'd said nothing about his marriage. He could be widowed, but he hadn't seemed particularly sad when he mentioned his wife in that offhand way.

"Do you remember Esme Harper, from the boat?" Charlotte asked. "I should say Esme Van Hausen. You did know she married Charles, not long after?"

"Oh yes."

How could he not? The "*Titanic* sweethearts" had been inescapable.

"I was in New York last year, and I paid her a visit," Charlotte said. Mr. Healy's eyes widened, just a bit.

"Mr. Van Hausen died last autumn, in an automobile crash. I went to pay my respects. She was rather a mess, which was understandable given the circumstances. The rotten thing is, she'd been unhappy for quite some time, long before he died. They were very much in love when they married—you could see she adored him in the boat, couldn't you? But they were never able to stop those rumors that he'd snuck onto the boat dressed as a woman or paid off the crew, even though it was complete nonsense. From the way Esme spoke, she and Charles never really escaped the sinking."

"I'm sorry to hear it."

"Here's the curious part," Charlotte said. "I left my card with Esme, to be polite, not because I expected to ever hear from her again. And then, months later, she received a letter from that Swedish girl, Anna. The one you pulled from the water."

"You don't say?"

"She lives in Minnesota. Up north somewhere." Charlotte had meant to look it up on a map, but she'd never gotten around to it. "She's married, with three children. Apparently, she's been trying to find me for years, but she didn't know my surname, only that I was called Charlotte. When she saw a notice of Charles's death, she thought Esme might know where I was. She wrote to Esme, Esme sent Anna my address, and Anna wrote to me."

"That's quite a story." Mr. Healy looked interested, which was encouraging.

"I gave Anna a coat, on the lifeboat," Charlotte explained. "You remember how drenched she was—I wanted to warm her up. She tried to give the coat back, on the *Carpathia*, but you could see just from looking at her that she was desperately poor and needed it far more than me. I told her to keep it and didn't give it another thought from then on. What I didn't know was that Reg, my husband . . ." Charlotte stumbled over the word. Should she tell him? Would it make any difference? "He'd hidden fifty pounds in the lining."

"Goodness." It was a considerable sum, even today, but it would have been a fortune to a young sailor in 1912.

"Anna intended to return it, but she didn't know how to find me. Eventually, she gave the money to her husband, and he used it to start his own building firm. Apparently, he's been very successful. She said it's all due to me, which of course it isn't, but I suppose it's true that the money helped him on his way."

"Your husband never told you?" Mr. Healy asked.

Charlotte pictured Reg on the day they'd met, showing off the hidden compartment in his jacket where pickpockets couldn't get to his banknotes. Not long before he had flagged down the lifeboat, Reg had muttered in her ear as he draped his coat around her shoulders. She'd been too angry to pay attention. Was that what he'd been trying to tell her? If so, her stubbornness had denied her the knowledge of his final gift.

"He tried to, I think," Charlotte said. "But I didn't hear him. Anna said it would be a weight off her soul if she gave the money back. The only difficulty is, I don't feel right keeping it."

"If the money was your husband's . . ."

"I was never married."

Four simple words, dissolving the lie Charlotte had lived with for two decades. She wasn't sure why she'd admitted it.

"I was very much in love with Mr. Evers, despite the fact that he was a swindler and a thief," Charlotte said. If she was going to be honest, she might as well be thorough. "Or perhaps *because* he was a swindler and a thief. But he had no interest in marriage. He asked me to pose as his wife so he'd appear more respectable during the voyage. After we were rescued, and the officers were taking down names, I gave mine as Mrs. Reginald Evers because I knew that's how it appeared on the passenger lists. And then, in New York, I found there were advantages to being a widow. A measure of independence I rather enjoyed. So I remained Mrs. Evers from then on."

Mr. Healy was silent for a moment, and Charlotte was sure she'd shocked him. Then his lips twitched into the beginning of a smile.

"If you're not Mrs. Evers, then what shall I call you?"

Charlotte Digby, she thought, but it sounded like a stranger's name, nothing to do with her. "My friends call me Charlotte."

She realized instantly that the offer, the sort of flirtatious suggestion she'd have made at a smart London party, was all wrong for this prim working-class home. Mr. Healy dropped his eyes and fiddled with his teacup. Charlotte was aware of having crossed a line—dashed over it, really—and wondered how she'd find her way back.

"Then you must call me Edmund," he said quietly. "If we are to be friends."

"Splendid." Even if Charlotte never saw him again, she liked knowing he thought of her that way. "I promise, I shall be very careful to address you in public as Captain Healy."

Edmund shook his head, looking perilously close to blushing. The social banter that was Charlotte's second tongue was, for him, a foreign language. Best to be direct.

"I don't need the money," she said. "It feels tainted by Reg's death. I'd much rather it do some good in the world. I was thinking perhaps a charity, something to do with sailors, and I was hoping you could help me. There must have been a relief fund for the families of *Titanic* crewmen who died?"

"There were funds, at the time," Edmund said. "But it's been twenty years—I doubt any of them are still active."

Of course, Charlotte thought. Many of the children who had lost their fathers on the *Titanic* would have become parents themselves by now.

"There is one charity you might consider," Edmund said. "The Tipton Aid Society. It was started by the widow of a sea captain. A few of my mates were lost in the war, and Mrs. Tipton saw their families were taken care of. Paid the school fees for one promising lad, and now he's at university."

"Yes, that sounds perfect," said Charlotte. Reg had always fancied himself a bit of a Robin Hood; he'd have enjoyed knowing that the money he'd stolen from rich fools would go to deserving children. "I'll write to her, shall I?"

"I could introduce you, if you like."

"Well, I can't stay long today . . ."

"Another time?"

It was an invitation, offered with a tentative hand.

"Very well," Charlotte said. Then, because she hadn't gotten where she was by avoiding difficult questions, "Perhaps I could also meet Mrs. Healy?"

Edmund raised his shoulders in a faint attempt at a shrug. "She's at her mother's in Liverpool."

Charlotte granted him the silence to explain, if he chose to.

"Sailors don't make good husbands, as a rule," Edmund said. His voice was quiet and tinged with disappointment. "My wife wasn't born into that life as my mother and grandmother were. It was hard on her, with me gone a month at a time. And even when I was home, I wasn't much for talking. I'd grown accustomed to being on my own.

"We didn't have children, which might have helped. I don't feel the lack of them, myself, but it would have made her less lonely. In any case—she has sisters and nieces and nephews in Liverpool. She's happy there. So that's the arrangement we've come to."

Should Charlotte feel sorry for him? She couldn't tell if he was upset by the state of his marriage or relieved to have his wife out of the way. Perhaps it was a bit of both. If Edmund and his wife had been actors or singers, they'd have been divorced long ago and well into their second or third marriages. But Charlotte knew divorce was still unthinkable for people like the Healys. Though they led separate lives, their marriage—on paper—would endure.

"When do you sail next?" Charlotte asked, a social kindness to shift the conversation back to safer ground.

"A week tomorrow. It's usually three weeks on, one week off. I'll be back at the end of May."

"So we might schedule a visit with Mrs. Tipton then?"

"I'll call her later today. She'll be very grateful for your kindness."

Charlotte could feel the momentum gathering toward an ending. *Very good, thank you. It's been a pleasure.* She should be standing up and gathering her things. But she didn't want to leave. And from the way Edmund was sitting—relaxed against the back of his chair, the teacup perched on one knee—she sensed his grateful ease. He didn't want her to go, either. Thoughts welled up into words, unleashed by his tolerant understanding.

"What I said before, about putting the *Titanic* behind me. I had—or rather, I thought I had. I never spoke of it, tried never to think of it. But it turns out the memories were still there. Preserved."

Had Lady Upton's letter set all this in motion? Charlie Van Hausen's death? Perhaps it was simply the march of time. The older Charlotte got, the more she longed for her past self. The woman she'd been with Reg, who'd never shied away from adventure. A woman with endless possibilities ahead of her.

"Does it ever seem as if time bends around, as you grow older?" Charlotte asked. "I can barely remember who I lunched with last week, yet scenes from that night are so clear in my memory, I practically shiver. I can see all their faces—Anna and Esme and that dreadful Mr. Wells . . ."

Edmund managed a chuckle. "Blowing his smoke in Mrs. McBride's face!"

Charlotte imitated the woman's strident bark. "I will *not* be treated in this manner!"

"Yes, it's as you said. All perfectly clear."

"I never thanked you properly, for saving our lives."

Edmund looked uncomfortable, as she'd expected he would. "I hardly deserve that."

"You were following orders. We might well have been swamped if we'd rowed back, and I'm very sorry for the way I spoke to you. I've been meaning to apologize for a very long time."

"No need," Edmund said stiffly.

"All those inquiries and awful stories in the papers . . . they could never explain what it was really like, could they? Having to make a decision of life and death when you're freezing and knackered and afraid you're about to die. Things happen so quickly, and you haven't time to think. And later, when you're called to account for what you've done, how can you possibly make anyone else understand?"

"We should have saved him."

How calmly he said it! Yet Charlotte could hear the chill of self-accusation. "The man in the water?" she asked.

"I still think of him. Do you?"

"I try not to." The heartless truth.

"What makes it worse was that I knew him."

"You did?" Charlotte remembered how sure she'd been that it was Reg. How she'd talked herself out of believing it.

"He turned his face, when I held up the lantern. I didn't know his name, but I'd seen him in the canteen. He was a steward. He had a mother and a sweetheart, and he'd say, 'When I get back to my ladies . . . ,' and the others would say, 'Oh, go on, then,' and he'd keep smiling and boast that they were the finest examples of womanhood ever seen. Always cheerful, always smiling.

"He'd have lived if I had had control of the boat. I went over those minutes again and again, all those nights at my parents' house, when I couldn't sleep. What I'd done wrong. How I might have spared those women their grief."

"You can't take all that upon yourself." Charlotte felt a ridiculous urge to press her hands against Edmund's cheeks. To pull him close and whisper her forgiveness. "You did your best. We both did."

Edmund took a deep breath. "No point going on about it. What's done is done."

"Do you know, I'd never done anything selfless before that night," Charlotte said. She couldn't allow this conversation to sink into despair. "I was a liar and a thief, pining after a man who'd never have married me. I hate to think where I'd have ended up if the *Titanic* hadn't sunk. Prison, most likely. It's terrible to say, given the loss of life, but it was the making of me. I'd never have known what I was capable of, otherwise."

"I changed as well," Edmund said. "Though I can't say if it was for the better. I wasn't the boldest lad, growing up, and I was used to following orders, not giving them. I wasn't as strong as I should have been." He brushed away Charlotte's attempt to protest. "I wasn't, and I learned from it. By the time I went back to sea, I was a better sailor. More disciplined."

And something precious was lost: the impulsive decency that made Edmund throw a line to a dying man. The self-possessed man sitting opposite Charlotte would carefully weigh the costs and benefits of such a rescue; he valued caution over action. But wasn't that true of everyone, as they aged?

"There's something freeing about surviving the worst," Edmund said. "There were chaps who worried about German submarines, during the war, and I'd find myself thinking, what if we are hit? If I live, I live; if I die, I die. It's out of my hands."

"That sounds like a rather useful approach to life."

"It can be."

Charlotte wondered whether Edmund had applied that same mind-set to his marriage. *If we're happy, then we're happy; if we're not, so be it.* His imperturbability must be a great asset when commanding a ship, but how did it affect his private life? Her most recent lover, a theater director, had been a tempest of moods, ranging from buoyant elation to self-pitying misery. It had been rather thrilling, at first, but exhausting by the end. How much easier to come home to a man who was always quintessentially himself.

"I have my regrets, as anyone would," said Charlotte. "But I've made my peace with it all. We survived. That's enough."

Edmund looked at her tentatively, seeming to gather up his nerve. "May I speak honestly?" he asked.

Haven't you already? Charlotte wondered, but she simply nodded.

"I was curious when I received your letter, but I expected this meeting to be rather uncomfortable. I didn't think there was anything to be gained by discussing the past. But I've enjoyed talking to you very much."

"Thank you."

"You have a way of inspiring confidences. I suppose that's why you're so good at your job."

Edmund gave Charlotte a pointed look. An attempt to tease her, she hoped, but she didn't want him to question her motives.

"I told you before, I don't intend to write anything about the *Titanic*," she said. "I'm not here as a reporter. I'm here as a friend."

It felt strange, saying it out loud, but right.

Charlotte glanced at her watch, shocked by how much time had passed. She usually kept to a strict schedule, her mind always calculating where she needed to be next. Edmund's parlor had shielded her from the chaos of her everyday life.

"I'm so sorry," she exclaimed, rising from the sofa. "I've got to catch the three o'clock train back to town. There's a dinner tonight . . ."

A dinner she'd been looking forward to. Noel Coward was going to be there, and that gorgeous Laurence Olivier. She'd been looking forward to it for weeks, savoring the anticipation each time she glanced through her diary. Now, to her surprise, it felt like a burden. The rush back to her flat, choosing the right dress, preening in front of the mirror, all so she could sit through the same gossipy conversations, the same judgmental pronouncements. It all seemed so pointless.

"Please, don't let me keep you."

Edmund was standing, too, flustered. He hurriedly placed his teacup on the tray and went into the hall to fetch Charlotte's hat. She wished her departure weren't so rushed. It felt wrong to follow a heartfelt conversation with such a superficial parting.

"I'll arrange a visit with Mrs. Tipton," Edmund said, and Charlotte replied, "Yes, please do," and then the door was open, and Charlotte was standing with one foot inside the house and one foot out, and it felt, for one swooning second, that they were together again in the lifeboat, the *Carpathia* looming above them. Now, as then, they reached for one another, and Edmund clasped Charlotte's hands, just as he had when she was about to climb up the ladder. It wasn't goodbye. It was a promise.

Edmund's house wasn't far from the station, but Charlotte hailed a taxi, just to be safe. She found herself already anticipating her next visit. Tea and biscuits in the parlor. Speaking freely about her worries. Edmund's understanding nods. The relief of his undemanding company.

Charlotte pictured herself leaning in toward Edmund and kissing him. Not the next time, but perhaps the time after that. He'd be gentleman enough to hesitate, at first, but that might give way to longing, a willingness to follow where she led. She liked the idea of showing him a few bedroom tricks his wife was unlikely to know. They could have a lovely, life-brightening affair, and when the spark died out, as it inevitably would, there'd be no blame or regret. She'd look back on their time together with wistful fondness, grateful for whatever hours of happiness they'd shared.

But what if her attraction went deeper and turned into something more? Charlotte had never wanted to be married, because no matter what a potential husband might say, he'd always expect his wife's needs to be subservient to his own. But Edmund, like Charlotte, was content with solitude. They could come to their own unconventional arrangement, living largely separate lives and coming together at month's end, their affection renewed by distance. It would be a partnership built on companionship and understanding, where their pasts wouldn't need to be hidden or explained. Lazy mornings with coffee and the papers, walks in the country on Sunday afternoons. Simple routines Charlotte had never admitted she longed for.

It was ridiculous, of course. Edmund was already married, and she had a life of her own, one that would hardly tempt a reserved sea captain. Imagine, Edmund at tonight's dinner party! Yet Charlotte found she could imagine it: there'd be a few eye-rolls, at first, and a fuss over Edmund's novelty. He'd be shocked by Isobel Galloway's latest hijinks—which would please Isobel to no end—and he'd listen respectfully to the old theater bores telling the same stories they'd told at the previous dinner. And in the end, his politeness and self-possession would win them all over. Isobel would tell Charlotte he was lovely and absolutely perfect for her, and Charlotte would know it was true.

Or there could be another path entirely. Charlotte could reach for Edmund, only to have him turn away. He might still be in love with his wife, or have a stronger moral compass than she did. If he showed no interest in her advances, Charlotte would laugh them off in a way that preserved their tentative friendship. She would still make occasional visits to Southampton, and she would encourage him to come to London and meet her for tea at Brown's or the Ritz. He'd marvel at the prices while she teased him for being provincial. He might even resolve the problems in his marriage and introduce Charlotte to his wife, and she would be genuinely happy for them both. Without a new romance to distract her, Charlotte might finally write the novel she'd always intended to, skewering country society and its pretensions, and Edmund would read it and send her a letter telling her he'd enjoyed it. And when she saw his name on the envelope, she'd feel the heartening warmth that comes from knowing a person you care for has been thinking of you.

Charlotte had always been a storyteller, but only in fiction do events sort themselves into a tidy conclusion. All of these futures with Edmund were possible; all of them could be equally true. She would make her offer, like tossing a stone in the sea, and the repercussions would ripple outward, beyond her control. No matter what happened, Charlotte and Edmund would always be bound together. He was a part of her past, a part of her future, the man who would always make her feel safe.

AUTHOR'S NOTE

Years before the blockbuster movie came out, I read Walter Lord's classic account of the *Titanic* sinking, *A Night to Remember*. Like so many others, I was immediately transfixed by the ship's combination of glamour and tragedy. But it was another book, *The Titanic: End of a Dream*, by Wyn Craig Wade, that helped me understand why the ship still fascinates us today. Relying heavily on the US Congressional hearings that were held soon after the tragedy, Wade's book puts the sinking in a larger cultural context, revealing how much social class, ethnocentric snobbery, and technological change influenced the course of events. While Lifeboat 21 and its passengers are fictional, I stuck close to the historical record when describing the events before and after the launching of the lifeboats.

The *Titanic* sailed with enough lifeboat space for only half the people on board, the result of an antiquated safety code that hadn't kept pace with the growing size of ocean liners. Yet some of those lifeboats were lowered half full. Not everyone realized the seriousness of the situation, especially early on, and some survivors later testified that there were hardly any people on deck when their lifeboats were loaded. On one side of the ship, male passengers were allowed to board if there was space; on the other side, they were kept out, even if there were open seats.

When newspapers began reporting that first-class men had been rescued while third-class women and children had drowned, it sparked universal outrage. Had third-class passengers been barred from reaching the lifeboats? Officially, no. Once the captain gave the order to launch the lifeboats, third-class women and children were supposed to be given access to the upper decks; a few stewards even led passengers directly to the boats. However, some women refused to leave their husbands—which, tragically, resulted in a number of entire families being lost. Others were simply too hesitant or frightened to venture beyond their assigned quarters; eyewitnesses described huddles of immigrants praying in the third-class common rooms, seemingly resigned to their fate. Others, like Anna, climbed cranes to reach the upper decks when they found their way blocked or were unable to navigate the confusing route to the boat deck. It's important to remember that evacuating a ship as huge as the *Titanic* wasn't an orderly process. The crewmen were new to the ship, and many had little or no training in emergency procedures. A lifeboat drill scheduled for the morning of the sinking was cancelled (for unknown reasons). About 80 percent of the *Titanic* crew died that night—nearly seven hundred men and three women. Some performed heroically in their last hours, others didn't, but the odds of survival were clearly stacked against them.

I've often wondered what it must have been like in one of those half-empty lifeboats when the ship finally went under. There were hundreds of people in the water, screaming for help as they slowly froze to death. In some boats, crewmen who suggested pulling people from the water were dissuaded by their terrified passengers; in other boats, women begged to go back but were told it was too dangerous by the sailors in charge. The desperate screams of the drowning went on for more than an hour; in one lifeboat, passengers and crew sang loudly to cover up the sound. Only Lifeboat Number 14, commanded by Fifth Officer Harold Lowe, attempted a rescue. "If anybody had struggled out of the mass, I was there to pick them up, but it was useless for me to go into the mass," he later testified. "It would have been suicide." He waited for the crowd to "thin out"—for the weakest to die—but underestimated the lethal effect of the freezing water. By the time he returned, he found only four people alive, one of whom died not long after.

While the excerpts of Congressional testimony in this book are my own creation, the questions and responses were inspired by the actual hearings, which began the day after the *Titanic* survivors arrived in New York. The complete transcripts of the US and British inquiries into the disaster are available online at www.titanicinquiry.org, and those exchanges were a great help in understanding the conventions of the time. (It was an era of stiff upper lips, not tearful oversharing.) I was also struck by whose stories were deemed important; the people who testified were overwhelmingly crew members and first-class passengers. Only a few third-class passengers were questioned, none of them women, and there was no testimony at all from second-class passengers.

Titanic researchers have no shortage of sources, and I consulted many of them during the writing of this book. The *Encyclopedia Titanica* (www.encyclopedia-titanica.org) is an extensive, well-maintained site that includes passenger and crew bios, deck plans, and links to current *Titanic* scholarship. One particularly helpful reference was *Titanic: An Illustrated History*, by Don Lynch, which I consulted constantly while writing shipboard descriptions. *Titanic Voices*, by Hannah Holman, includes more than sixty first-person accounts of the disaster, offering a wide range of perspectives. *Voyagers of the Titanic: Passengers, Sailors, Shipbuilders, Aristocrats, and the Worlds They Came From*, by Richard Davenport-Hines, introduced me to the fascinating backstories of the ship's lesser-known passengers. Yes, the *Titanic* had more than its fair share of aristocrats and millionaires, but it also carried people with secrets: husbands traveling with "wives" who were really their mistresses, card sharks, a father who'd kidnapped his children from his estranged wife, and men who were traveling discreetly with their male partners. In sum—a wealth of ideas for a novelist.

ACKNOWLEDGMENTS

Many people cheered me along during the writing of this book. Here are a few who deserve special thanks:

My parents, Mike and Judy Canning; my sister, Rachel; and my husband, Bob, who were there when I came up with the initial concept during a family vacation and never once said, "Aren't there enough *Titanic* books already?"

My agent, Danielle Egan-Miller, who also believed in this idea from the very beginning.

Jodi Warshaw, for giving the OK to a pitch that began, "The *Titanic*, but not cheesy."

Jenna Land Free, for caring about my characters almost as much as I do.

My daughter, Clara, for her advice on character names.

My sons, Alan and James, for making me laugh every single day.

Kim Bold, my official British consultant, for her suggestions on Charlotte's story line.

Veronica Robinson at the Swedish American Museum in Chicago, who provided me with resources on Swedish immigration to the United States.

The Glenview Public Library and Northbrook Public Library in suburban Chicago, where much of this book was written.

Librarians everywhere, for sharing their love of books. You are my tribe.

Some people are constants in your life; others circle in and out. I'm grateful for the friends who've been there during all the stages of my career as a writer, as well as those I've reconnected with in recent years. We all tell ourselves stories about our lives, but once you start comparing notes with others who were there, you sometimes discover that the truth is more layered than you thought. That realization became an underlying theme of this book, in part because I was living it. So my final thanks go to the people who helped me figure that out—and made this more than just a *Titanic* book.

ABOUT THE AUTHOR

Photo © 2013 Heidi Jo Brady / HJB Photo

Elizabeth Blackwell is the author of *In the Shadow of Lakecrest* and *While Beauty Slept*. A graduate of Northwestern University and the Columbia University Graduate School of Journalism, she lives outside Chicago with her family and piles of books she is absolutely, positively going to read someday.